Praise for
The Other Woman

"Love, sex, betrayal, friendship, redemption . . . [An] engaging tale about the pitfalls of modern romance."
—*The Dallas Morning News*

"Dickey has developed a knack for creating characters who elicit both rage and sympathy . . . Dickey taps the intimate emotions of a woman whose hurt we feel viscerally."
—*Entertainment Weekly*

"A fast-paced tale."
—*Essence*

"[A] sharp-edged, sizzling novel . . . Dickey offers plenty of straight-on sex and violence, but also probes questions of contemporary morals and the psychology of betrayal, writing compellingly and believably from his heroine's point of view . . . another crowd pleaser"
—*Publishers Weekly*

"The prediction here is that *The Other Woman* will show up on beaches all over the country this summer."
—*Forth Worth Star Telegram*

"Good and gritty storytelling."
—*Kirkus Reviews*

Thieves' Paradise

"Smartly paced . . . heart-pumping . . . electrifying . . . In his compelling picture of another world, Dickey believably shows how even in the underbelly of society, loyalty, respect, and love have their place."
—*Publishers Weekly*

"Dickey delves deep and brings light into a world where crime has its own set of rules."
—*Baltimore Afro-American*

"Passionate, sensual, rhythmic, comical . . . If Eric's previous novels are food for the soul, *Thieves' Paradise* is the nectar and ambrosia of life."
—*Chicago Defender*

continued . . .

Between Lovers

"A witty, sexy romp."   —*Sunday Denver Post*

"A hip, funny, and realistically bittersweet love story of our times."   —*Washington Sun*

"Provocative and complex."   —*Ebony*

Liar's Game

"Steamy romance, betrayal, and redemption. Dickey at his best."   —*USA Today*

"Fast-paced . . . sexy, sassy . . . a high-spirited roller-coaster ride of a novel."   —*Florida Star* (Jacksonville)

"Skillful . . . scandalous . . . a rich gumbo of narrative twists."
                                            —*Minneapolis Star Tribune*

Cheaters

"A deftly crafted tale about the games people play and the lies they tell on their search for love."   —*Ebony*

"Wonderfully written . . . smooth, unique, and genuine."
                                        —*The Washington Post Book World*

"Hot, sexy, and funny."   —*Library Journal*

Friends and Lovers

"Fluid as a rap song. Dickey can stand alone among modern novelists in capturing the flavor, rhythm, and pace of African-American speak." —*Fort Lauderdale Sun-Sentinel*

"Dickey uses humor, poignancy, and a fresh, creative writing style." —*USA Today*

"A colorful, sexy tale." —*Marie Claire*

Milk in My Coffee

"Rich *Coffee* steams away clichés of interracial romance . . . a true-to-life, complex story of relationships." —*USA Today*

"Heartwarming and hilarious." —*The Cincinnati Enquirer*

"Dickey scores with characters who come to feel like old friends." —*Essence*

Sister, Sister

"Genuine emotional depth." —*The Boston Globe*

"Vibrant . . . marks the debut of a true talent."
—*The Atlanta Journal-Constitution*

"Bold and sassy . . . brims with humor, outrageousness, and the generosity of affection." —*Publishers Weekly*

ALSO BY ERIC JEROME DICKEY

Drive Me Crazy

The Other Woman

Thieves' Paradise

Between Lovers

Liar's Game

Cheaters

Milk in My Coffee

Friends and Lovers

Sister, Sister

ANTHOLOGIES

Got to Be Real

Mothers and Sons

River Crossings: Voices of the Diaspora

Griots Beneath the Baobab

Black Silk: A Collection of African American Erotica

Gumbo: A Celebration of African American Writing

Cappuccino (Movie)—Original Story

ERIC JEROME DICKEY

naughty or nice

 NEW AMERICAN LIBRARY

New American Library
Published by New American Library, a division of
Penguin Group (USA) Inc., 375 Hudson Street,
New York, New York 10014, USA
Penguin Group (Canada), 90 Eglinton Avenue East, Suite 700, Toronto,
Ontario M4P 2Y3, Canada (a division of Pearson Penguin Canada Inc.)
Penguin Books Ltd., 80 Strand, London WC2R 0RL, England
Penguin Ireland, 25 St Stephen's Green, Dublin 2,
Ireland (a division of Penguin Books Ltd.)
Penguin Group (Australia), 250 Camberwell Road, Camberwell, Victoria 3124,
Australia (a division of Pearson Australia Group Pty. Ltd.)
Penguin Books India Pvt. Ltd., 11 Community Centre, Panchsheel Park,
New Delhi – 110 017, India
Penguin Group (NZ), 67 Apollo Drive, Rosedale, North Shore 0632,
New Zealand (a division of Pearson New Zealand Ltd.)
Penguin Books (South Africa) (Pty.) Ltd., 24 Sturdee Avenue,
Rosebank, Johannesburg 2196, South Africa

Penguin Books Ltd., Registered Offices:
80 Strand, London WC2R 0RL, England

Published by New American Library,
a division of Penguin Group (USA) Inc.
Previously published in a Dutton edition.

First New American Library Printing, October 2004
10 9 8 7 6

 REGISTERED TRADEMARK—MARCA REGISTRADA

New American Library Trade Paperback ISBN: 978-0-451-21298-6

The Library of Congress has catalogued the hardcover edition of this title as follows:

Dickey, Eric Jerome.
Naughty or nice / by Eric Jerome Dickey.
p. cm.
ISBN 0-525-94776-0
I. Title.
PS3554.I319N38 2003
813'.54—dc21   2003013456

Printed in the United States of America

naughty or nice

For every action there is an
equal and opposite reaction.

*Learned that in physics, the day I was
actually paying attention.*

Livvy, Tommie,
and Frankie

$\mathcal{L}$ivvy

I was reevaluating my life. I'd been keeping busy at work, teaching skincare and body-care therapists the correct treatment protocol, product knowledge classes, taking out-of-town trips to teach business classes on how to be successful in the skincare industry.

The irony was that I smiled at my nine-to-five and taught people how to get it together when my marriage was ragged and everything in my world was falling apart.

I went to my hotel window, looked at the never-ending whiteness falling from above, at the mountains of snow that lined the street, folded my arms, and went back to my laptop.

The ad read ARE YOU A WOMAN BETRAYED? It was from a Web site for discreet encounters. The Web page had popped up on my screen while I was surfing the Net.

For the most part, I was a West Coast gal with most of the Ten Commandments carved in my heart. But this weekday seemed to be one of my weak days, the kind of day that made me gaze at my wedding ring and ask myself some hard questions.

My cellular phone rang and pulled me away from the computer.

It was Tommie, my younger sister. There were three of us McBroom girls. Now McBroom women. Frankie was the oldest.

I was the baby of the family until Tommie came along and made me a middle child. They were my bookends, my support.

In her haunting, soulful voice, she said, "Whassup, Sticky Fingers?"

I laughed. "Don't start with that."

Most of the time Tommie was pure sunshine. But with all she's been through, I should be calling to check on her three or four times a day. Loving somebody makes you worry about them twenty-four-seven. But her voice had that motherly tone that worked my nerves.

She asked, "Where are you today?"

I told her I was in Newark, Delaware. America's first city.

She asked, "How did it go today?"

"Wasted trip. Classes were canceled. We're snowed in."

"Still snowing back that way?"

"More like a blizzard. As soon as the trucks plow it away, it's right back."

"How cold?"

I told her that it was six degrees out. So cold that the snow looked like it had been crystallized, and was as hard as ice. I'd gone outside to touch it and damn near froze to death.

"What's there to do back there?"

"Grow old and die."

"Look, I have issues with you being gone and nobody knows where you are on any given day. I don't know what hotel you're at, what city you're in. That's kinda jacked up."

Tommie wanted to know if I'd been working out, if I'd been eating three squares a day. I told her they had put me up at the Embassy Suites and there was a TGIF attached to the hotel. That was their only room service. I'd thrown on my gray sweats and worked out in the rinky-dink gym for two hours, then went over to the restaurant, ordered a low-fat salad, sat in the lobby in front of the fireplace, ate, and watched the hotel employees decorate a Christmas tree.

She said, "You have to keep your health up."

Tommie was talking and I was back at my computer, looking

through those personal ads, every now and then punctuating the conversation with "uh huh" or "okay" or "right."

My fascination was with the cyber world. There were a lot of explicit ads on that site.

MAHOGANY WOMAN SEEKS IVORY LOVER
FOR ORAL PLEASURES.

I read them, and I saw the people, doing things that illicit lovers do.

BI-CURIOUS ISO THREESOME WITH BOYFRIEND.

I blinked away from those images. I asked Tommie, "Where is Frankie?"

"Think she went to look at some more property."

"You seen her?"

The television was on in my hotel room. Ten o'clock news. The city and the airports were shut down. I was trapped inside this four-star cave being tortured with local news about "pot-hole patrols," and a bulletin letting the city know that Home Depot was out of salt and shovels.

Tommie said, "We worked out at Sand Dune Park this morning, then we drove to Hermosa Beach and had brunch on the boardwalk at a bistro café."

"Don't rub it in." I cleared my throat, tried to stay focused. "You work today?"

"I'm at Pier 1 now. On break. Heading over to Barnes & Noble so I can get a cup of tea. It's crazy today. Old Navy has a sale, and I think we're getting a lot of their customers."

"All sunshine in Manhattan Beach, huh?"

"Let's kill the chitchat and cut to the chase," Tommie said. "Staying on the road isn't going to make Tony's paternity suit go away, Livvy."

That hit me hard, a blow to my stomach and my throat at the same time.

She said, "Everybody who was at your dinner party . . . Well, you know how people talk."

"Tell them I said fuck off."

The fact that Tony had had an affair was bad enough, but the fact that the baby might be his, my life had become a bad dream that I couldn't shake. My head throbbed. And what I felt, it all came back just like that, that feeling that there was no word to describe.

"All I'm saying is running away will not make it go away."

I snapped, "I'm not staying on the road to make it go away."

I rubbed my temples, took a hard breath, and told her that one of our instructors was sick and Dermalogica had asked me to travel for a couple of weeks and teach some classes: Seven Steps to Success, Environmental Control, Spa Body Therapies, and Hormones and Menopause.

"Get real. You're not the only friggin' overpriced-lotion-pushing instructor they have."

"I'm not a lotion pusher. I'm trained to teach over fifty class—"

"Yeah, yeah, whatever." She told me to hold on while she ordered a ginger-peppermint tea and a muffin. The server's voice came through Tommie's mouthpiece, told Tommie she looked very Christmassy in her red top and green pants. After that she came back to the phone. "You're using avoidance behavior as a defense mechanism. Stop being a coward and face—"

"Well, fuck you too. Don't spit that Norma Rae therapy bullshit at me. You went to Galveston, spent a few months with Nurse Ratched, and came back a regular Freud."

Tommie introduced me to the click.

She'd brought up my pain and I'd brought up her therapy issues.

I slapped the phone against my head, cursed.

I closed my eyes. Wished I were riding down Pacific Coast Highway in a convertible, top down, all of my cares blowing into the ocean breeze as I headed up into wine country, maybe to Oakland. I'd always wanted a convertible as a second car, my weekend car. Shit, as much money as we spent on friggin' attorney fees on this damn paternity suit, I could've had one.

I took a breath, tried not to get too worked up, tried not to cry any more useless tears.

I called Tommie back.

She answered, "What?"

"Tommie, what I just said . . . I apologize." Everything about me was heavy. "Don't sit on my nerves like that. Remember who you're talking to. I used to change your Pampers."

"And I'll be changing your Depends."

"Oh, please. I'm only six years older than you."

"Six dog years." Sounded like she was sipping on her tea, eating her muffin. "So be nice or I'll come to whatever convalescent home you're in and kick out the plug on your life support."

That eased the tension a little, but not much.

She asked, "Well, since everybody is asking, and you won't say, I guess I have to ask—"

"Don't."

"Have you heard anything about Tony's DNA test? She his baby momma or what?"

"Where are you?"

"In the kiddie section of the bookstore."

"You saying that to fuck with me?"

"What? Oh, no, no. Straight up, I'm buying a book for . . . for my neighbor's little girl. And don't trip, nobody can hear me talking about family business. Whassup with the DNA?"

I took a hard breath. "Tommie, will you give it a break?"

"We need to face this, Livvy."

"I don't want to do this."

"Stop walking around the pink elephant."

I snapped, "Stop stressing me the fuck out."

She snapped back, "You're stressing me out too."

"I don't call you to stress you out. I'm not there to stress you out."

"You're flying all over the country and with all these crazy people in the world blowing up buildings I keep thinking you're going to end up on a plane with Bin Laden."

"Baby, Bin Laden doesn't want to fuck with me right about now."

Both of us backed down.

ARE YOU A WOMAN BETRAYED? taunted me.

I took a hard breath, sat on the floor, my head between my knees, eyes closed. "I'm just . . . all this drama . . . these attorney fees . . . eight fucking thousand in attorney fees . . . court papers because he fucked around and . . . shit . . ."

That was when the tears came. I shivered and choked. I was feeling lonely and fat and unattractive. I'd gained so much weight that my body didn't feel like it was my body anymore.

After I told Tommie all of that, I wiped my eyes, grabbed a tissue, and blew my nose.

She softened her tone, "It's gonna be okay."

"Can we please get off the phone now?"

"Hold on."

She was at the cash register paying for a book. The cashier's voice came through and I heard her complimenting Tommie on her frosted makeup and reindeer socks. Then she asked Tommie if she played basketball. I could see my little sister now, tall and dressed in solid colors, long-sleeve shirt, her long hair braided and hanging down her back.

I went to the bathroom and grabbed some tissue, blew my nose again.

She came back on the line. "Stop blowing snot bubbles in my earpiece."

"Wait . . . wait. You're wearing frosted makeup?"

"Don't start. I know it can be bad for my skin."

"That is . . . Damn, Tommie. Make sure you cleanse so you don't break out."

"Don't change the subject. You're making the ugly crying face?"

"Wait. Red shirt, green pants, frosted makeup, and ugly reindeer socks?"

"Hey, I work at Pier 1. It's the Christmas sale. What do you expect?"

"That's so fugly." I chuckled. *Fugly* was one of our family phrases. It meant "fucking ugly." "And yeah, I'm making the ugly crying face."

We talked while she hurried down to Farmer's Market to get a banana, then as she hustled back into Pier 1. Customer after customer stopped her for decorating suggestions. If they only knew how hideous her apartment looked. Sounded like the store was crowded. It took her a moment to make it back to the break room. She was moving a lot, no doubt putting on her blue apron and name tag and that cheesy button that says "ASK ME HOW YOU CAN GET 10% OFF!"

She asked me, "What's the worst thing that could happen with you and Tony?"

"God." I sniffled, wiped my eyes with my palm. "You sound like Momma."

"Would your world end?"

I blew my nose again. "Can we end this conversation, or at least change the subject?"

"You gonna be okay, Livvy?"

"Head hurts. I need a sleeping pill."

"Take a Tylenol PM."

"No, I need one six feet tall with nice-sized hands and feet."

My baby sister howled.

"I'm not joking." I blew my nose again. "Need an orgasm to get rid of this headache."

"What do those feel like?"

"Headaches or orgasms?"

"That works?"

"Headaches, cramps, depression, you'd be surprised what a good O can fix."

Tommie just turned twenty-three and hadn't had one decent sexual experience. When I was her age, I had my esthetician license, was shacking up with Tony, playing wifey, making love like rabbits, and making plans for us to get married.

Her break was over. She had to hit the floor and smile at the customers. Now I wanted to keep talking to her. But I told her I had to pack and get ready for the morning.

We ended the conversation with kisses and I love yous.

I walked to the front window, looked down at the courtyard. People were in front of the fireplace, but I didn't see anyone I might be interested in having a conversation with. Slow night. The Christmas tree was almost decorated. Right after that my cell phone rang again. I thought Tommie was calling back, or maybe it was Frankie's turn to call and harass me.

Antonio Barrera popped up on the caller ID. My husband was calling.

Numbness ran through me. The room turned colder.

I didn't answer. Just paced the suite, phone glowing, vibrating in my hand.

When the vibrating was done, I held the phone another minute. It didn't beep; he didn't leave a voice message. Minutes later I called him back. I let it ring once, long enough for my cellular number to display on his caller ID. Then I hung up. Our way of communicating without talking. His: *Are you okay? I miss you.* Mine: *Life is great. I'm doing okay.*

I held down the red button until the cell phone turned off.

I kept going back to the ad that stirred me, read it over and over.

ARE YOU A WOMAN BETRAYED? I'M A MAN CHEATED ON TRYING TO UNDERSTAND HIS PAIN. ISO HAND-HOLDING AND PASSION. ONLY THE SERIOUS NEED APPLY.

I stared at that screen, my fingers hovering over the keyboard, moving in bicycle motions, like anxious legs suspended in air, getting closer to the keys with each breath.

I clicked the ad.

The stranger's objective was for consenting adults to meet and "To get together during the day and both go home with a smile and a twinkle in our eyes. This would be my first time being involved in an indiscretion. My purpose is not to hurt anyone, but there comes a time when the pain has to be stopped. I'm searching for that excitement again, that special feeling of passion. I need passionate kisses, hand-holding, cuddling. Maybe I am dreaming."

I mumbled, "Excitement. Searching for excitement."

My fingers in my locks, I walked away from the computer, showered, looked over my changing body, pinched more than an inch of fat, damned how the pounds had come on so fast, damned Tony and that skinny bitch. When I made it through that wave of anger and sadness, I washed my face with a special gel, then smoothed on skin renewal booster before using a cream around my eyes and lips to keep my skin from wrinkling too soon, tied a satin scarf over my locks, put on my pajamas and thick socks.

I cleaned up my room, folded my gray uniform, flossed again, packed everything I wouldn't need, kept moving so I could keep unwanted thoughts from clinging to my mind.

There was only so much I could do.

I went back to my computer. I was about to turn it off.

ONLY THE SERIOUS NEED APPLY.

I typed in my e-mail address, paused, then typed in my message.

FROM: BIRD
I AM A WOMAN BETRAYED. I HAVE BEEN CHEATED ON. I DON'T
UNDERSTAND. NOT SURE IF I EVER WILL. I CANNOT FLY. I CAN-
NOT SIT. I AM RESTLESS.

Livvy

The tears came as soon as I hit ENTER.

Regret became the platinum ring around my throat.

Head in my hands, eyes closed, I remembered when Momma used to stress over men. Couldn't remember all the uncles we had until she found the man who loved her unconditionally.

When I was much younger, I asked Momma what was marriage all about.

She said, "The end."

Then I asked what that meant. She smiled and gave no answer.

"Does that mean it's about children, getting a big house, stuff like that?"

"Children ain't guaranteed. A house ain't home. In the big picture, it's about the end."

"I'm confused. You gonna tell me what that means?"

"Momma can't do all of your thinking for you, Livvy. You'll figure that out on your own. All you need to know is this, when all is said and done, it's about the end."

"That's okay. I'll ask Frankie."

"If Miss Know It All had a clue, she wouldn't keep getting herself in situations. Momma say don't do it, Frankie does it anyway, and you're following right behind her. You might as well ask Tommie. Hell, Tommie is the only one who listens and might ever figure it out."

"Tommie's like . . . She's not old enough to know nothing about nothing."

"You still arguing instead of listening."

"I am listening."

She said, "Grown folks are often blind to what a child sees."

"You sound like that old man on *Kung Fu*."

My thoughts moved away from Momma, back to my husband. For a while I closed my eyes and wished I could go back in time to the day before I met him, change everything.

I was twenty-two. That year I'd gone solo to this Halloween party in Ladera Heights, the biggest house at the end of the block with a huge backyard overlooking La Cienega Boulevard. An adults-only party thrown by this mogul in the music industry who did it up big time. Either dim lighting or tea lights were everywhere. African art, both sculptures and paintings. Stuffed cats and jack-o'-lanterns lining the walkways. Spooky and sexy all at once.

And inside, on both levels, it was pretty dark. Dry ice machines created smoke. Lots of exotic foods and plenty of booze, enough alcohol to make everyone want to sign up for rehab by sunrise. Costumes ranged from the absurd to the near childish, fantasies and fetishes represented in full force: schoolgirl uniforms, bondage clothes, and adult versions of superhero costumes.

I had on my devil costume: leather bustier and leather pants. Every man I walked by would tell me that he had been bad and wanted to visit my hot spot.

As soon as I made it to the room that was the official dance floor for the party, I saw a sister in a big Afro, miniskirt, and thigh-high boots on the dance floor doing her thing.

That was Frankie. My other big and tall sister.

I made my way through the crowd and asked her, "You supposed to be Angela Davis?"

"I'm Foxy Brown."

"You look like Angela Davis."

"Whatever."

"Some of these sisters are kinda skanky."

"They have prizes for best costumes."

"Is naked a costume?"

"It is tonight. The most naked girl with the best body always wins."

"Damn. So this the kinda place you hang out at."

"Stop cock-blocking and dance with somebody."

I started dancing with someone dressed like a pimp: pink polyester suit with a red shirt, matching hat, white patent leather stack-heel shoes with goldfish in the heels, the whole nine.

I told him, "Nice costume."

"What costume?"

"Oh shit. Never mind."

Me and Frankie were side by side, rocking the room McBroom style.

Frankie told me that it was the kind of party where school-teachers wore masks and makeup, had three shots and let the whore in them run free. *Blackula* was playing on television screens in almost every room. Music was loud, bumping hard, lots of nasty dancing, and with all the masks and costumes, you didn't know who you were dancing with. It was like Mardi Gras.

Then I saw Dracula, his foreign eyes watching me. Golden skin, wavy hair slicked back.

Dracula adjusted his mask, followed me. The living dead followed the fallen angel.

Drink in hand, I left Frankie on the floor and strolled outside, admired the property and moved beyond the waterfalls in the backyard. A circular bar with bartenders in costumes was in the far corner. People were grabbing drinks and vanishing out into that private part of the yard, only their laughs and sensual sounds letting you know what spots were already taken.

The golden-skinned Dracula in the midnight mask stayed on my footsteps.

I stumbled over a woman. She had on a cat's mask, a black

see-through cat suit, her hair funky and Afrocentric. Cat Woman with dark skin. She was on her knees, pleasing Batman.

He jerked. "Ouch."

I shrieked. "Oh, damn . . . oh, damn . . . I am so so so sorry."

Cat Woman laughed and I saw her braces. She went back to handling her business.

I was so embarrassed, had never seen anything like that, and I broke away from my wide-eyed stare and hurried back to the rest of the party, pretty much ran into Dracula. He had his mask pulled back, showing his chiseled face. His hair was wavy, combed back.

I told him, "You might not want to go over there."

"Pretty wild, huh?"

"Think I almost made Batman get circumcised by Cat Woman."

Again, I walked away. When I was at the back door, I looked back. He had an accent that sounded provocative. He'd only said a few words, but they were hot, sensual.

He was so different from what I was used to. Very erotic.

I smiled, held the door open. Dracula pulled his cape away and followed.

He asked, "What's your name?"

"Beelzebub. Where you from?"

"Transylvania."

We played that game and laughed our way to the pool room. A lady dressed like a witch was on the pool table with her legs wrapped around a shirtless man in army fatigues. G.I. Joe was tonguing and grinding the hell out of the Wicked Witch of the West in front of a room filled with French maids, Spider-man, Darth Vader, and Wonder Woman.

That wasn't my kind of party, but I loved it all the same.

Dracula followed me wherever I went. He brought me drinks, food, spoiled me.

He said, "I want to know all about you."

"Not much to know."

He asked me what I did for a living. I told him that I had just started working as an educator for Dermalogica, a skincare company. He told me that he was a vascular surgeon at UCLA.

"What's a vascular surgeon?"

"I operate on the cardiovascular system. Routine operations."

"Like what?"

"Arterial blood vessel bypass surgery, repair of abdominal aortic aneurysms, insertion of synthetic grafts for dialysis access."

"With all those ten-dollar words, bet you did good on your SAT."

Again he asked me my name. I told him I was Olivia, but people called me Livvy.

His name was Antonio, but everyone called him Tony.

Anonymity was gone and we were no longer strangers.

I told him I was from Inglewood by way of good old South Central.

He was born in Quito, Ecuador, raised in Hermosa Beach since he was a teenager.

I said, "That explains the accent."

"You have the accent."

We danced a little while, and for a few songs he taught me how to salsa.

Then we walked around the side of the house. A basketball and a hoop were there.

I picked up the ball, dribbled, wanted to drive in for a layup, but shot from where I was.

Swoosh.

He said, "Easy shot with nobody guarding you."

I groaned. "If I didn't have on heels and leather . . ."

I was slimmer, quicker back then, an insecure woman who used arrogance as her shield.

He didn't back away. "Sounds like shorty is a shit talker."

"Shorty? You're barely taller than I am."

"Tall enough to . . . Damn you're quick."

"Shit, think I just broke my heel."

I didn't. I took my pumps off anyway, put them to the side, walked the driveway barefoot and picked up the ball, dribbled, did a few crossovers, went to the free-throw line, got my shoulders square to the basket, cocked my right wrist, left hand on the side of the ball and right hand behind, right foot in front of left, feet shoulder-wide, focused on the whole basket.

Swoosh.

He clapped his hands. "Impressive."

"You don't want none of this."

He grinned like he wanted all of this. I chewed my bottom lip and blushed.

Right about then, Frankie came outside looking for me. I introduced her to Tony.

She asked, "You have any brothers?"

I gave her the look, the one that told her to stop cock-blocking.

She left, laughing, drink in hand, wagging her ass back toward the party.

A slow record came on and we danced the dance of people high on the spirits. Tony flattered me, touched me, put his face close to mine, his beard grazing my neck as he whispered in my ear, his accent so provocative and as erotic as his words, as stimulating as his promises. He put his heavy hand on my shoulder, let his fingers trace down my back to my butt.

We kissed.

And just like that, we became inseparable.

You've got mail.

That came from my computer, startled me. It was the response from a man betrayed.

I e-mailed him again. He had insomnia, was stressing. Just like me.

He invited me into a private chat room.

In the back of my mind, I heard Momma telling me that it was about the end.

Tommie

"Hi, young lady. I'd like to look at this rug."

"No problem," I tell her.

I'm just getting on the floor at work before a middle-aged black woman spots me, maneuvers around all the white girls on the floor, and comes over to me. She's short, salt-and-pepper hair, a round woman wearing thick glasses; reminds me of my paternal grandmother.

I ask her, "What size do you need?"

She tells me, "Six by nine."

"We have those right . . . right . . . Here you go. Would you like to see a rug pad?"

"Love your voice. It's pretty, like a singer. Sarah Vaughan comes to mind."

"Thank you. Would you like to get a rug pad, also? They only cost five dollars, and you can cut them so you can use them under different rugs if you like."

"I'll take one. My Lord, my Lord. How did you get that burn on your face?"

She cringes, then sounds sad, and that rattles me for a moment.

I struggle with a smile.

I say, "Happened . . . The burn is from a long time ago."

"You're too pretty to have something like that marking your face."

"Uh . . ." I lose my momentum, then regroup. "Do you . . . Do you have any kids?"

"No man is ever gonna want you with your face like that."

I ask her, "Do you have any kids?"

"Kids. Of course I have kids. And a husband. And grand-children. And—"

"Then the rug . . . I mean the rug pads will be perfect for you."

She scrunches her face. "Rug pads?"

"Keeps the rug from sliding, so your kids . . . I guess your grandkids'll have fewer accidents if they run through . . . You get the picture."

"Lord, have mercy. Was that burn an accident?"

I ignore her and ask, "What colors do you have in the room?"

"I dunno. Let me think . . . peach, yellow, mauve . . ."

"Know what pillows would look great with that rug? Let me show you."

I keep talking, never giving her time to ask any more questions. By the time I get in control and finish doing the "up sale" routine, pushing as much merchandise as I can, she's buying three rugs, rug pads, all kinds of candles, candle trays, pillows, and two bar stools.

Everyone in the store is busy, so I have to take her mountain of merchandise to her car.

She gives me a five-dollar tip and tells me, "And I'm telling you this, old black woman to young black woman. Get a perm; get rid of that African hairstyle. Put some color in your hair, and get that earring out of your eyebrow if you want to make it in this world. Maybe see a doctor about your face because the right man ain't gonna look at you twice if—"

"Thanks, but I have to get back inside. Our seasonal sale is keeping us busy."

She nods. "Remember what I told you."

"Thanks. Happy holidays."

I hurry by cars and see my reflection, the history on my face keeping up with me no matter how fast I move. My image meets me in the reflection of the glass doors as I rush back inside Pier 1, smiling. Then a hundred mirrors echo the burn on my face.

First chance I get, I leave the floor and go to the break room. My left hand wants to shake, but I won't let it. The memory tries to come back, and I can't stop it.

Some days history is silent.

Today history screams.

$\mathcal{F}$rankie

Running. Riesling. Sex.
  Those are my three vices.

First and last, I'm a runaholic. I started pounding the pavement right after my divorce. That was seven years and damn near seventy pounds ago. I was married at twenty-six. By the new millennium standards, a bona fide child bride. That screeched to a halt when this heifer—a bulimic bitch from Boston—sent me a Polaroid of her and my husband butt-ass naked in my bed. Bitch was nice enough to make sure the Fed Ex man left the porno pic on my doorstep on Christmas Eve. Even put the photo inside a very nice Hallmark card, wishing me happy holidays and a prosperous new year. Manipulating skanks can be so cold and calculating. I asked my lovey-dovey-hubby who the fuck that was, and all he could do was look like he was about to have a stroke and shout, *"Where you get that?"*

And boy did we argue and fight.

He started coming at me with crap like, "Well, whoever she is, she ain't fat enough to have her own zip code. Look at your chain-smoking ass. You walk around smelling like the butt of a cigarette and, what, you expect me to pass that up? You're a dead fuck anyway. Learn to suck a dick and move your ass and you might be worth something. Hell, fucking you is one step below jacking off."

Five seconds later I had to call the paramedics because I had shoved my chubby foot so far up his narrow butt he had to get an ass-ectomy in order to get my three-inch pump surgically removed.

But, hey, when I look back at those photos, I was a little on the fat side, the sister he dumped me for wasn't. Didn't matter. We were both immature and loving on borrowed time. Actually I should thank him for the motivation. I tossed the pork out the fridge, gave the red meat to a neighbor I couldn't stand, bought some running shoes, put one foot in front of the other, and changed my own life. Reebok and some open road is better than Jenny Craig any damn day.

Wine is simple. I love me a glass of Riesling.

And sex, well, ain't a lot been jumping off. I don't think any woman wants to spend that time between Thanksgiving and Valentine's Day living and loving a capella, while everybody else was getting presents and flowers. Too many parties to go to, the kind where people show up in couples. Hmmm. Well, the last man I was seeing (the last one I considered a boyfriend, meaning he was on the A-list, meaning I was seen in public with him, my sisters met him, and my friends knew him), that ended eight months back. A long time to be without fondness, compliments, and genuine affection.

That's not to say that I've been using all of this real estate for a paperweight. Time to time, I gets mine. My old A-list boyfriend is not to be confused with the ones who fit into the B-list category. The B-list is the occasional date and sex category.

The C-lists were the dicks in a glass jar, straight-up booty calls who came to my rescue and put out a raging fire, the ones who showed up after dark and left before the morning newspaper was tossed on the front porch. Booty calls don't count. Those were all about tension relief, when a man stunt doubled for a worn-out dildo and hooked you up before you went postal. Those were the sexual escapades that would never make it on your résumé of carnal activities. You denied them the way Bill denied Monica. No photos, no videos, no stained dresses, no proof.

After almost three seasons of C-listing, I was ready to find me a potential for the A-list. The problem was that I was thirty-plus, the age where a woman wanted to find a man so she could have a child. The problem with that was that men my age were trying to find a child to make their woman.

I said nothing from nothing left nothing, posted my info out at Yahoo!, BlackVoices, NetNoir, Match-dot-com. That had me as nervous as a felon in a high-speed chase because I was scared that somebody I knew, maybe an ex—especially an ex—would see my picture out there with that cute header *RUBY DEE SEEKS HER OSSIE*. But at least I wasn't as direct as the sisters who had pictures of themselves with their lips wrapped around bananas. If my ex (pick one) ever saw some crap like that, he would call me up laughing so hard that he'd be barely able to get out his words, "Is it that bad? Have you stooped down that low? Damn, Frankie. Shit so bad you have to advertise to meet a man?"

So anyway, I wiped my apprehension on my jeans, dipped into my reservoir of courage and downloaded my cute little picture. Silver bracelets, skin tanned from working out in the sun. Five-foot-nine, down to one-hundred-sixty pounds (actually one-hundred-seventy, but what's the point of being on the Internet if you're not going to lie?), sexy legs, in search of single, widowed, or divorced—the last two being the types of men that, ten years ago, I wouldn't have touched with a ten-foot pole. Especially the widowed. Last thing I wanted was a widow man who had the ghost of a dead soul mate following him around like Michael Myers on Halloween.

Then I sat back and waited.

The first day, not a single e-mail. Talk about feeling cyber-rejected like a mofo. Even e-mailed myself to make sure it was working.

I mean *zero* e-mails.

Then the next day, I logged on and, wow, over sixty e-mails. Forty-five with pictures attached. Half sent photos of themselves butt naked, holding on to their coffee stirrers. If that was the way a brother said hello, taking me to Bible study wasn't the first thing on his mind.

Three were from women who wanted to know ARE YOU LIB-ERAL? and LET ME LOVE YOU LIKE NO MAN CAN and WANT TO MEET ME AND MY HUSBAND IN LAGUNA NIGEL?

Delete. Deeeeee-lete. De-fucking-lete.

Talk about being a magnet for losers.

And to make things worse, I should've been more specific and said no Jheri curls, brothers who wear pink curlers, played-out pimps, wanna-be gangstas, street pharmacists, or gold-tooth-wearing hustlers. The list was shorter, but would never be that damn short.

I didn't delete the cute ones. Or the ones that had coffee stir-rers the size of my arm. Talk about a leg-crossing challenge. I kept a copy of those perverts in my Personal Filing Cabinet, added them to my own private collection. Never know when I might be alone on a cold, rainy night, sipping wine and need-ing a little visual stimulation to get my juices flowing.

And the white men, they e-mailed in droves. Sent all kinds of virtual cards, called me two hundred kinds of beautiful. Damn. But I had to update my profile to let them know that Willie Wonka wouldn't be getting into this chocolate factory.

Then, this brother sends me this pic and damn, he looked like Denzel on his Oscar-winning night. I moaned out a sweet hallelujah and smiled. I did not hesitate to e-mail him back. He was the kind of brother you'd want to put on a Santa suit and come down your chimney every night of the year. First we were talking about investment strategies, mutual funds, going over all sorts of red-hot funds that sizzled. After a few late-night con-versations our exchanges became pretty hot and heavy. What's the point of being online if you're not going to dim the lights and talk some freaky talk?

Then he typed, "Let's meet."

"You don't waste any time."

"Not when I see what I want."

"You haven't seen me yet."

"Meet me at Reign on Friday night."

I typed, "Around eight sound cool?"

"Perfect. I'll be the one holding the yellow roses."

I valet-parked and stepped into Reign, my sashay as smooth as butter pecan ice cream, glam to the bone. The place was humming. Reign was a New York–style, trendy hangout made of marble, polished steel, and plastic smiles. A 90210 watering hole where broke-ass people congregated over apple martinis and pretended they weren't broke-ass people; social drinkers about to socialize their way into an AA meeting. Brothers had Maxwell and D'Angelo demeanors. Sisters were divafied, weaves as seamless as their panty lines, most of them lounging at the bar, where the bad lighting hid every flaw.

Five after eight. No Denzel in sight.

Then this sister in a short dress sashayed in, a B-list actress strutting in full diva mode, her backside so well defined, so big and round that brothers stopped breathing and started watching her moneymaker like it was the NBA finals. Every woman gave her the "that slut ho bitch" look.

The claws came out and the mumbles began.

"Bitch can't even act."

"Only reason she works is because she licks coke off the director's dick."

"She wears more makeup than a transvestite."

I crept to the ladies' room and checked myself out, hoping my outfit didn't make my teaspoon of rooty tooty fresh and fruity booty look flatter than Arkansas after a tornado. I was in a hot spot filled with man-hungry women and women-hungry men, people who were preoccupied with superficial attraction, so all of this 38-32-42 was in the mirror for a few moments, doing some last-minute primping.

I walked around the bar comparing my natural locks to all the fake hair, my café au lait complexion to the ones that looked like a whiter shade of pale, then to the ones that were dark and lovely, wondering how my black dress compared to their shiny, stretchy, and tight clothes.

Still no sign of my damn Denzel. Ten after eight. He was ten minutes late.

I was taking out my cellular phone when somebody said, "Frankie?"

I turned around and saw a face from my past. Felt like I'd been injected with potassium chloride. He was fine as hell, dressed in grays and blacks under a leather jacket, hair short and neat.

I said, "Nick?"

Nicolas Coleman. An old A-list lover. A very A-list lover. Always awkward running into somebody you'd been intimate with, especially when you had hoped he wanted more from you.

I made myself smile. "Hey, stranger."

"Didn't recognize you at first." He looked surprised, like he had said my name, but still wasn't sure that it was me. He finally got his words together. "Damn. You are looking good."

"You too."

Then he moved into my personal space, touched me, hugged me. I wasn't ready for that. All of a sudden whatever karma we had shared, the energy he had left inside me, tingled to life.

"Look at you," I said, pulling away. "I see your books all over. Big baller shot caller."

"Your locks . . . wow . . . nice. You . . . damn." Again, his expression told me that he was surprised I'd lost so much weight, but he didn't know how to phrase his thoughts. "You are looking good."

I gave up a morsel of a nervous laugh. "You just said that."

Our hair let us know how long it had been since we'd seen each other. Last time I saw him his hair was in twisties and my hair was in a bob. Since then, I've cut it all damn near to the bone and it's grown back, framed my face and hung down my back and over my shoulders, colored deep brown with golden tips. Back then his hair was longer, hip and bohemian, and now he was clean-cut.

I said, "I see a wedding ring."

He smiled.

I asked, "Nicole?"

"Nah." The spark in his eyes dwindled, then came back. "Somebody else."

"Somebody else?"

Back then, his whole world was about this girl Nicole. Always Nick and Nicole.

He got off the subject, asked me how my sisters were doing, yada, yada.

I went back to what was on my mind. "So you and Nicole finally parted ways."

"We did."

There was a moment of silence between us, a slice of quiet so small, yet it was louder than the clatter in this joint. In that silence I thought about that night he was having so many problems. The night he was coming unglued. His family was tripping, his preacher-man father didn't like his work. Nicole was driving him insane. And he called me, needed to talk.

We met for drinks.

Conversation.

Back to my place.

More drinks.

The fourth glass of Riesling kicked in and I jumped bold, told him to *snap the fuck out of it, that confused, selfish bitch doesn't care about you*, then kissed him and risked rejection. Bold enough to kick off my shoes, slap my titty in his mouth, put my hands in his pants, and lead him into my bed. I straight up offered my body as a salve for his anguish. Or took his to salve my own.

Penetration changed everything, especially amongst friends.

Back then I had a boyfriend. A decent brother that I just couldn't get into, not on the level that I wanted, especially when I wanted somebody else. And I knew Nick was hooked on Nicole. So, Nick probably saw me as . . . Never mind, I'm not even going to go there.

And now he was wearing a wedding ring and I was surfing for prospects out on the Internet.

He asked, "What happened to your book?"

"Well, lots of rejections. Then I got into buying property. Had to help Livvy with her wedding. And Tommie . . ." I shrugged. That simple question about my book, especially coming from him, taunted me. "Did some traveling. Brazil. Amsterdam. Other places. Got sidetracked."

This brother in a black suit appeared down near the end of the bar. He smiled at me. I perked up and changed my body language, moved away from Nick, told him that I thought I saw my date. But when the black suit got closer, he tapped Nick on the shoulder. Both of them laughed then did that one-arm-man-hug thing that men do so people will know they're friends, but won't think they have sugar in their tanks, then they did a handshake, the kind that let you know they were fraternity brothers.

Nick introduced me to his homie, a guy named André. Told me he was a comedian. In Hollywood, actors, comedians, and singers came a dime a dozen, half-priced on Wednesday. Everybody was working on a screenplay or a one-person show in between waiting tables.

André said, "I was in the back chilling out at the bar. Lot of talent back there."

I said, "Oh, really?"

Talent meant eye candy that was somewhere between an eight and a dime piece.

André said, "And you working that dress like a Jamaican with ten jobs. I saw your fine ass walking around here giving brothers whiplash. You got a walk that could put Viagra out of bid'ness."

"Out of bid'ness?" I repeated, mocking him.

"Out of motherfucking bid'ness. I was about to slide you my damn number, fo' sheezy."

We all laughed. And just like that, I thought André was the coolest of the cool.

Nick apologized. "I didn't know there was another room."

André said, "That bar is hopping."

"Oh, damn," I said. "There's another bar?"

André pointed toward a narrow opening that I assumed was for employees only.

I should've rushed away and looked for my Denzel, but I couldn't leave. Something was anchoring me here with Nick. A strong current with an unbreakable undertow.

"Man, you missed it. This fat, gap-toothed motherfucker . . . looked like Yoko Ono with a jacked-up Afro . . ." André was on a roll, cracking up. ". . . like Professor Klump in a tight red suit . . . and a green polka-dot bow tie . . . motherfucker dressed like a Christmas present to a Muslim. I'm putting that shit in my script."

André couldn't stop laughing. He fanned himself and told Nick he'd be right back, headed toward the bathroom, left me and my old potential A-list lover by ourselves.

Nick said, "We need to keep in touch."

There was a moment between us, or maybe it was just me. Things we did together, the old pictures and birthday cards I still have in a shoebox, all those thoughts gave me a warm, fuzzy feeling.

My mouth opened to say we should keep in contact, that I missed him, stuff like that.

But I don't know what the hell happened; something went wrong . . . went south inside of me.

I said, "Well, I don't think I'd want my husband keeping in touch with women he used to sleep with. And, I'm here with somebody. So that would be disrespectful, don't you think?"

"As friends, that's all I was saying."

There was another moment of silence. Something about the way he said that made me feel so small. Like what had happened between us . . . like it didn't happen.

"We fucked, Nick." Those words came out of me so fast that I thought somebody was snapping out my thoughts. It jarred me as much as it did him. "Nick, keep it real, and we can walk away with a little respect. We were never friends. At least you were never mine."

"What? We ran together, we read each other's work—"

"I would've had the decency to tell you I was getting married, or invited you to the wedding. You know how I found out? Was flipping through *Ebony*, and bam, an article about you—and your wife. Kinda whacked. Even if I didn't invite you, I would've told you."

There it was. What was behind my smile. The resentment. I put it out there, very abrupt, very hard. There was bitterness, some I didn't really know about until now.

That hit him hard. But my own words had left me rattled.

The worst kind of ex was an ex who didn't know he was an ex.

He said, "So, if you saw the article in *Ebony* . . . then you knew I didn't marry Nicole."

Ooops. And just like that, my little faux pas had risen, and here I was—straight busted. Yeah, I knew about him and the African wife. And yeah, I reminded him about the woman who rejected his ass. Maybe the part of me that was hurting wanted to open up the part of him that used to hurt. Damn. There I was, being a petty bitch in high heels. An abrupt numbness made me feel two inches tall. For the first time in a long time, I was speechless.

"It's cool." He nodded. "Take care, Frankie."

"Wait. Nick." I opened my purse. "Here's my card. Keep in touch, if you like."

Nick raised his palms; his smile wounded, his eyes vexed, told me that it was nice seeing me again, wished me much success and moonwalked away, left me standing like a statue of rejection and holding my damn card in my hand.

Damned penetration always changed everything.

Nobody wanted to be on someone's B- or C-list, especially if they were on your A-list.

The secondary bar was hidden like Bruce Wayne's bat-cave. A larger crowd was back there lounging and flirting. I circled the bar twice, began feeling kind of stupid for being stood up. Stupid for running into Nick and tripping like that. In my head

I was rewriting that last friggin' moment, not switching into PMS mode and letting any of that old animosity out. Damn, on top of that, I'd been stood up, and didn't want to do an about-face and go back out there right now, didn't want to pass by him.

Then there was a tap on my shoulder.

A smooth, baritone voice said, "Frankie?"

This gap-toothed, nappy-headed, Buddha-belly brother in a fire red suit and polka-dot bow tie was standing in my face holding a dozen yellow roses.

All I could say was, "Uh, yeah?"

"I was getting worried." He chuckled with glee. "I was wondering if you got lost."

"I . . . well . . . I was up front." Everything inside my head started rocking like I was on the *Riverboat Queen* during a monsoon, no Dramamine in sight. Next thing I knew he had kissed my cheek and flowers were in my hand. "Wow. Thanks for the flowers."

He said, "Just in time. Let's head upstairs before we lose our reservations."

"Upstairs?" *Shit.* That meant I had to walk by everybody and be scrutinized by both the gold diggers and the wankstas. Everybody including Mr. A-List. "Oh, yeah. Dinner. Right."

"Follow me. My, my, you are looking lovely."

Yellow roses in hand, I ghost walked through the main area, past all the glam. Nick and André were at the bar; too busy talking to see me. Irritation was in Nick's face, enough for that smile to be turned upside down, so I knew he was telling his homie what had happened between us. I had done that with my bitterness. Felt bad, but that was what I was feeling. I pretended that I didn't see them.

"Holy shit," somebody mumbled, then chuckled. I looked over and it was André looking in my direction, his mouth wide open, laughter creeping up from his chest to his throat.

Nick saw me. Just as much surprise in his eyes. I couldn't look at him. Felt so damn foolish.

My date led me to the hostess; she took us upstairs to the area with dim lights and candles. All eyes were on us. I would've been more comfortable walking with a naked white man.

He pulled my chair out first, then squeezed into his seat and said, "You look stunning."

No, I'm just stunned.

He said, "You can put the flowers down."

"Oh. Yeah."

"After all of our late-night conversations and e-mails, I've looked forward to meeting you face-to-face. Nice to see the face that goes with all of those provocative conversations."

I looked at him and remembered what I wanted to forget, thought, oh God, oh God. We had cybersex. And I had actually thought about him—well that picture he had sent me—last night while I was lying in my bed, my hand between my legs, double-clicking my mouse, moaning and squirming and letting out sweet curses, and imagining that me and the man in my mind were going at it like rabbits.

"Well, how was your day, Frankie?"

"What?" I cleared my throat. "Oh. Pretty good."

"Outside of property, any good investments?"

We talked about technology stocks, then some blue chip names that weren't doing too bad, mentioned a few old-fashioned stocks, conversation about hot IPOs that were up four hundred percent.

I shook my head. "Keep away from old-fashioned stocks. I'd gamble on Tyco or Bank One."

"Especially Bank One. Very cheap stock."

That's one thing my choices of men and stock have always had in common. Their potential looked great—guess I've been buying low—but their value has always plummeted overnight.

The waiter came back with salads. That broke our discussion. We ate, sipped our wine, started talking about other things, moved to comfortable topics.

His chubby-cheeked smile was infinite. "Hard to believe that I met you on the Internet."

"Thanks, but you don't have to say that so loud."

He was trying to get his flirt on, but I had moved him from the list of romantic wishes over to the buddy-plan-friend list. Those are the brothers a sister calls when she needs help moving furniture. The men that women need to keep in contact with. Especially if the guy owns a truck.

Like I said, the list was short, but not that short.

He said, "Let me make a quick run to the bathroom."

As he wobbled away, I saw the tofu- and wheat grass-eating people stare at him, glance at me, then shake their heads. So many snickers and whispers.

And why was it when you were out with one guy, you saw all kinds of guys you'd want to share a drink with? If I had come down here by myself, it would've been a damn Urkel convention.

This sucked like a hooker on Sunset.

I wondered if it was like that when I was married, if that was what people did to my husband whenever I walked away from the table. I lowered my eyes, opened my flip phone, and a made a call.

Tommie answered, "You're calling. This is not good."

"Remember the Fat Bastard in that Austin Powers movie?"

"Is he that fugly?"

"Fucking ugly like a mofo."

"No! Frankie, run for the hills."

I looked at the yellow roses, an arrangement that probably cost at least half a C-note. I told her that he was a nice guy, very intelligent, but he's just not the reflection of what I'm looking for in a man, as shallow as it might sound, not physically, not at this moment in my life. Watching him sort of reminded me of my own issues. It cut down to the bone. And I remember how people used to treat me, the jokes, the looks from the skinny people. I'm not that small, not as fit and firm, and my sisters, never will be, so that's why I'm being real cool, very sensitive about how I handle this little fiasco.

"Oh, it gets worse," I told her. "Guess who is in the restaurant."

"Who?"

I ran down the whole thing, what Nick did, what I said, how I lost it. Well, my version.

She said, "The casual relationship between you and Nick has always caused you psychological stress. What you did was in response to your own grieving. You expected a particular response and—"

I pulled the phone from my ear and stared at it like Tommie had lost her mind, took a deep breath, toyed with the shells around my neck, and changed the subject. I asked, "Heard from Livvy?"

"Damn. Traffic is so bad."

"Where are you?"

"On Rosecrans trying to get on the stupid 405."

"Thought you had to work with the rest of the candle pushers."

"Things slowed down. Just got off. Should've gone down Sepulveda."

Tommie told me that she had talked to Livvy not too long ago. Told me that she was snowed in. Hard to believe it was that damn cold anywhere, being out on a cool night in Beverly Hills. She said Livvy broke down crying, but cheered up, cracked jokes, seemed to be holding it together.

I looked at my watch. It was almost nine. I asked, "You going in for the night?"

"Java Lounge at Club 'Bucks."

"Ground is shaking. He must be on the way back."

"Holla."

We hung up.

My date came back, smiling like I was the best thing since unleaded gasoline. I swear to God, he was floating like he was in the Thanksgiving Day parade. So happy to be with me. Just to be with me. I wish more men—well, the ones that I was happy to be with—felt that way about me.

But that's the way it always was. The men who were interested in you, you had no desire for. The ones you wanted didn't want you. And if you did hook up with them, they dumped you for a twenty-year-old, ended up fucking one of your so-called best friends, or chased lesbians.

Anyway. That summed up three of my heartbreaks.

The salads were taken away and our entrees came.

We finished our seafood dinners and he put the meal on his American Express. I offered to pay half. He wouldn't let me. I tried to leave the tip. He wouldn't let me do that either, said that he had asked me out. I thanked him, gathered up my yellow roses, let out a fake yawn, and grabbed my purse.

We left the table, me hiding behind that big bouquet, passing by the hoochies who looked like actresses at a cattle call, trying to audition for the casting couch stuffed with the most money. A corral of wounded queens still trying to figure out how to fuck a guy without getting fucked over.

Then I saw my reflection. New clothes, locks hooked up, thirty-something, smelling as good as good could get, no kids, no husband, nowhere to rush to on a cool night like tonight.

Robertson Boulevard was lit up, holiday lights making the street look like a low-budget version of Vegas at night. Valet pulled my car up and I wanted to run and jump in before it stopped rolling.

My date walked me to the car door. "Nice. My last car was a Benz."

"Thanks."

When brothers saw the streetlights reflecting off the side of my cabriolet, my stock went up; their eyes started looking at my caboose like they wanted to ride this train.

"Riding with the top down," my date said. "Won't you get cold?"

"I turn the heat on full blast."

Valet pulled his car up behind mine. A 7 Series BMW with personalized plates: FINE BLK MN.

Mr. Delusional must have a lot of fun-house mirrors at his crib.

This was the end of what I thought would be a Dionysian

evening that led to Riesling kisses and fuck-me smiles by Christmas, then us naked, holding champagne, saying happy New Year.

And just in case, as always, I had an overnight bag in the trunk of my car.

My date asked, "Would you like to continue this conversation some—"

"I really need to get home."

He said, "Call me and let me know you made it in."

"I will. Thanks for everything."

That was a lie. I sped down Robertson, my Inobe CD playing as loud as I could stand and as soulful as I wanted to become. I took a deep breath. I was a prisoner who had just been paroled.

$\mathcal{F}$rankie

Sheer pande-fucking-monium.

The restaurant next door to 'Bucks had more security than the Democratic National Convention. Orange cones blocked the entrance to the best parking like the velvet rope at an exclusive club. That side lot was stacked with high-end cars: 350ZXs, Escalades, BMW Z4s and X5s, Mercedes, Jags.

You'd think I'd pulled up at the Taj Mahal.

This was Java Lounge at 'Bucks; 'Bucks meaning Starbucks, the one in Ladera, an area filled with fast-food joints, strip malls, and car dealerships; where six lanes of traffic on La Cienega, six on La Tijera, and six on Centinela came to a grinding halt. Magic owned the coffeehouse, TGIF, and Fatburger, so the air was filled with the scent of exotic coffees, hot wings, and over-cooked hamburger meat. So you wouldn't forget who owned the spot, murals of Magic Johnson's grinning face were all over the place. Next door to 'Bucks was TGIF. That was where the chickenheads and wankstas hung out, sporting Sean John, Rocawear, Enyce, and Phat Farm like ghetto-fab Italian suits.

'Bucks was where the poets, chess players, and musicians came to spread enlightenment with spoken word, have mental wars, and share songs from the heart. Vendors were out front selling candles and cards for Kwanzaa, incense and oils, Kente cloth, other Afrocentric things.

Too wired to go home, too tired to go out, I'd come here to

wind down. And to hang out with Tommie. Needed to vent. I know it might sound stupid, but I was proud of myself for going through with the date and not insulting the fat fugly man and breaking for the door the first chance I got.

I said, "All of this to get an overpriced cup of caramel macchiato."

Tommie said, "Hook me up with a white chocolate mocha."

"Where you going?"

"Looking to see if somebody is here."

Tommie was five-foot-ten, the tallest of us all. I had my leather jacket on, but I was most definitely overdressed for this room. Tommie was a thrift store queen and blended in with the grunginess of the poets. She was wearing tight jeans, a midriff top, a large jean shirt wide open, her brown leather backpack strapped on, holding onto a beige notebook filled with her poetry.

I hadn't seen her in tight jeans in months. And she never showed her stomach, not like that.

She peeped outside, then walked out the side door near the chess players. She came back in the door facing the strip mall and the people smoking and sipping java underneath the outdoor heat lamps. A small performance area had been set up in a corner, and the place was standing room only. A sister was at the microphone, full-figured, D-cups, hair in a big funky Afro, long jean skirt, all that and as sassy as they came, doing her thing, a real sexy piece praising her vagina. She had on a red T-shirt with black letters that read PHAT: PRETTY, HOT, AND TEMPTING. Her words were music, between rap and song, the way she sang praises to her vagina, the faces she was making, the way she was moving, the subtle gestures, she had men licking their lips and fanning themselves.

You can lead a man to water, but you can't make him drink.

You can lead a man to good pussy, but you can't make him eat.

Sisters were laughing and who hooing and snapping fingers, the old schoolers raising candles, the true tech heads holding up their cell phones with their lights on. Some women were slapping hands, and at the same time wondering if their pussy was as good as hers.

Sister brought the house down. After the applause, I asked Tommie, "You performing?"

"Was . . . but . . . nah. Not tonight. Wanted to . . . well . . . I had invited this guy."

My sister wore braids the color of Epsom salt, sort of made me think of her as Storm from the X-Men, had silver earrings in her nose, belly button, and one in her left eyebrow. It all looked good on her, fit her personality. She was an Amazon queen on this block of the universe.

I asked, "A date?"

"Well . . . not exactly."

And in that moment, her slender face looked so sensitive. Her thick bottom lip became pouty, sucked on her top lip, then she chewed on her nut brown skin. Below her left eye, almost on her cheek, was a burn the size of the face of a Timex watch, the mark that reminded me of what I wanted to forget.

She was busy fidgeting, then asking me if she looked okay, making sure everything was in place.

We found a spot and listened to spoken word ranging from the political to the spiritual to the sexual. Most brothers did political pieces, either about oppression, unity, or black-on-black crimes.

Black people can't do nothing together but the Electric Slide.

I was growing tired, but my caramel macchiato would have me up awhile. Tommie was barely sipping on her white chocolate mocha, her eyes still going over the crowd, in search of some guy.

We browsed out front, looked over the things for Kwanzaa. The vendor was passing out conspiracy theory literature and selling T-shirts. I supported the cause and bought a couple, one for Tommie, one for me that said DON'T FORGET KIRSTIN HIGH AND KENITHIA SAAFIR.

We headed across the lot, walking through parked cars.

Tommie said, "I'm worried about Livvy."

"She's put on a lot of weight. I lose a pound, she gains two."

"The more she gains, the more she looks like Momma."

I took out my cell phone and dialed Livvy's number. It went straight to her voicemail. We left a high-spirited message, passing the phone back and forth, telling her we missed her like crazy.

She asked, "You think it's Tony's baby?"

I grunted. "Fucker."

"Momma always said you can't stop a man from cheating."

"But a baby? Too bad Livvy can't send his ass to jail for fucking her over like that."

Tommie laughed a little. "Like you tried to do to your ex-hubby-wubby."

I bumped her and joined in. "Tried my best."

My starter hubby was in the army. I raised hell, tried to get that ho locked up under article 143 of the UCMJ, one that was there to punish adulterers, but not a damn thing happened. Military looked out for their own. Fuck 'em. I wanted to join the army after high school, needed that college money, but because of height and weight standards . . . whatever. I just would've ended up brainwashed and out in a fucking desert trying to do my best not to become a friggin' POW. My ex-ho for a hubby cheated with that bulimic bitch he met in basic training. Couldn't count the number of times he called me fat.

Tommie said, "You hate Tony?"

"No, I love him. He's family." I shook my head. "I'm just so . . . disappointed."

"He did so much for me. This is such a major letdown."

I took a hard breath. "God, I need a cigarette."

"No, you don't."

"At least get me a milk shake and a dozen Krispy Kremes."

We walked at a slow pace, cool breeze blowing across the lot, street traffic punctuating the calm, leaving my memories behind with each step, knowing that they would all catch up with me later in life.

Tommie went on, "Livvy always shuts down when things get rough."

"Like when Momma died."

Tommie pulled her lips in. "I miss them sweet potato pies."

"Sho 'nuff."

"She made the best sweet potato pies in the whole wide world."

We held hands, our arms swinging back and forth.

I said, "Haveta keep tradition and visit the cemetery."

"Been getting your breasts checked?"

"Not yet."

"Frankie—"

"I know, I know."

"That's where it starts. Remember Aunt Amy, Auntie Alex . . ."

"Guess it . . . guess it scares me. Maybe I'd rather not know."

"Not knowing isn't going to make it go away, not going to make you live longer."

I'd parked near the sheriff's substation. She hopped in my car. I started letting the top down and noticed all the colorful signs, streamers, and frosted decorations advertising Christmas sales in every store window. Hell, Christmas decorations had been up before Halloween. And Thanksgiving decorations probably went up right after the Fourth of July. Holidays overlapped like relationships.

"Wow." Tommie turned around and picked up my bouquet. "Frankie, these are nice roses."

"You want 'em?"

"Nah. That wouldn't be right."

"Lying about how you look should be a felony."

"What did the fugly man say about not looking like his picture?"

"Think I was too stunned to ask. Seeing Nick—"

"Big Dick Nick had you going woo woo woo."

"Hell, yeah." I laughed. "Had to pop a Percodan when he was through with me."

"Somebooty is still sprung on the woo woo woo."

"Seeing Nick, acting like a fool, then seeing fugly standing there with roses . . . it was too much."

I drove around the lot, parked between Ross and Subway. That's where she'd left my old Jeep Wrangler. Well, it was her Jeep now. I'd given it to her as a present after she came back home. She hadn't washed it once since she'd had it. I didn't say anything. I wanted to, but I didn't.

"All that security at TGIF." I pulled my locks into a ponytail. "We turn anything into a club."

"Too bad they don't support the businesses in Leimert Park like this."

I motioned at TGIF. "This'll last 'til somebooty gets shot."

"You are so negative."

"Why does every black club close?" I yawned. "Somebody gets shot."

"Not always."

"Oh really?"

Tommie yawned back. "Sometimes they get stabbed."

"True."

"Speaking of getting shot and stabbed, we gonna invite the rest of the family over?"

I rolled my eyes, something I rarely did. "Half of those fools are Crips, half of 'em Bloods. We put them in the same place we'll end up with a bunch of bloody crippled people."

"Hadn't thought about that. Maybe we can rent Kevlar vests, roll up in there 50 Cent style."

"We'll do our private thing, then maybe—and I do mean maybe—we'll go visit one or two of the older relatives. Maybe hit Blood City on Christmas Eve, roll through Cripville on Christmas."

We sat there for a moment, yawning the night away.

I asked, "What are your long-term plans?"

"Get back in Cal State L.A. Finish up. My New Year's resolution, special for Daddy."

"Get off your ass and don't end up thirty with no skills and no education."

Our parents didn't finish high school, so it's been up to us girls to push each other. No brothers or strong male figures were around to guide and protect us since Daddy died, so we had to guide and protect each other. We didn't grow up in a Norman Rockwell painting, didn't have any doctors or lawyers in our family, never had those kind of role models, so I took responsibility, made sure Livvy had her education and some sort of a marketable skill, and wanted all of us to be the role models for the next generation. Every generation should be better than the one before.

Tommie patted my hand. "I'm going to start paying you more rent next year."

"Just work on getting your shit together."

"Well, maybe I could move to a cheaper area so you can rent your place out."

"No, you're not."

"You can't keep spending and lending me money."

"I don't lend money. I never give more money than I can afford to lose."

She leaned over and kissed my cheek. A couple of brothers passing by saw that and looked at us like we were Rosie O'Donnell and Ellen DeGeneres.

I yelled, "Ain't that kinda party."

One of them yelled back, "Not a party unless a dick's invited."

"We're sisters, asshole. Keep stepping and don't mess up our family moment."

They moved on.

Tommie yawned. "What you want for Christmas?"

"A fallout shelter."

"Get me a shovel and a pick and I'll start on that first thing in the morning."

I chuckled. "What do you want Santa to bring you?"

"Whatever you get me is fine."

She was still looking around, still searching for the mystery man.

Tommie fidgeted. "I've been having real erotic dreams."

"Welcome to the club."

"About this guy."

"Uh huh. The guy you've been looking for all evening."

She laughed and shook her head. "Was I that obvious?"

"What does he look like? What does he do? Give me the juice."

"He has a nice personality. Very caring."

"Is he nice looking? Light, dark, brown, what?"

"A creamy vanilla with a nappy head."

"Maybe we should drive around and look for his ass."

She laughed. "Kinda like Common with an LL body."

"Damn. What's his name and does he have an older brother?"

She blushed.

I smiled, gave her a you-go-girl nudge. She was so innocent when it came to affairs of the heart. She believed in love the way I used to believe in Santa Claus and the Tooth Fairy.

She asked, "Can you be in love with someone and they don't know you exist on that level?"

Once again, I thought about Nick. About evenings spent at bookstores reading each other's work. About something I had initiated and got pissed off when it wasn't fully reciprocated. Yeah, I tripped. It was all about my own expectations, not his desire. Maybe I expected him to be loyal to me, but I knew that people were loyal to their needs, to the emotions that helped them build their dreams.

The bottom line: I owed him an apology. I really did. But they'd be drinking lemonade and ice-skating in hell before he got one.

Tommie interrupted my thoughts, told me, "I wanna be ballin' like you one day."

"Baby, ain't no fun being a queen living in a kingless castle."

"Let down the drawbridge."

"I did. Nobody's coming over but court jesters and peasants with bad credit."

"Then you'd better put a doorbell on the other side of the moat."

"Why is it so hard to find a decent brother?"

"Because you're looking." She cocked her head, thinking. "One time I asked Daddy how he met Momma and he told me that when you stopped looking for your keys, you would find your keys."

"Sounds like some off-the-wall philosophical shit out of *Matrix*."

"Daddy and Momma looked at too much *Kung Fu*."

Not long after that, Tommie kissed my lips, got out, and climbed into her dirty Jeep. I waited for her to fire up her ride and back out before I did the same. Her Pink CD was playing loud and strong as she sped east toward one of the duplexes I owned in old Ladera. I cranked up Inobe and she sang me around the corner to the Mail Connexion. I looked at the sign and laughed, wondered if there was a place called *Male* Connexion. Anyway, I needed to check my post office box. Then Inobe sang me west toward LAX and my crib in Westchester.

I made it home in ten minutes.

I kicked off my shoes then turned off the house alarm. The universal remote was by the door. I picked it up and pushed a few buttons, selected which lights I wanted turned on, then dimmed them. Another button and soft music came though the ceiling speakers throughout the crib; another turned on the fireplace and adjusted the temperature in the house to seventy-five degrees.

All the white walls and ethnic art made me feel like I was living in a cultural museum. Sometimes I thought about renting the big crib out to a family and downsizing into one of the smaller properties. Hell, maybe that was why I loved for someone to be here with me at night, until the sun started coming up. Made me feel feeble to admit my weakness. Sometimes I heard shit going bump in the night. Could be my imagination, could be real, but either way, it would make me feel better if I had a

defense system made of about two hundred pounds of testos-
terone and a .357 Magnum by his side.

Five minutes after that I had stripped down to boy shorts
and a tank top.

Out of habit, I turned on my speakerphone and checked my
messages while I signed onto AOL. Always had to check my
e-mail. My buddy list popped up and I saw that Livvy was still
logged on. It was almost midnight here. I sent her an instant
message, told her that we had been hanging out and we missed
her. She sent a smiley face. I asked if she had insomnia, or
needed me to call so we could talk. Actually, I was the one who
needed conversation. It took her two minutes to answer and tell
me that she was chatting with somebody. I sent her a smiley
face and asked who.

No response.

I asked her to call me and let me know about her flight so
somebody could pick her up.

No response.

I checked my cyber mail: forty-two spams and twelve
e-mails from other dating hopefuls.

A few other people on my buddy list were floating around in
that cyber mesosphere. Pretty soon I was juggling somewhere between six and eight screens, at least five of them guys, two of them
former booty calls, trying to decide if I was going to lower myself
to my C-list and let one of them come over and tie me to a bedpost.
Could use a good tongue bath and toe sucking right about now.

I'd kicked off my shoes and been online an hour when another IM popped in my screen.

"Glad to see you're home safe." It was my fugly date. "I was
waiting for your call."

I didn't respond.

Livvy was still online, not responding to my IMs. Her away
message still wasn't on. After four in the morning on the East
Coast and she was still online chatting with somebody.

Another message from Fugly popped in my screen: "I would
like to see you again."

I signed off.

It was bedtime for this Bonzo, so I used the remote to turn everything off, put one fluffy pillow under my head, another between my legs, pulled the covers up to my neck, and welcomed the Sandman.

In my dream I saw Momma. We were in our old house in Inglewood.

She sat on the edge of her bed, called me over to her, "Frankie."

"Yeah, Momma."

"Come here. Feel this."

"Momma . . . you have a lump in your breast. It's hard."

"It doesn't hurt."

"Your skin . . . these veins . . . How long have you had this?"

The skin on her breast and underarm looked swollen. Veins were prominent on one breast. Her nipple looked funny, almost inverted. And she had a rash.

Her voice trembled, sounded like I'd never heard her sound before. Momma was afraid.

She said, "I've been having some discharge."

The phone rang and woke me up, took Momma away. I was crying when I answered.

My blurry eyes looked at the caller ID. I cleared my throat, answered, "Hello?"

"Frankie?"

"Yeah."

"It's Nick."

"I know."

Tommie

The lights in his living room are on. I see them as I turn left from 63rd to South Fairfax.

I slow down in front of his duplex, think about pulling into my driveway and calling it a night, think about not being bothered with him, but I don't make that turn, something won't let me, makes me sit in front of his building and stare at the lights in his window.

My cell phone rests in my lap. I push the number three and it speed-dials his number.

He answers, "Yo, Thomasina McBroom."

"I hate caller ID."

"It betrays anonymity."

Happiness floods my lungs when I hear his voice, so deep and resonant.

"Whassup, Blue?"

"How'd it go tonight?"

I say, "'Bucks was off the chains."

"You perform?"

"Changed my mind."

Blue pauses for a moment. His thick voice softens. "Sorry I couldn't make it."

"What happened?"

"Baby momma drama."

"Sorry to hear."

"Unless you have a hookup at Mobil, gas is too high to burn up like that."

He's in his bay window, looking down at me, watching me idle in front of his building. I turn my wheels, shift to first, and park where I am. His lives in a duplex owned by Frankie too. Not too many people know that because it's handled through a management company.

He says, "C'mon up."

He vanishes and his porch light comes on. I take out my lipstick, start freshening up.

I ask, "Need me to bring anything?"

"Nah. Thanks."

I change my mind about leaving my Jeep right there, make a hard turn and park across the street, in front of the duplex made of light gray stucco, Frankie's oldest property. Blue lives right across the street from me, upstairs on the east side of South Fairfax. I live upstairs on the west side. The way the buildings line up, when my lights are off and his blinds are open, I can lounge on my beanbag and watch him and his daughter playing and walking around their place. I can see when his baby momma comes over. I can see them arguing. I can see when she leaves. I can see him pacing, see how upset he is whenever she comes to see her daughter.

Purse and notebook in hand, I'm getting out of my Jeep when bright headlights come down Fairfax, then the vehicle slows down. My hand tightens, fingers adjust to the button on the Mace on my key ring, only to relax when I see it's my next-door neighbors, Womack and Rosa Lee. A Charlie Brown Christmas tree is on the roof of their SUV.

Womack speaks and starts small talking, eventually asks, "How is Livvy?"

I say, "She's doing okay."

Rosa chews her bottom lip. "We called her a few times—she never called back."

They were at the dinner party when all of her drama started.

I tell them, "She's been . . . She's not really talking to many people, you know?"

Rosa Lee says, "Tell her not to be a stranger. The boys miss shooting hoop with her."

Their three boys and their daughter are all in the backseat, everybody sleeping. We say our good nights and they ease down their narrow driveway. I wait until they are out of sight before I jog across Fairfax. When I get to the bottom of the stairs, I take light and easy steps. I'm halfway up when the porch light turns off and Blue opens his front door. He's barefoot. I can't stop my smile. His creamy vanilla complexion lights up. He runs his fingers through his nappy hair and yawns. Common with an LL body. In Levi's and a tank top. He's always casual.

I whisper, "Hey."

"Don't you look good."

Blue gives me a one-armed hug, something that disappoints me because it feels too brotherly. He kisses me on my cheek, right on the history that marks my skin, and my jazzy heart beats like hardcore hip-hop. My lips ache for the same as I hug him with two arms.

He's my friend and I love him.

We stand close enough to tell that he's just rushed and brushed his teeth. His eyes continue to compliment me on my look. My jeans, my midriff top, the jean shirt I'm wearing wide open, my silver navel ring, my silver jewelry, the whole nine.

I whisper, "Looks like a tornado came through here."

"She's sleeping. You don't have to whisper."

"Don't want to wake her."

I walk in and sit on the edge of the futon. He does the same.

I say, "Looks like you've had a kiddie party in here."

"You don't usually dress up like this."

"You like?"

"Like the way those jeans are fitting you."

I blush a little. "Thanks."

"You must've been on a mission tonight."

"Well, I was looking for somebody at 'Bucks."

"You're a wonderful woman. Hope he appreciated it."

I pull my lips in, hold in a sigh.

He says, "Sorry I missed it."

"It's cool. What happened?"

He gives me a simple shrug. "Shit happens."

"Yeah, shit happens."

What floats in my mind is simple, I wanted you to see me tonight, to witness my passion, to get to know me better through the words from my soul. I wanted to perform for you at 'Bucks. I wanted to say things in a crowd that I can't tell you when we're one on one.

And now I want to touch you, Blue. I want you to touch me.

The teapot sings, interrupts that moment. I follow him toward the kitchen. CDs are scattered on the carpet: Bobby Bland, VeggieTales, Darius Rucker, Learning to Read, Blue's Clues. There are too many dolls, kiddie books, and toys to count. I maneuver through the hodgepodge of clutter like I'm walking a minefield in the desert. I stumble on a Scooby-Doo doll. Scooby's voice is activated and he yells for Shaggy to give him a Scooby snack.

He grumbles, "I told her a hundred times to clean up her mess."

"She's four. Let her be four."

"She has to learn responsibility now."

"And she's still four."

Pictures of Blue, his daughter, and her mom are in the living room on the wall, greeting people as they come in the door, as if he were waiting for her to come back. Even in a photograph, her energy is negative. Her eyes follow me. I look back at her. I think that picture should be in the bedroom, in a space as private as his thoughts.

His laptop is on his small kitchen table. He powers it down, moves it to the counter, then turns his small CD-radio on to KJLH. Nat King Cole's classic holiday offering goes off as En Vogue comes on singing a funkdafied version of "Silent Night."

I ask, "How's the screenplay coming along?"

He shakes his head. "Slow. Not a lot of free time to write."

"Still no bites on the one you sent out?"

"My wannabe agent thinks I should change the characters."

"In what way?"

"From black to white. Impossible to sell a black drama to Hollywood."

"You know what they say about selling a black film, 'No money if ain't funny.' "

I go to use his bathroom, then stop by the bedroom and peep in. Monica is sleeping wild and twisted, a tiny lump on a twin-size futon resting under white sheets and green covers. An old maple dresser rests against another wall. The dresser is forty years old. Used to belong to Blue's old man. His dad was a postal carrier and his mom worked food service at a high school.

On the way back to the kitchen I step on Scooby-Doo. He talks to Velma this time.

Blue's putting lemon cookies on a plate and making our ginger-peppermint tea.

I ask, "What happened this time?"

He shrugs. "Her mother was supposed to pick her up at noon."

"What did she say?"

"No-call, no-show."

"You have to work and she left you hanging again."

"I know. She lacks selflessness and emotional maturity."

"Why don't you say something?"

"Throwing gas on a fire never helps."

I sit down at his kitchen table. Sticky rings from where some-one has put a glass or a cup on the table are on the side with the booster seat and the Blue's Clues place mats. I get up and get paper towels and glass cleaner, maneuver around Blue, wipe down his table, then open his refrigerator to get out a lemon. Three- and four-letter kiddie words are on the refrigerator—one of my gifts to his daughter—along with preschool art projects, most unrecognizable.

Blue continues talking. "She's not mother material. Never has been maternal."

"Not every woman is."

He puts a cup of tea in front of me, sits the honey on the side. We sit. We season our tea with honey and lemon. We stir. We sip. We eat lemon cookies.

"Would be easier if I had a son."

"Don't say that."

"I love Mo. Wouldn't trade her for a sixty-four-and-a-half Mustang."

"That's good to know."

"But she's a girl. Girls need to be around girls. And women. I just think I'd do better with a boy. I understand football and basketball better than Barbie and SpongeBob."

"She needs her daddy too. We all need our daddies."

"I'm doing my best."

"You stay strong and at least she won't have the same men issues."

"I know." He shakes his head, rattling his memories. "Can't count the number of women I've dated who hate their daddies. They have deep wounds that won't heal, so it's like no man will ever live up to their unreal expectations."

"Same goes for the brothers who didn't have a daddy. They end up treating . . . more like mistreating women the way they saw their mommas being mistreated."

"It goes back to the foundation. Our foundation has been destroyed."

We slip into conversations we've had before about the history of our people. From slavery to oppression to life beyond the Industrial Revolution, Blue knows all about the evolution of the black man, understands how hard it is to raise up an oppressed culture, and has helped me to not be so hard on our people, but to understand how and why many of us ended up feeling hopeless and on alcohol and drugs, and as a result, homeless or in jail or the cemetery. Depression makes people cling to what makes them feel good. So much depression amongst our people, and rightfully so, I've pointed that out to him. He's a good conversationalist, not just on topics about

black people, but about people in general. We talk about everything from child prostitution in Thailand to the president's war
on reproductive rights.

He turns the radio off, asks me to read him some poetry,
wants to know what he missed. The erotic piece inspired by my
dreams, I don't have the courage to read it now, when he is
close, so I read a sociopolitical piece that ends in "When the ma-
jority gets treated like they are minorities, they call it injustice.
We call it Monday, Tuesday, Wednesday . . ."

He likes that one.

Then I share with him a short political antiwar piece of work,
something I wrote the day the troops invaded Baghdad. Old
news, but I like it because it shows my anger in how they said
it wasn't about oil, but protected the oil, and allowed the muse-
ums to be looted and culture destroyed, the same way parts of
our culture and art were stolen and destroyed.

He loves the writing, but disagrees with it conceptually.

I tell Blue, "Nothing you say can convince me that Iraq
needed us over—"

"You don't understand fully what was going on."

"I understand right and wrong. Violence is never the answer."

Whenever we talk, even like this, his smooth voice is pleasure to my ears. Our exchanges create an ebb and flow that I feel
in my body. He's moving in and out of me.

"I bet our ancestors"—Blue sips his tea—"wished someone
had come to liberate them."

"That was different."

He shakes his head. "Oppression is oppression. Just like the
slaves, Iraqis didn't ask to be liberated because anyone caught
doing such a thing would be tortured and executed."

I sip my tea, feeling naïve again, wishing we were talking
about something else, about infinite possibilities between us.
"Why do you think no one came to liberate the slaves?"

"They didn't have CNN."

We laugh.

He says, "They didn't have oil."

"To get saved, you have to be viewed as worth saving."

He nods and motions at my notebook. "Read me something else."

The next page is "Erotic Dreams in Shades of Blue." Our conservation makes it hard to segue to that sensuality. I stare at the page and my emotions stare at me in black ink.

Eyes closed . . . I want to touch myself . . . want to imagine what it's like to feel you . . . my eyes glowing every time I see you . . . my heartbeat between my thighs . . . becoming a celibate cat in heat

That last part, celibate cat in heat, not sure if that's the right image I'm going—

"Tommie, you're over here." I jump and close my notebook when I hear Monica's voice.

She runs a sleepy run, almost falls, comes to me and grabs my legs, catches me off guard. She's small for her size, but strong. She is barefoot, in too-big white pajamas with yellow ducks.

I push my notebook aside and pick her up. "Hey, Boobie."

Her hair is long and thick; skin a bronzy yellow, eyes the hue of a new penny.

I say, "The ponytails are holding up."

She says, "I want my hair braided, not in ponytails. I want six braids."

"If your daddy says it's cool, I'll hook you up tomorrow if we have time, okay?"

"Okay."

Blue asks, "Why are you out of bed, Mo?"

"I heard Scooby-Doo." She wears a sad look on her face. "Is it morning time yet?"

"Come here."

She goes to him. He hugs her. Sad look gone. An actress in training. A daddy's girl. With Monica, Blue changes. His voice is filled with love, but it's the firm love of a parent.

"Sun is still sleeping." He kisses her forehead. "Still night-time."

"Mommy coming to get me?"

Then there is silence. A moment of sadness.

He sighs. "Mommy . . . she . . . something came up."

"She said she was coming to get me for lunchtime. Lunchtime and dinnertime are over."

"I know."

Monica is anxious. Blue hugs her, tries to take her disappointment away.

"Daddy, can I tell Tommie I'm learning *allllll* about Kwanzaa on the computer?" She rubs her eyes, yawns, struggles with the word, "Ooooo-moe-jah and—"

"Tomorrow, Monica. Time to go night-night."

"May I have some water, Daddy?"

"You had water before you went to bed."

"I want water out of my green cup."

Blue puts her in my lap and gets her green cup. "Water, then back to bed, understand?"

"Tommie, are you going to braid my hair like 'Licia Keys?"

"Alicia Keys it is."

"I'm I'm I'm doing a spoken word project at school."

"Really?"

"When I grow up I'm going to be a poem writer just like you, and you can help me!"

She drinks the water, then asks if she can do this, can she do that, tries her best to keep talking, but Blue makes her give me a good-night hug, then takes her to the bathroom and lets her use it before taking her back to the bedroom. I hear them talking. So much love is in this space.

I sit at the table for a while, waiting and thinking, feeling like I should go.

I met Blue because of Monica. I used to see him going out in the morning, struggling to get her in the car seat so he could get her to the sitter and get to work on time. Monica's hair would be jacked up, halfway plaited, halfway Afro. Crooked parts. No oil or moisturizer. Even when Monica's mother had her and dropped her off, her hair was jacked up. Actually, she did a worse job than Blue. Blue and I were on the way out at the same time one morning and we both waved. He was in his driveway and I was backing out so I could get to 'Bucks and write a bit before I went to open at Pier 1. I drove down the street, then turned back around, pulled up in front of his place, introduced myself as a neighbor, told him that I wasn't trying to get in his business, then asked if he needed me to do her hair. He offered to pay me. I told him it was pro bono. He told me that his baby momma wasn't good at styling hair, either that or wasn't patient enough to try and learn how to plait and braid hair as gifted as Monica's, so he did his best. Had the poor child looking like Buckwheat in the electric chair. I have to give him credit for trying to hold his own. That was how we met. That was how we became friends. Through Monica.

Twenty minutes goes by before he comes back, that parental irritation all over his face.

I ask, "She sleep?"

"Yeah. Had to make sure no monsters were under her bed."

"She makes a sucker out of you."

"I know. That damn *Monsters, Inc.* movie . . ."

We laugh and yawn.

I ask, "What are you gonna do about work tomorrow?"

He makes another cup of tea, sits down again. "I'll have to call in."

"You can't keep doing that."

"No choice."

"You could lose your job."

"Old Navy ain't all that. It's only seasonal part-time work so I can get that discount. Need to buy Mo a few things and save a few dollars for when I'm off track at Unified. When her mom jacks me over on a Friday night at the last minute, I don't really have a backup plan."

"Yes you do."

"It's not your problem, Tommie."

"Bring Monica over."

"Don't you have to work?"

"Don't have to be at Pier 1 until three."

"I don't get off until five."

"Maybe I can change my hours."

"That's not being responsible." He tugs at his hair. "You can't do that."

"Blue, it takes a village. Understand that."

Blue has cable and I don't. So a couple of times a week I come over to braid or plait his daughter's hair. Our little ritual. I do her hair. I eat with them. He bathes her while I wash his dishes. I play with her and read to her so he can get a break. Blue puts her in the bed by nine. Then he makes us ginger-peppermint tea and we watch cable for an hour or so.

Tonight we just talk.

He opens up the futon in the living room and I rest next to him, not touching but wanting to. The words stop and the yawns come on strong.

He asks, "Running in the morning?"

"If Frankie calls. Don't have to."

Being on a futon, anything that resembles a bed with a man is a huge step for me. It means I trust him. My sex and guilt issues don't exist with Blue.

My eyelids get as heavy as Blue's breathing.

I pull the covers up to my neck. Blue moves his heat closer to me, almost spooning.

Sleep finds me.

Then I hear feet; feel a tiny body crawl up on the futon, climbing over us like we're a mountain. Monica gets under the covers, snuggles her cool body between me and her daddy's warmth. She looks at her daddy, sees he's sleeping, then moves over and looks in my face.

She whispers, "Tommie?"

"Yeah, Monica?"

"When is morning time?"

"Not too long. Close your eyes and it'll be here before you know it."

"I forgot to tell you I love you."

"Love you too."

She says, "G'night."

"G'night."

I massage her back; calm her the way my momma used to do me. Her breathing becomes heavy and smooth. I get up in the darkness, put my shoes on, pick up my purse, grab my keys.

I'm at the door, turning the lock when Blue's voice follows me. "Leaving?"

"Thanks for the tea."

He never says, but I can tell that he's not comfortable when Monica comes in and sleeps between us, if only for a moment. I understand the message he doesn't want to give his child. And she's at that age where she tells everything. And her momma gives Blue enough drama.

We pause. Darkness hides the truth as unspoken words fill the air.

He says, "Tommie . . ."

Something is on his mind. The way he said my name gives me awkward energy.

I ask, "Whassup?"

It takes him a moment. "I'm really sorry I didn't make it to 'Bucks."

"No big deal."

"Yes, it is. You do so much for Mo and I couldn't make it around the corner to support you. After I realized her momma wasn't coming . . . could've brought Monica with me, she would've loved to see you—"

"No, it's cool. I understand. If you need me in the morning, holla."

"We can work it out over here."

That pronoun builds a wall between us, reminds me that I'm not part of their *we*-ness.

I say, "Blue, you do things for me all the time. You change the oil in my Jeep, you flush out the radiator."

He doesn't respond to my sprawling words, just gets up and comes to the door. He hugs me with both arms, holds on to me. I hug him tight, hold on to him.

He knows.

And I know he knows.

He tells me, "You're a beautiful young woman, Tommie."

"I'm a grown woman, Blue."

"I know you are."

This is our pink elephant.

I don't know if the elephant looms and breathes because of my therapy, my two years of abstinence, or my abuse and trust issues that he knows a little about, or our age difference.

Or if it's because we're friends, and there are lines friends don't cross.

My palms become rivers while my throat turns into a desert. People think that therapy makes it easier to put things on the table, to say what you mean and mean what you say, but it only teaches you how to hide your own problems while you become better at fixing other people.

It's hard to put my arms around him because at the end of the hug is another good-bye. I know I'll have to let go. I know I'll have to move on. That we'll have to go through this again and again. The only thing waiting for me across the street is thoughts of him and Monica.

Again we're face-to-face, and I wonder if he's going to kiss me. I want him to. I don't want him to. He lets me go and the room turns cold. I turn the door handle. But I don't leave.

I say his name. Emotions ride out of my body on my voice.

I whisper, "Can I ask you a question?"

He shifts. "Sure."

"What are we doing?"

He struggles with my question. "What do you mean?"

"Blue, don't . . . you know what I mean."

"We're friends."

"I know."

"Tommie, you're twenty-three. I'm thirty-eight. Renting a duplex. A single parent. A struggling screenwriter. A schoolteacher at L.A. Unified, where sometimes I get my check on time, and sometimes I don't. I work at Old Navy on the weekends to make ends meet."

I let him go until he's done. All the things he tells me are the reasons I admire him.

I say, "My daddy was a janitor, a plumber, did whatever he had to do."

"I'm not your daddy, Tommie."

"And I don't expect you to be. I'm just asking . . . Whassup?"

"My life is complicated, Tommie."

We're standing there looking at each other, the pink elephant moving back and forth, then sitting in a corner, giving us enough room to do this circle dance.

"Life is complicated for everybody, Blue."

"And I'm damaged goods."

"We're all damaged, Blue."

Lights are coming down Fairfax, somebody driving too fast for this residential area. The car slows down and whips into Blue's driveway. It's a dirty, white Pontiac Grand Am.

Erotic feelings dwindle as tension rises.

I say, "She's here."

Blue curses her. "Not even a phone call to say she's going to be fourteen hours late."

"Don't get upset."

"She's damn near forty and as irresponsible as a fucking—"

I shush him and motion at his sleeping child. "Lower your voice."

His voice becomes a harsh whisper, "She gets me every time."

"Don't give her that power. And Monica doesn't need to see that either."

"This is ridiculous."

"Shhh. And don't say anything negative about her in front of Monica."

The car parks and she gets out. We step out the door. She sees us up top and stops.

Blue says, "Funny how you can have a child with someone and have zero connection. I look at her, feel nothing, other than that's my child's mother. Don't even know her."

"How did you . . . I mean . . . you and her . . ."

"How did we have a baby?"

"Yeah."

"Shit happens." That's his answer to the unanswerable.

I say, "I'm out, Blue. Holla if you need me."

I head down the stairs, smell her perfume before I get to her. She waits at the bottom.

She has on hip-hugger jeans, Birkenstocks, a Dave Matthews Band sweatshirt. I doubt if she is five feet tall. Her blue eyes cut me up and down, and she flips her blond hair away and gives me an expression that makes me think that Sister Moon is tugging at her ovarian walls.

I speak to her as I pass. "Assaluym alakiam."

She says nothing, just heads up the stairs.

DISSONANCE

ℒivvy

I was snowed in for two more days. For two days, I was online, chatting with the man who had created the cyber ad, the man who wanted to talk to a woman who had been betrayed.

We didn't exchange phone numbers, kept it online, and talked about hooking up.

That excited and scared me.

The airport in Philly opened at the crack of dawn, and I bundled up and rode a cold and crowded shuttle, then fought the madness at the ticket counter for three hours, only to get put on standby and wait two more hours before finally getting on a cross-country flight to LAX. And of course I had to take what I could get, a three-hour layover. Seemed like the world was slipping back into the Ice Age. Flew over ice and snow for hours. Lots of turbulence, no sleep.

The anxiety of my real life started to dampen my palms over San Bernadino County, not long after the windmills, sand, and palm trees in Palm Springs. The number of snow-covered mountains lessened long before then, but that was where the smog started to welcome me home.

"You sure are reading a lot of comic books." The man next to me said that.

I was crammed in the back row, the one right before the bathrooms, worst seats in the house because they didn't recline and there was nonstop traffic. I was sitting with two men who looked like retired linebackers, both too big for their seats. The guy next to me had snored the first hour, then woke up and started reading his paper; the other guy played his Walkman too loud. I had a window seat, so for that final leg of my journey back to reality, I was a lioness in a cage, mentally pacing back and forth, wanting to break free.

I shifted and tried to stretch my back, said, "A few. *Spider-Man, Daredevil, Superman.*"

"Used to read 'em when I was a kid."

"Me too. They've changed."

"How so?"

"Profanity. Pregnancies. Real people problems."

He went back to his paper.

I went back to *Daredevil.*

I wasn't really focused, my mind drifting back to my late-night and all-day cyber exchanges with that stranger. Carpe Diem 0707. That was his screen name. We sat up and swapped emotions for hours. It was good. He told me that he was thirty-seven, a combination of black, white, and Cuban. In my mind, I saw a mature man with an extraordinary face. Funny thing about the Internet, you could be in Iowa and he could be in Alaska, but you felt like you were on a beach in the Virgin Islands having tropical drinks. We talked, in general terms, about life. Love. Marriage. Betrayal. I didn't give him the specifics of what Tony had done, only let him know that it had fucked me up. We both had our televisions on CNN. We talked politics. Like reading a good book, it becomes real, you feel it, you see it, and the movie plays in your head. Close to sunrise, the conversation moved from politics to talking about sex in general, then about sex in specifics. It was so easy to type out your inner thoughts. It was nice. It was a new kind of freedom. I told Carpe Diem 0707 all the things I liked, how I loved being dominant, but at the same time I loved being in submissive positions, doggie style being at the top of the list. Guess I went with the flow and loved to mix it up, sometimes tender, sometimes rough. Loved for a man to take control, slap the ass and tell me what to do. I loved the idea of being tied up with silk scarves, blind-folded, handcuffs, the whole nine. I'd been sucked into a zone and I told him things my best friends didn't know. I told him things my own husband didn't know. Anonymity made a person uninhibited and bold; brought the fantasies out in the open. He asked questions and I was excited to answer.

Couldn't believe I had that conversation. Didn't know I could feel that way with a stranger. I didn't know him, but I gave him a face, a body, and I imagined things.

Carpe Diem 0707. Seize the day.

And while we typed, I put my hand in my sweats, started touching myself.

Then Frankie popped in my screen while I was having a long-overdue orgasm. Scared the hell out of me and made me lose my momentum. Took me a while to get back to the edge.

It wasn't funny then, but I laughed now. It felt like Frankie had walked in on me. Reminded me of a time when I woke up in the middle of the night, heard soft whimpers, and walked in on Momma, spread eagle, her man on top of her, moving slow, creaking the bed. Momma had it going on in a major way. I was in elementary school then. Momma had her Saturday night ways, the ways of a woman who didn't have a steady man but had constant needs. I'd be lying if I said she didn't come in after getting her Friday night party on, smelling like she'd been swimming in a bottle of Bacardi, cigarette on the tip of her lips, giggling and holding hands with a late-night visitor, trying to tiptoe him into her bedroom, her cures for late night loneliness. I could see her right now. Always so sensual, so curvy and lady-like, brown skin that was always baby smooth, long black hair always pressed.

I was missing my momma. Wishing I could talk to her, ask her what to do with myself.

She'd light up a cigarette, blow smoke out the corner of her mouth while she put out the match and say, "Fuck 'im or leave 'im. Don't matter. Same problems you got with this one you gonna have with the next one. Only thing is since this one in the doghouse, you got the upper hand. He know he done done wrong so he ain't gonna ride down that street no more."

The flight attendant came by picking up the last of our trash. I sighed.

Whenever this plane landed in Los Angeles, I could vanish from that cyber world by deleting my screen name, and just like that, the pseudonym *Bird* would no longer exist.

Or I could become Bird.

All night and most of the morning we sent messages, asking questions, giving answers. He told me he was an only child, born in Houston. I told him I was an L.A. girl, had two sisters.

"In preparation for our landing, the captain has turned on . . ."

It was eerie watching the air change color, become shades of brown and gray as the plane moved across the desert closer to the ocean, knowing I'd be breathing that carbon monoxide in less than an hour. I looked down at all the grids, but we were too high to tell who had Christmas lights up already. In the darkness, traffic looked like red and white ants moving back and forth. Even late on a Sunday night there were so many cars on the 605, 710, and 110.

I sighed and closed my eyes for a moment. Almost home.

Then we were descending over Inglewood, passing the Great Western Forum, Hollywood Park, and the 4-oh-my-God-why-is-there-always-so-much-damn-traffic-5, the last jam-packed freeway we crossed before touching ground. Just looking at it made my head hurt.

As soon as we rolled to the gate, from first class to coach, damn near everybody turned on their cellular phones and started making calls. Impatient people were cramming the aisles, getting luggage from overhead, and leaving the plane, the flight attendants telling everybody to have a happy holiday, while I stared out the window at the tarmac and thought about what was waiting for me here in L.A. I called my job and left a message, told them the plane had landed without incident, then let them know that I was tired, and asked if they could get someone else to cover San Diego. I had a lot of comp time on the books and I needed to stay home, put in some quality time with my family, and deal with some personal issues.

I hung up.

My row finally started to move. The big guy on the end got out, stood there, waiting for people to get out of his way so he could get his luggage.

The big guy next to me took forever to get up, kept me captive until damn near everybody was gone. He grabbed his laptop from under the seat, pulled his other bag from the overhead storage, then got up. I put my bulky laptop case on the seat, then reached in the overhead for my bag and coat. No problem getting my coat, but my luggage was so tight that I couldn't yank it out. My headache escalated and I thought I was about to explode. I took a hard breath, rubbed my temples again, closed my eyes, and said something indecipherable. Simple things were going wrong. Simple things like that made me want to scream.

"You look like you need a hand."

I looked up and it was the big guy who had been sitting next to me. He'd seen me struggling, came back and helped me get my overpacked luggage.

I said, "Thank you."

"You're welcome."

There was an awkward moment when we made eye contact. He looked at me, smiled. "Whatever it is, it'll get better."

My dominant mood had been written all over my face. Didn't realize that until now. I pulled my lips in, then made myself smile. "Have a merry Christmas."

He raised a brow. "I'm Jewish."

Then we both laughed and headed down the aisle.

I told him, "Happy holidays, happy Hanukkah . . . okay, you got me."

"That's better. You're smiling. Happy holidays to you too."

I caught a taxi and blended in with the madness of airport traffic that spilled out into the City of Fallen Angels. I closed my eyes to the madness. Ten minutes later the driver turned off Slauson and drove into Ladera Heights. A few of the houses had their curtains open, lights on Christmas trees creating a colorful night. One block had decorations up outside. One home had a nativity scene; another had a waving snowman, a sleigh and reindeer on top of the house, and elves throughout the front yard, the whole nine. My hands became fists. Breath was getting short, like all the air had been sucked out of the car.

I leaned forward and said, "Driver . . ."

"Yes?"

I was ready to tell him to turn around, that there had been a change of plans.

Then I heard Tommie's firm voice telling me to *stop running*.

"Nothing . . . just . . . just slow down."

He cruised by the triplexes and ranch-style homes at the foot of Ladera. As we went up the hill, single-level homes built between the forties and the seventies gave way to a tract of new millennium two-story homes built on small lots with modern floor plans, all made of beige stucco and reddish tile roofs, the kind that keep fires from spreading.

When we were growing up, we'd look at homes like these and get so jealous. We had some rough times. Momma would be up all night cursing at those damn bills, trying to figure out how to stretch every dollar, knowing there wasn't enough money to eat and pay them all, so Momma would put them in a hat, close her eyes, and pull them out one at time until she was out of bill money. If it was a really bad month, she'd throw them in the air and say whatever bill doesn't come down gets paid. Momma would curse the bills, grab her cigarettes, and tell her girls to get dressed.

"*Where we going?*"

"*We're running away to Disneyland.*"

"*The one in the backyard?*"

"*No, the one down the 5. Get your shit. We're outta here.*"

That's what I wanted to do, throw my problems in the air and run away to Disneyland.

*   *   *

The taxi pulled away and I stood on my front porch for another five minutes, as motionless as the palm trees, before I
opened the door. The television was on. Down the hallway, I
heard another noise. Roomba was humming back and forth
across the hardwood floor. Roomba was one of Tony's robotic
toys, an automated vacuum cleaner for lazy people. Our house
was filled with his gadgets from every Sharper Image and
Brookstone in L.A.

I called out, "Tony?"

No answer.

I rolled my luggage into the foyer, then went into the family
room. Nothing in there but white walls and African artifacts
bought at Ross and made in Mexico. Our furniture was soft and
earth tone. Lots of decorative mirrors and plants throughout the
house.

A glass was on the island in the kitchen. Two plates and silverware in the sink.

Tony wasn't down here.

I called his name again. No answer.

I stepped around Roomba and went upstairs.

He wasn't in the bedroom or the office either. I went back
downstairs, lowered the volume on the television and went to
the refrigerator. That was where we posted our work schedules.
Tony's work schedule said he had had a long day yesterday and
was back at the hospital tonight. He'd left the television on so
there would be noises in the house.

I picked up the home phone, dialed his cell phone, let it ring
once, enough for the home number to show on his caller ID.
Again, communicating without talking. *I'm home.*

Then I went outside to the mailbox. Tony never brought the
mail in. That never used to bother me. Tonight it added to my
irritation. There were the usual bills and bulk mail.

A large white envelope was crammed inside, turned sideways and pushed all the way to the back. It was stiff, made of
cardboard, had the words PHOTO MAILER and DO NOT BEND in

large block letters along each side. It had a Marina Del Rey post-
mark. No return address.

I went back inside, opened a drawer looking for scissors. The
knob came off the drawer. I stood there, holding it, eyes wide
open, my hand shaking. They had advertised these homes as
the Black Beverly Hills. Outside, they were eye-catching, but inside they were falling apart.

I took a breath, rubbed my temples, stood at the counter,
ripped the package open.

Baby pictures. She had sent pictures of the baby. Her name,
Miesha. Pictures of the sonogram, photos of the baby wrapped
in a blanket. There were other photos, several close-ups.

Roomba bumped into my foot. I kicked it as hard as I could.

I slapped the pictures on the counter. Stared at them for a
long while. My trance was broken when the phone rang. Tony's
cellular number lighting up the ID. I let it ring.

I washed dishes in total silence, dried them, and put them
away.

I went back to the pictures, stared at the magnet of my humiliation.

I wrote a simple note: *She looks like you.*

Then I packed more clothes and headed for my truck. I'd
driven down the hill, away from my home before I gave in and
allowed the tears to cloud my eyes.

Livvy

San Diego was less than a two-hour drive from my life in Los Angeles. The same for him. If things didn't work out for either of us, or if there was simply a change of heart, if I didn't like the way he looked, or if for whatever reason he didn't like my hair, or if I wasn't thin enough for his taste, we agreed to be honest and go our separate ways, as if we never met.

My cellular rang. It wasn't the man I was planning to meet. Frankie's number was on my caller ID. She'd called at least ten times and wasn't going to stop until I answered.

I answered, "Hey."

"Don't make me put your picture on the side of a milk carton."

"Where are you?"

The first voice was Frankie. The second was Tommie. They had me on a three-way.

I adjusted the bags in my hand, said, "At Fashion Valley Mall. Stress shopping."

I loved them, but hearing them did nothing for me right now.

Tommie asked, "How many pairs of shoes you buy?"

"Who said I bought shoes?"

Frankie tisked. "Oh, please."

Via Spiga. Pliner. Pelle Moda. I had done some serious damage to my charge card, all in the name of therapy. My bookends knew me better than I knew myself. Still, I denied every single pair of shoes I had in these bags, and the three pair I had already taken to the truck.

They let me know that Tony had been calling all over looking for me. He had been home, my husband had seen the pictures. After I'd left Ladera, I'd gone by Frankie's place.

I said, "Frankie, you really should close your living room windows at night."

"What are you talking about?"

Last night I was going to stay with her. I'd called and there was no answer. As I was heading down her walkway, the sweet sounds of a McBroom woman living in pleasure, on the edge of ecstasy, came to me. And unless Sharper Image made talking vibrators, I heard Frankie's lover too, their passion slipping out into the night.

I said, "You sounded like a damn cat with its tail caught in the door."

Frankie cursed me for busting her out like that.

Tommie laughed. "Frankie, you know your butt be woo woo wooing."

I said, "She didn't make it to the bedroom, Tommie. She was in the living room with the damn windows open."

"Whatever," Frankie snapped. "All you had to do was knock, Livvy."

"And your friend would've thought he was getting a two-for-one."

"Hell, I could've used some help."

I asked, "Who was over there riding you like the Lone Ranger?"

Frankie wouldn't reveal the identity of her orgasm donor.

Tommie asked, "Was it the fugly man?"

Frankie cursed Tommie out, then Tommie tried to tell me about Frankie's blind date, about her running into some guy she used to be crazy about. The phone wasn't even up to my ear, all of their words going out into the wind. I wasn't up for this kind of conversation.

I looked at my watch, then lied to them, "Gotta go. Teaching a class."

Frankie said, "Kind of late in the day to have a class."

"Look, I'm working so . . . guess I'll call you back when I get some free time."

Frankie asked, "What do you want me to tell Tony if he calls again?"

"Tell him it's not your problem. That's goes for you too, Tommie."

Tommie responded, "Okay, okay."

"Tell Tony it's not your problem."

"I understood it the first time."

I let them go, took a few deep breaths, then headed outside.

I stopped underneath the sign for the JCPenney package pickup, a few feet away from the Salvation Army people who were ringing bells at every entrance. My eyes went to the sky. Darkness was sitting on the city. I looked at my watch and waited a few more minutes. I was dressed in all black, a dozen bags at my feet. First a Mexican lady passed by, her child in a stroller. Then a man passed by with his child on his shoulders. This time last year I had baby fever so bad, it was ridiculous. I knew it was my time. They were all over the mall. Some of them were pretty cute. Pisses me off to think I was sitting up with Tony, having that "let's get pregnant" conversation and he already had a bastard on the way.

A black Nissan pulled up and slowed down. He waved. I waved back. It was him. Had to be. Not many black people were down this way.

My hair was pulled back into a ponytail, like I had told him.

He said, "Bird?"

I smiled. "Carpe?"

He laughed. "Let me park."

"Okay."

I rocked from foot to foot, bounced my Gap and Banana Republic bags against my leg. He vanished down at the end of the lot, near the golf course. Right after he disappeared, a red Miata slowed down by me, another shopper looking for parking. The back window had been torn, maybe slashed, then repaired with duct tape. Convertibles always made me smile and imagine riding down the coast, music up, and my hair dancing in the breeze. When you wanted something, you saw it everywhere. Dream homes. Good relationships.

My dream car sped down the aisle, mixed with the rest of the people looking for parking.

Minutes went by.

When I thought Carpe might've had a change of heart and driven away, he appeared between the cars at the end of the lot, hurrying my way.

He said, "Parking sucks."

"I know."

Like we had agreed, he was dressed in blacks too. He was tall, around six-four, his hair short with a goatee, and he had told me that he weighed around 185.

One look at him and I doubt if he had ten percent fat on his body.

I shook his hand. Our first touch. Our first time hearing each other's voices. My first time smelling the sweet patchouli on his skin. His first time smelling the soft perfume on mine.

He said, "Getting your Christmas shopping done?"

I held on to my smile. "Got a couple of presents . . . for my sisters."

"Wow. Talk about shoes."

"My fetish."

"I see. You must've shut down the mall."

"I know, I know. Women and shopping. Strange thing about Christmas shopping is that, well, call me selfish, but somehow I always end up buying more stuff for me than for other people."

He chuckled. "Must be crowded in there."

"Kinda weird. Lot of cars, but nobody's really lining up for the cash register."

"It's like that all over."

"Yep. Economy is really bad. People are losing jobs and holding on to their chips."

He nodded. "How was your drive?"

In Southern Cali, when people felt awkward and didn't know what to talk about, they always talked about two things: traffic and weather.

"Easy," I said. "Came down the 405 then took the toll road to the 5."

"I've never taken the toll road."

"Three bucks saves you thirty minutes."

He motioned at the bags sitting at my feet. "How long have you been here?"

"Came down late last night. Needed to get away from L.A."

"I feel you."

There were things we could do to get comfortable, places we could walk and talk: Seaport Village, Fashion Valley Mall, or take the 5 across the border and hang out in Tijuana.

He said, "Hungry?"

"People on a diet are always hungry."

"What do you want?"

We stood there, smiling awkwardly at each other. It was very bizarre, this moment that made him more than words and a name on a computer screen. He'd gone from being virtual to real. I was trying to be cool, but I was tense, nervous as hell.

I said, "You heard of the Gaslamp District?"

"Don't think I've been down there."

"It's a hot spot. Restaurants, jazz joints, night clubs, whatever."

"Which way?"

"Not far."

"You want to ride with me or—?"

"Follow me."

"No problem."

"Let's eat and . . . take it from there."

He nodded.

I caught the 8 down at Hotel Circle. Carpe followed me to the Historic District and we parked in Horton Plaza, the outdoor mall facing the Gaslamp. I thought I'd get lost, but I didn't.

I'd looked this up online and printed out the directions before I went to meet Carpe. The area was a miniaturized version of Bourbon Street mixed with a little of New York's Soho, landscaped by evergreen and palm trees to give it that bona fide West Coast flavor.

He said, "Nice Victorian architecture down here."

I agreed with a nod, then asked, "What do you want to eat?"

The moment I said that, my question felt sexual. It didn't sound that way, but it felt that way. That wasn't a question to ask a man. Too open ended.

I rushed my words, "There are over eighty restaurants over sixteen blocks."

He said, "I'm open."

"Well, there's Japanese, Italian, Mexican . . ."

"Let's just walk and be adventurous."

"Okee doke."

"See something you like, we'll check it out."

We crossed the street, two restless people in search of something better, blended with the crowd, passed by clubs playing cool jazz, rhythm and blues, and folk music, stopped in the Hard Rock Cafe for a moment, moved on by cigar shops and billiard rooms, saw some salsa dancing, even passed by a disco complete with strobe lights and mirrored balls.

He said, "You look nice."

"Thanks. You too."

"I didn't expect . . . You're beautiful, if you don't mind my saying so."

I smiled. He said that in a soft and soothing, reassuring way. "Thanks."

I was wearing an angora sweater and velvet jeans, the kind of clothes that felt good to the touch. Clothes that were sexy without being hoochie.

He said, "Your husband cheated?"

I put my hands in the pocket of my leather jacket, then one hand came up to my hair, rubbing it back when it needed no rubbing. My humiliation was easier to talk about online. When

Carpe had no face, no voice, no aroma, I had found comfort in his anonymity.

I said, "He had an affair."

"How'd you find out?"

"What do you mean?"

"She call you? Did you hire a service to follow him? . . ."

"We were having a dinner party, celebrating my husband's promotion with friends, family, a few neighbors. The doorbell rang. There was this beautiful woman asking for him."

"She came to the door?"

"No, it was the process server. And of course when a beautiful woman comes to your door looking for your husband, you don't leave. I waited. He came to the door, and she slapped the papers in his hand, told us to have a good night, and walked away."

"Wow. At a dinner party?"

"My sisters, our friends, lots of people were there. It fucked me up. I went nuclear, started yelling, made everybody leave. It just . . . damn. Really made an ass of myself."

"Can only imagine. How old is the kid?"

The image of those baby pictures were engraved in my mind. I took my hands out of my pocket, then put them right back in.

I answered, "Six months."

"How long have you been married?"

"Five years."

"Kids?"

"We'd been trying . . . then this . . . Can we talk about something else?"

At one time I was so clear about what I wanted to do with my life. Now I wasn't so clear anymore.

He put his hand on my shoulder for a moment. "How about them Raiders?"

I laughed. "Raider fan?"

"Yup."

"Cool."

We walked and talked sports. Both of us were down with the

Lakers, straight ride-or-die. And I lived for March Madness. I told him I played basketball in college.

He asked, "What position?"

"Mostly small forward and running guard."

"No wonder your body is so nice."

"Not even. Back then they had me down to twelve percent body fat."

He asked, "Were you any good?"

"I can take you to the hoop."

"Don't talk it if you can't back it up."

"Oh, I can back it up."

"We're gonna have to find a court so I can take you to school."

I said, "Scored twenty-eight points in one game."

"Who were you playing, the Clippers?"

We laughed.

He asked, "You like sushi?"

"Love it."

He pointed across the street at Sushi Bar Nippon.

I nodded. "Cool."

We ordered spicy tuna rolls, shrimp tempura rolls, California rolls, eel, sake, and plum wine. The food was great, the conversation was easy, and the wine was making the world seem lighter. The sun was deep inside the ocean, blue skies as dark as my growing desires.

It was a struggle not to, but I fought the urge to take out my card and see how many points this meal would be, added it all up in my head. If I went over my limit . . . I wouldn't go over my limit. Well, not too far. I wouldn't dress in mourning the rest of my life.

I asked, "Your wife cheated on you?"

"Thought we were keeping away from those topics."

"Okay, I'm nosy."

"Why?"

"Because . . . you're . . . you're very handsome."

He smiled.

I asked, "Where did you meet her?"

"In the Caribbean. She had just finished her studies at Baruch."

"An island girl."

"Yeah."

I ate another California roll.

He asked, "You're going to tell me what you do for a living?"

"Nope."

"Your real name?"

"Nope. Just call me Bird. And I'll call you Carpe."

We laughed.

"With an ex," he told me. "Guy she was with right before me, actually."

"Sorry to hear that."

"He was in law enforcement."

"An officer of the law committing crimes of the heart. The plot thickens."

"He was the one who moved her out here. She was pregnant. Quit her job. Had her furniture shipped. Drove out here by herself. Guy didn't help her at all. Relocated her whole life for the guy. When she got here, she found out he had another woman."

"Sounds like she was put on the bench."

We shouldn't have, at least I shouldn't have, but we laughed again.

I asked, "She had the baby?"

"She sent it down the toilet."

"You caught her when she fell." I tisked, shook my head. "And she got back with him?"

"Oh, yeah. As soon as he called, she was running back to him."

"How did you find out?"

"Got the code to her cellular. Heard the messages. They were meeting at a hotel."

"What did you do?"

"Went there. Found her car. Blocked her in and waited until she came out."

"Damn."

He took a breath and said, "You're right."

"What?"

"We should talk about something else."

His angst made lines in his forehead. I reached over and touched his hand. I said, "You should keep a journal. Write it all down, what you're going through."

"Is that what you're doing?"

"You could say that. My younger sister told me to journal."

"Writing down negative feelings . . . that helps?"

"It's not about being negative. It's about honesty with yourself. Helps me try to understand what I'm feeling."

"Do you?"

"Not really. Right now it looks about as coherent as something Algernon would write."

"Who?"

"Oh. My bad. *Flowers for Algernon* is a book about a retarded guy named Charlie and Algernon was actually a mouse . . . and . . . never mind. Long story."

"I get it."

I asked, "More sake?"

"Sounds good to me."

We sipped our poison and talked.

He said, "The nightlife is kicking down here."

"Lot of clubs down here with live music, if you're interested."

"Sounds like a plan."

Our waitress came over to check on us. A short and dark sister, beautiful face and wonderful petite shape. I doubted if she was out of college yet. Didn't have adult problems yet, not the kind that wore you out and robbed you of your right to sleep. All of the other workers at this Japanese sushi bar were Mexican, and she was the only person here who spoke English. Black woman in charge of Mexican cooks at a Japanese restaurant. It was kind of funny. It gave me and my date something to chuckle and whisper about.

He said, "Have to be honest . . . this is awkward."

I blew air and nodded. "It is."

"Wanna . . . stop?"

I said, "Let's just stop bullshitting each other."

"Aw, man." He nudged me. "Sure you want to? We were having so much fun."

"No." I laughed. "Not unless you do."

"You keep touching your hair, your face."

"Do I?"

He nodded. "You're all over the place."

"Your leg keeps bouncing," I told him. "The change in your pocket is talking to me."

"Trust me." He had a nervous grin. "I'm over here hoping I'm funny, hoping that I'm impressing you in some way, hoping I'm a good date so far, hoping we have a good time."

I raised a brow. "You're trying to impress me?"

"You're beautiful. Good personality. Not what I expected."

I nudged him. "Stop stealing my thoughts."

He laughed again.

I said, "I'm over here trying to think of open-ended questions to keep us talking."

We laughed together.

"What we said . . ." I let my words hang, then shifted, didn't know what to do with my hands, so I swallowed some more sake. "Did you want to . . . do something else?"

"Yeah. If you want to. No pressure. I'm free for the night."

He gave me a boyish smile, reached across the table, took my hand, rubbed my skin.

He said, "Ready to go?"

"Lead the way."

We left Nippon, hand in hand, opening the door between us a little wider.

A lot of traffic was going into Horton Plaza, a combination of seasonal shoppers and moviegoers. Military sentiment and support was on bumper stickers, in store windows. This was a military town and a lot of the men had the buzz cuts to prove it.

Carpe asked, "What kinda music do you like?"

"Doesn't matter. I'm open. You dance?"

"Little bit."

We heard blues playing and went into Croce's, a shotgun-style bar that had a small stage up front. We sipped beers, ate peanuts, were having a great time. Two Heinekens later I was thinking, fuck Weight Watchers and fuck the rest of the calorie-counting world. The music resurrected my soul, and it felt like I was nineteen again, reliving my college days, wild and loose, throwing caution to the wind, going after whatever made me feel good at the moment.

I didn't know any of the songs, but I was rocking and clapping my hands and loving every minute of it. We'd been there about an hour when a couple of nice-looking sisters came in and sat at the bar. Fine women with big legs in short skirts. Carpe rubbed my leg, told me he'd be right back, then went to those women. It was interesting watching him introduce himself, interesting watching the way they reacted to him with smiles, and just like that they were in a conversation. Not more than a minute went by before he came back to me.

He said, "There's a hip-hop club around the corner."

"Yeah?"

"You said you wanted to dance."

"So, anything I ask for, you can make it happen."

"I'll do my best."

"A sister could get used to being treated like this."

As soon as we walked into the club, we took off our coats and made our way to the crowded floor, found some elbow room, and danced to the remixed and hard beats of Too Short telling *motherfuckers* to *quit hatin'*, then bounced to 50 Cent, DMX, Nas, Snoop, and a few others. We danced until I felt sweat covering my arms and back. We rested long enough to wipe our brows, get more drinks, then went back to the dance floor.

A camera kept flashing. It was a red-haired white girl, snapping away.

She came out on the floor, a brother dancing all up on her, licking his lips and smiling like he wanted to use her to end racism, at least until the sun came up. San Diego looked like that kind of town, where Mayflower descendants had *Amistad* fetishes, and vice versa. She was drunk as hell, whoo hooing, in full tourist mode, taking pictures of everybody and everything.

She laughed and pointed the camera at me. "Smile."

I gave her the "move bitch" face. "Do you mind?"

"I'm from out of town. Just trying to have a little fun."

I ignored her. Turned my back and let her rude and drunk ass photograph other people.

She was trying to out-dance me, but my ethnic pride refused to let me be out-danced.

Carpe said, "Damn. You are working it."

I laughed. "I haven't even warmed up yet."

The camera flashed, that drunken girl taking pictures of herself, the guy she was dancing with, then everything. The brother she was with was all over her, holding her shoulders, helping her stagger off the dance floor. Looked like she was heading to the bathroom to toss her cookies.

I shook my head, wiped the sweat from my brow, went back to my own fun.

Atomic Dog came on and the room went wild, sent the house into freak-me mode. With the sensual moves and sexual energy, with all the whites and Mexicans and Asians in the crowd, it was like being in the middle of one big international orgy. I joined in, put my hands on my thighs, backed my pride and joy up into Carpe, my backside rolling up against his groin.

My date was with me, slapping my ass, dry humping me to the beat, rocking me booty song after booty song. With every touch we were opening a door I didn't want to close. When the booty songs faded, I ran my fingers through the sweat on my skin. He stayed behind me, held me close, dancing up against me, the kind of dancing that was more sex than anything else, his fingers moving up and down my body. And I felt him. Felt his heat and desire to live inside me harden against my ass. I closed my eyes, pressed against him, and danced my angst away.

I turned around, faced him, wondered how he moved in bed, how long it lasted.

He took my hand, rubbed my skin with his. My nipples were hard, aching.

I swallowed my own fire. "Let's change the temperature."

"Okay."

I touched his face, tiptoed, and we kissed. Not long, just enough tongue exchange to let us know where this might be going. It was a nervous kiss, a good kiss, slow and deliberate, his tongue feeling and tasting damn good, the kind of kiss a woman wants to fall into.

We stopped and stared at each other.

Then he let his tongue dance with mine.

I wiped my lipstick away from his mouth and we danced like we owned the city.

My problems were fading away and I was at Disneyland. My other life didn't matter anymore. Livvy didn't exist, only Bird. I loved the way Bird was feeling.

We danced until last call. Then sipped on water until the lights came on. I was tipsy, sweaty, tired, feet hurt, but not ready for Disneyland to shut down the ride.

He picked up our coats and led me through the thinning crowd.

He said, "It's after two."

"Already?"

It was the end of the night and we both knew what was next.

With sweat drying on my skin, the night air felt cooler. The nightlife was closing down, but people were hyped, trying to couple up and find their own one-on-one after-party to go to.

We held hands all the way back to my SUV. He was parked next to me. We stood between our vehicles and kissed some more. Kissed and he rubbed my breasts.

"What you said . . ." I let my warm words hang on the coolness of the night breeze, then shifted, didn't know what to do with my hands. "Did you want to—?"

"End the night with a smile on your face?"

"Yeah."

Our tongues danced again, this time longer. He rubbed against me, sent me a hard question. I rubbed back, sent him my wet answer. Then we stopped kissing, held each other, got ready to figure out how we were going to handle the next transition, the widening of this door.

He pulled my hair from my face. "Would you like to . . . the Hotel del Coronado?"

"Nice resort. Pretty expensive."

"I'll put it on my American Express."

I kissed him again. "I already have a room."

"You do?"

"Comfort Inn. Suite 2218."

His smile was almost as anxious as mine. Still, this had me bouncing my leg.

He followed me back toward I-8. Hotel Row. Miles of places built for indiscretions.

Room 2218 was upstairs, away from the office and street traffic.

The room was just that, a room. King-sized bed that had a little sag in the middle, old cover in blues and earth tones, industrial green carpet, a chair with no arms next to the dresser at the foot of the bed, another chair with arms at the small desk next to the bed. Heavy golden curtains and some sort of atrocious green and gray wallpaper throughout. There was barely enough room to walk by the foot of the bed and the dresser. A mirrored closet was on the other side of a small nightstand, a reflection that would reverberate whatever happened on that bed.

The door closed behind him.

There were no more words between us.

No words meant no more bullshit.

I pulled the curtains up, left a sliver of light.

He turned the little radio on, found soft music, then came

over to me. Our kiss took us to the bed. He grew against me and I shifted him so he was on the right spot, then bit my lips and moved against that growth. I pulled his shirt off; he did the same with my top, my breasts rising with my breathing. He took the ponytail holder away and my hair fell, framed my face.

This liquid sensation ran through me, one I'd had before. It was warm, tickled me all over. The same sensation I embraced the night I lost my virginity. When I wanted to experience something I had never experienced before. Anticipation of a new pleasure excited me.

He whispered, "What do you like?"

So many erotic images went through my mind.

I swallowed. "Surprise me."

He moved my hair from my eyes and I touched his chest. He was strong. He touched my breasts with both hands. I tingled. A fire grew inside me. He lowered his head and I closed my eyes, felt his tongue moving back and forth over my left nipple, then my right, making my breasts shine with his saliva. My eyes tightened; my first moan escaped me, followed by squirms, then more sounds that let him hear that dark and erotic side of me.

I touched his back, raked my nails over his flesh. His patchouli scent was seeping into me, into my skin, and his hair smelled like lavender. I loved lavender. It oozed sexuality. We had other odors, the ones that came from dancing and sweating, and those were just as erotic.

He asked, "Still nervous?"

"Don't stop."

To tell the truth I was terrified, like when the roller coaster was at the top and I could look down and see that first drop. He tugged my pants down over my hips, my thighs, and they bunched at my ankles for a moment, then he took my shoes off, dropped both, each thump sounding like my heartbeat, and pulled my clothes away from my feet.

Cool air covered my skin, telling me that I was naked.

He touched around my vagina. "Brazilian wax."

"Yeah."

"It's beautiful."

"Thanks."

"You smell so damn good. Love it when a woman takes care of herself."

He tongued my hip bone, my pelvis, took my toes in his mouth. I squirmed and moaned, God, how I squirmed and moaned. He was on his knees, holding the back of my thighs, pulling me into his mouth, praising me with his tongue, flesh that was very gentle, as smooth as water, a rhythm that made me hold the sheets and float, float, float.

It felt so good that three-letter sounds became four-letter words.

My shudders and twitches told me that this was real.

Now a stream of ten-letter moans and four-letter words came from me.

This was awesome. He was going to eat his way to China.

He moved away from me, left me twitching and breathless, heat rising between my legs, struggling to open my eyes, then panting and watching him take his clothes off.

My cellular phone started vibrating against the dresser, a blinking blue light in the darkness. It had to be three in the morning. Only one person would look for me at that hour.

In the blink of an eye, a thousand thoughts came and went. I thought about my husband, all of our ups and downs as a couple, about my life so far, about morality and immorality.

He said, "It's okay to answer it."

My cellular hummed again, danced across the dresser until it fell on the floor, then vibrated against the carpet. I watched it until the blue light quit flashing like a warning.

"Bird, you okay?"

I nodded. My words caught in my throat. "I want to watch you touch yourself."

He sat in the armless chair, stroking himself. I was curious what he would feel like inside me, to taste him, to become . . . official . . . I think that's a good word . . . to become official with him.

I sat on the edge of the bed, still tingling, my hands squeezing my breasts.

He told me, "Touch yourself, Bird."

I did. We entertained each other.

I said, "Hope you brought something."

He walked across the room, his dick bobbing up and down. I watched the solidness in his legs, in his back. I wanted my body to look that solid again. He dug in his pants and pulled out a Magnum. That made my vagina tingle and purr. A woman always hoped a man wore Magnum. Not only wore them, but was qualified to wear them. In that moment I remembered an ex who bought Magnums, but him wearing them was like me putting on a dress four sizes too large.

I asked, "Can I put it on for you?"

He smiled and came to me. I got on my knees, touched his offering. It was darker than the rest of his body, hot chocolate with thick veins running down the sides, one big muscle.

I said, "Open it up for me."

While he tore the wrapper, I primed him. I've always loved holding a man like that, his heat in my hand, looking deep into his eyes, hearing his breathing thicken, watching him lose control. Even when he handed the condom to me, I kept stroking him, feeling his energy rise until he closed his eyes and moaned. I was tempted to make him orgasm like that, not invite him inside me. I had the power to make him feel good in any way I chose. *That look* was on his face, the one that said this was so good.

His mouth parted and he licked his lips over his ragged breathing.

I said, "You're thick."

He smiled, touched my locks. My words boosted his ego, showed in his eyes. Always compliment a man on his penis. That was his vanity.

I put the condom on him, made sure it was there to stay.

I said, "Sit on the chair."

I straddled him, kissed him, his warm body against mine, his hand grabbing my ass. I was so wet. He stretched my walls, hard and strong, slipped deep inside, surprised me. The shock of a new lover being inside me made me shudder and gasp, then we were hanging onto each other. He pulled my hair, eased in and out of me, moved me away from pain.

Moans rose.

He pulled my hair, kissed me hard, slapped my backside and I was lost in . . . lost in . . . moving up . . . down . . . fucking him. I swallowed, panted, found enough wind and control to chant over and over. He was deep, rigid, hungry. Didn't expect it to be like this. The back of the chair slapped the wall. People next door had to hear. People passing by had to hear.

I lost it, said so many pornographic things.

His grip on me, so tight. My movements so . . . so . . . powerful. That was how I felt. Powerful. That rush of control had me so heady . . . so high. Then he hardened . . . grew inside me . . . his release . . . damn . . . so hot . . . again . . . leg trembled . . . back arched . . . saw a thousand flickering stars . . . soared on the wings of an angel . . . disconnected from this world and fell back into that place that owned no pain, that place that made me feel so alive and so close to death all at once, and I tried to stay there. Inside Orgasm lies healing. The zenith lifted the soul above all pain. But even a bird could only fly for so long. On the other side of every orgasm was reality. The truth I needed to avoid. My descent came back a breath at a time, and I struggled against it, moved against him with a fever, like I was in a hot-air balloon, easing back toward the ground.

I rested on him, his hands moving up and down my back, my hands doing the same to him. He was sweating a little and I was perspiring. Moisture gave his skin a nice glow. I rocked and moved against him, felt him go from firm to flaccid, then he softened and slipped out of me. I took his hand, put his finger on my spot, helped him massage me to the other side of the edge.

My shudders and twitches decreased. No more moans or four-letter words.

The ride was almost over.

When my breathing calmed a bit, I whispered, "God . . . that was . . . really good."

His hand played in my hair. "No, that was you."

"I was just responding to what . . . to . . . damn."

"You've got my head spinning."

"Best first-time sex I ever had."

"We're not done."

"Shit. I'm in trouble."

We kissed again.

I asked, "Want me to get up?"

"Not yet."

I reached down and touched his penis. The condom was still on.

We were back to being clumsy, naked, realizing how exposed we were, having a certain lack of grace. Two people who had been intimate and didn't know what to say.

I had committed adultery.

$\mathcal{L}$ivvy

Carpe carried me to the bed. We pulled the ugly covers up to our waists, our odors perfuming the room, me on my stomach, him on his side, our legs touching. I rubbed my leg against his the way a woman did when she wanted her lover to hurry and recuperate.

He touched my face, said, "You have beautiful lips."

"And you have a beautiful dick. Oh, you meant these lips, thought you meant those lips."

Carpe rubbed my body, admired me all over. "What size are you?"

"Five-five and I weigh one-thirty-eight, okay?"

"That's not big."

"For me it is. Gained eighteen pounds."

"The average size of a woman in America is twenty-two."

"But if you take out Oklahoma and Texas, it drops down to size nine."

He laughed.

I told him things I didn't want to. Good sex made a person talk. People were most honest in the first ten minutes after sex. Good dick was liquid Ecstasy and truth serum.

I said, "Gained most of my weight in the last four months. My hips and ass."

"How?"

"Had a Depo-Provera shot."

"What's that?"

"Birth control. Weight gain is one of the side effects."

I was wondering how he saw me, knowing that I was married, knowing that we had just met, knowing that he had conquered, never thinking that I had conquered as well. I think men saw us all as whores. Maybe damn near every woman was someone's whore: her husband's, her boyfriend's, always reduced to being someone's whore.

My cellular hummed again, irritated me and danced in the carpet and lit up the room.

I looked at the mirror, saw myself in bed with another woman's husband.

I crawled to the foot of the bed and picked my phone up, answered.

"Yes, Tony. What? What? What do you want?"

"What the fuck is going on, Livvy?"

"What the fuck you think, Tony?"

He said nothing for a moment. "Two weeks."

"I know. I have a calendar."

"Two weeks and you can't leave a message. I'm going crazy."

"Do you know what time it is? It's late Tony. After three in the morning. It's late and I'm tired. I have to teach in the morning."

"Livvy, don't—" He took a hard breath. "I went by Dermalogica today."

I knew what he was about to say. "How did you like the baby pictures?"

"You used your comp days and took the rest of the year off. So why are you lying about working?"

"Any word on the DNA test?"

"You took the rest of the fucking year off and . . . Where are you?"

"Did you tell me where you were when you were fucking that bitch?"

Thought that when I heard Tony's voice I'd quiver and cry. I was naked, with another man. Guilt was there, but it didn't smother me. No thick catch of regret was in my voice.

He asked, "Where are you?"

"Why? You wondering if I'm being naughty or nice? Ask Santa."

"Just tell me—"

"I am where I am and that's where I'll be until . . . until I'm somewhere else."

"I miss you, Livvy. That song 'Always' by Pebbles . . . our song . . . it's playing in my head twenty-four-seven and . . . look . . . let me . . . please . . . can I come where you are?"

"Nnnnnnnnnnno."

"Livvy," Tony said, exasperated. "I'd shove my head up my ass if I could."

Carpe had my foot in his mouth, sucking my toes over and over.

"You've already done . . ." I struggled with my breathing. "You've . . . damn . . . you've done that. At the dinner party . . . in front of everybody."

"I know, but I had no idea . . . Olivia, I love you. I'm sorry. I miss you. Come home."

"When will . . . when will . . ." A wave of tingles warmed my spine. "Oh, God . . . Jesus . . ."

"Livvy—?"

"When will . . . you know if the baby is yours?"

"I haven't heard anything, Livvy. I told you over and over, it might not be mine."

"But you still . . . you still . . . fucked . . . fucked . . . fucked her."

"We've gone over that."

Carpe had his finger inside me, stroking my swollen spot. I squirmed. Wanted to push his hand away. That finger followed me until there was nowhere to run. I closed my eyes, imagined his hand was Tony's hand, let myself get lost in Tony, fought to swallow my moan.

"I'm . . . I'm hanging up, Tony."

My husband called my name.

My love was coming down and I was losing my motor skills,

fumbling with my cellular, couldn't find the button to turn the damn thing off, so I broke it in half and let the pieces fall.

More heat and electricity curved my back, and I moaned, "Oh, God. Shit, nigga. Fuck."

My leg wobbled. An orgasm rampaged through me. It was so damn strong.

When it was over, I struggled to breathe, stared at Carpe, shook my head in disbelief.

Carpe took my foot in his mouth again, asked, "What size shoe do you wear?"

"Eight."

He asked me that like there had been no phone call to interrupt our conversation. I answered the same way. Tommie's voice was inside my head, whispering about pink elephants.

Carpe said, "You have a body that could make an army surrender."

"Mmmmm."

"They could've sent you to Baghdad and ended that war in fifteen minutes."

Carpe put his mouth on my breasts, tried to arouse me away from all bad thoughts.

I was angry at Tony. I was missing Tony. I was feeling emotional, another side effect from the Depo. Part of me was feeling dirty, ready to go home, another part not wanting to go home, and needing to get back to that place where nothing mattered, all of that at the same time.

I closed my eyes, imagined I was with Tony, cradled his erection in my mouth, and tasted us. I knew how to tell a man that he'd walked into a den of insatiability. This wasn't Tony. Not our flavor. Tony's call had stolen my high. I needed to get as far away from Tony and these thoughts as I could, find my way back to the edge.

I asked, "We're not finished, right?"

"Tell me what you need, Bird."

I whispered, "You ever rent a car?"

"Yeah."

"You drive it different than you did your own car?"

"Yeah."

"How so?"

"Drove it harder, faster. Pushed it to the limits."

"That's what I want right now. Rental car sex. Put me through the paces."

He kissed me, put on a condom, eased on top of me, entered me slow, and took me back to that place where there was no thought, no pain, that place that owned no reality.

The second fuck was always the best. I'd learned that over the years. Never to expect much from a man's first fuck. Never expect it to be too timeconsuming. It was the second one, the one that was nice and long, the one where they had to work longer and harder to get off, that was the sex I always craved. He sank in me and I shivered, let out so many sexy, melodic, and harmonic sounds. First we moved slow, then went from cool and calm movements to being gritty and guttural. He fucked me hard and I fucked him back with the same enthusiasm.

THE McBROOMS

The McBrooms

Livvy

"Why is it so hard to get good service at a black restaurant?" Frankie snapped.

It was late morning. We had run the hills of Inglewood at the crack of dawn, then gone to Tommie's place and showered. Now we were at one of the urban greasy-chicken and gummy-waffle houses, one that had pictures of all the out-of-work African American celebrities plastered on every wall like this was their shrine of unemployment. People were here, but the restaurant wasn't crowded.

"Frankie, chill the hell out." That was Tommie.

"Forget that," Frankie said. "We've been waiting twenty-five minutes and not one waitress has even come by to ask if we want a glass of damn water."

Across from us, a baby was laughing as her mother fed her grits and sausage. The baby smiled at me. I turned away, pretended I was looking at the framed black-and-white egos posted on the walls.

Tommie said, "Frankie, shut up."

"Look, he has chicken and waffles, those sisters have chicken and waffles, everybody has chicken and waffles but us. Excuse me, Miss Waitress. You see that? The heifer kept going."

Frankie grabbed her purse and headed toward the front door. She had on faded dungarees, sandals, a black sleeveless T-shirt that had NIETZSCHE HAD IT EASY in red letters on the front.

Tommie said, "She's gonna kill somebody if we don't get her some food."

Tommie was right behind Frankie. She was dressed in low-rise jeans, a sun-yellow T-shirt that had the phrases FORGET ART and $AVE THE OIL! framing President George W.'s grin.

I was dressed in sandals, jeans, and a light sweatshirt, everything black.

Tommie turned back to me. "C'mon. We're shaking this spot."

That baby was holding a chicken drumstick, eating grits, and smiling at me.

By the time I made it to the front, Frankie was at the cash register complaining.

Frankie snapped, "I shouldn't have to sit here and starve for twenty-five minutes, not even a biscuit or glass of water or somebody saying they'll be with us. What, am I invisible? You know what, *fuck a fucking chicken and waffle*. I'll give my money to CPK before I ever come up in here again."

Tommie was already outside, fluffing her eccentric hair, then shaking her head and pretending she wasn't with Frankie. I went out the door, Frankie behind me, shaking her head, cursing chicken and damning waffles. She slapped on her shades, made a right and stormed down Pico toward La Brea, a boulevard lined with potholes and worn strip malls, most having signs in English and Spanish.

Tommie asked, "You gonna tell her?"

"Hell no. Hope she walks to World on Wheels."

We stood there. Frankie slowed down when she realized we were parked in the other direction.

Frankie did an about face, marched back toward the ragged, uneven lot next to the restaurant.

I asked Frankie, "Wanna hit Roscoe's in Hollywood?"

"Fuck a fucking chicken and waffle."

Tommie said, "El Pollo Loco?"

"Fuck El Pollo Loco, fuck Popeye's, and fuck Golden Bird. And fuck Foster Farm."

Frankie kept going. Me and Tommie were walking slow and cracking up.

"Both of you c'mon dammit. I'm hungry. I gotta get some food. I told you before we drove all the way over here I was hungry dammit. We could've ate at Simply Wholesome and beat the rush and been shopping by now, but noooooooooo. You bitches just had to have some damn chicken and waffles."

Me and Tommie laughed so hard people passing by thought we were fit to be tied. Every time we stopped laughing, one of us cracked on Frankie and we started back howling.

Tommie struggled to pull it together. "Glad you're in a better mood."

"Whew. Stomach is hurting. Can't stop laughing at that fool."

"Good. You've been acting strange all morning."

We started walking, sucking up smog and sunshine, taking slow steps.

I wiped a laugh-tear from my eye with the back of my hand. "Lot on my mind, that's all."

"Tony? Did the DNA come? . . ."

I shake my head. "It's . . . well . . . San Diego. Did something I shouldn't have."

"Something tells me I don't wanna know what or who you were doing."

I sighed. "Tommie, you're the best. Wish I were more like you."

"What, celibate, in therapy, no man, and sales associate of the month at Pier 1?"

Again, laughter.

Tommie said, "I think I blew it big time."

"What?"

"Let me rewind. Okay, there is this guy. . . ."

"Oh, really?"

"I told him, in so many words, I'm feeling him."

"Has he told you he was feeling you?"

"Not exactly. Well . . . no. Not in the way I'm feeling him."

"Major mess up, Tommie. You know the game. No confessions."

"I know. And . . . and . . . well . . . He's almost forty. Has a kid."

"Damn, Tommie. That felon has two strikes."

"You're right. Don't tell Frankie. He's one of her renters."

"So, you seeing him?"

"Not since I told him. I'm letting it go before he thinks I'm a bugaboo."

She took my hand in hers and we made our way across the ragged lot. Frankie was letting the top down on her bourgeois-mobile, threatening to leave us if we didn't hurry up.

Tommie whispered, "San Diego . . . you were shagging?"

"We'll talk. Don't tell Frankie."

Tommie was surprised. She knows I've never hopped in bed with a stranger. I've always asked a ton of questions, and when we were done I asked a ton more.

Tommie tisked and I smirked as she got in the front. I relaxed in the backseat like always.

Frankie drove us down La Brea toward the 10. *The* 10. People in Los Angeles always put *the* in front of the freeways. *The* 10. *The* 5. *The* 110. Anyway, we didn't ask where we were going.

Frankie had shut up. That meant she was beyond hungry and mad.

Tommie and I left Frankie alone and got back to talking about our Christmas plans. We had started that discussion during our workout this morning, and still hadn't resolved where we were having family dinner since Tony and I were in a state of flux, the gift exchange, decorating trees, what to get close friends, who not to buy shit for, making cookies and gingerbread houses for our friends' children.

Tommie said, "For the dinner, we should invite extra people."

Frankie jumped in, "I'm not feeding skid row."

"Not our relatives, just some decent people we know."

Frankie asked, "Who?"

"Like . . . like . . . maybe people who can't get back home to their families, maybe the people we know whose life at home is not exactly the picture of a loving environment."

My attention wasn't with them, not at all. My new cellular phone had started vibrating and I faded out of the conversation. There was a new text message: *Bird, I want to see you again.*

I sent my reply: *We should leave San Diego in San Diego.*

He sent me another message. *Can't get you off my mind.*

I replied, *Same here.*

I want to be inside you.

My vagina jumped. It was still sore, and very happy. That next morning in San Diego, we had our good-bye sex. Sober sex. The quickie that was supposed to put the end to our one-night affair ignited a new fire. He laid me down, ate my pussy like he was on death row and I was his last meal, then stood me up, sexed me against the dresser. All over the room, this body was his. We ended up ordering pizza and staying there all day. The tingles, the heat that wouldn't die, it told me that I just needed to be fucked. To be reminded that this pussy still worked. He had me going crazy. I would've let him fuck me anywhere, side of the road, in a window, on the bed. Just fuck me and keep fucking me like he was a hunter and pussy season just began.

I closed my eyes and he was inside me, had me crossing and uncrossing my legs.

I opened my eyes, chewed my lip, and tingled while I typed out my thoughts.

I do miss u . . . your fingers inside me . . . your mouth on my breast . . . u riding me slow

Then I erased the message, didn't send it.

I couldn't go there again. Too much good sex and I'd start to feel the need to own.

Frankie said, "Livvy, you hear me?"

I snapped my phone shut. "Huh?"

Tommie said, "She's back there sending messages to some-booty."

I cleared my throat. "Work stuff. Somebody was asking where a few products were."

Tommie made that sarcastic *uh huh* sound.

Frankie peeped at me. "Am I missing something here, or am I missing something here?"

I said, "No."

Frankie nodded. "Yeah, I'm missing something. Your sneaky butt up to no good."

I stared at Carpe's last text message. *I want to be inside you.*

I felt him stirring my spot. My eyes closed and I tried to see what existed for us on the other side of Orgasm. I saw a blackness that was thick and never-ending.

My phone vibrated again. I didn't read the message. My panties were already wet.

We ended up on Hawthorne and 119th at Chips, a family-owned greasy spoon on the *Se Habla Español* side of town. Pictures of Bogart, James Dean, and Elvis were on the walls. All the workers were Hispanic, or Mexican, depending on what they liked to be called in the new millennium.

Service was fast. In no time flat we had a combination of breakfast and lunch food on our table.

We lowered our heads, and Frankie took over. "Dear Lord, thank you for this food we're about to receive. I pray for wisdom to understand men. Love to forgive them for being assholes. Patience for their moods. Because, Lord, if I pray for strength, the way I'm feeling, I'll beat one to death. Amen."

I sang, "Amen and Aaaaaa-woman."

Tommie tisked and shook her head. "From here on out, I bless the food."

Then we started pigging out and talking up a storm.

Tommie went on, "I want to invite two people over for dinner."

Frankie pressed on, "Don't piss me off with that . . . that feed-the-homeless babble."

"Well, Scrooge, you could always invite the fugly man."

I asked, "What fugly man?"

Tommie made a face like I was stupid. "I told you about him

when you were in San Diego. My bad, you were . . . Guess you were distracted in San Diego. So let me remind you all about her fugly—"

Frankie snapped, "Shut up, Tommie."

Tommie laughed. "And she didn't tell you she was with fugly and ran into Nicolas Coleman?"

I howled. "Big Dick Nick? The woo woo woo man?"

"I'm through talking to you, Tommie." Frankie frowned. "You know what, smart-ass? I'm raising your rent. Gonna charge you the same thing I charge everybody else."

Tommie took some of Frankie's pancakes. "Don't hate on me 'cause he was fugly."

Frankie pulled her plate away from Tommie. "What ya want for Christmas, Livvy?"

I swallowed a spoonful of oatmeal, thought about a lot of things.

I told Frankie, "Tony's paternity suit to come back negative."

Then there was a serious silence.

Tommie shrugged. "Compared to that, digging Frankie's fallout shelter is going to be easy."

We all laughed.

Frankie looked out the window, said, "This is our old stomping ground."

We grew up around the corner in an area that had more Spanish signs than English. All black and brown skin. Momma used to tell us to keep away from the Mexicans, but I used to admire their accents, had a crush on so many Latin boys. It was just something about them that did it for me.

Tommie said, "Remember when all of us used to climb up on top of our old garage when we were living on 110th, then jump off and land on an old mattress."

Frankie laughed. "We were crazy as hell."

"No, we were broke as hell."

We talked and ate off each other's plates. "Feliz Navidad" was playing on the radio. All of us stopped and sang along, had the Mexicans smiling and looking at us like we were insane.

Tommie pulled her braids back. "God, the years have flown by."

We paid the check and on the way to the car we kept pushing on each other, never stopped ragging on each other. The talking took me back. Took all of us back. That was why Frankie drove up Imperial Highway to Prairie and breezed through our old neighborhood.

She slowed in front of our old two-bedroom house on 110th. It had been painted from dark blue to peach. Looked better than it did when we lived and loved there, but the crowd of Mexicans out front let us know that our ghetto pass had been revoked.

Tommie locked her door. "It used to seem so much bigger."

I nodded. "And, damn, all these two-lane streets seemed hella wider."

We moved on, but kept looking back.

Tommie said, "That was our house, Sticky Fingers."

I leaned forward and popped Tommie upside the head. "What did I tell you about that?"

Both of those fools cackled like hens and started ragging on me again.

Frankie said, "Leave Tommie alone, Sticky. You know you used to go into Home Depot and steal everything you could get your grubby little paws on."

"Frankie, remember how she'd come home with nails, paint brushes, light switches—"

It was two against one. All I could do was fold my arms and try to talk louder.

I yelled, "Because I wanted to fix that raggedy house up. I wanted a nice damn house."

Frankie said, "Momma saw all the stuff you stole and freaked out."

Tommie imitated Momma, "If anybody in this house ever ends up at the police station, don't expect me or Bernard to have any pity on your black ass. Whoever got sticky fingers gonna be getting three hots and a cot like your dope-smoking cousins from the East Side."

"Her dumb ass got caught trying to steal a gallon of paint."

"Shut up, Frankie."

"And she was crying . . . the police brought her home . . . she was . . . Lord, she was confessing like she was on Perry Mason . . . begging Momma not to let them take her to Sybil Brand . . ."

"Shut up, Tommie."

Tommie wouldn't quit. "What do you get when you cross Winona Ryder with Bob Vila? You get Sticky Fingers at Home Depot."

Frankie howled. "Lord my side is hurting from laughing so hard."

I said, "You know what? Both of you bitches are getting on my nerves."

"Did she just call us bitches?"

We fought traffic and headed down on La Cienega and Third, became shopping warriors and battled to grab bargains at Old Navy, then hurried over to the Beverly Center. That was the spot to shop. Because when it got dark, the old fat Santa was replaced with a shirtless, sculpted Santa who had a lean Chippendale body. Just like all the other women with pornographic fantasies unabashedly asking Santa if they could sit on his North Pole, we were buck wild, touching his arms and pecs, joking and telling him we wanted him to come down our chimneys.

We shopped and talked for hours, until we were dead on our feet, then rode Sunset and cruised through ritzy neighborhoods looking to see who had the best lights. We always went by this one house in Hollywood Hills that had a live nativity scene. They hired out-of-work actors to dress up like Mary, Joseph, the three wise men, and perform in their front yard once a week.

Frankie said, "These people are half a brain cell from being retarded."

I said, "Don't say *retarded*. Say *Algernon*. It's literary and people'll think you're smart."

"Then shut up, Algernon."

We were all over the city, but a big chunk of my mind was still on our old house back on 110th, thinking about when I was in the third grade and Frankie was in the seventh, the day we came home and saw a beautiful Christmas tree sitting in the corner, waiting to get decorated. Momma had said we wouldn't be able to get us a tree that year. Money was tight.

Momma was sitting in the chair, her cafeteria uniform still on, hands in her lap, tears in her eyes. I hadn't seen her cry like that since Big Momma had died.

I was scared; the first thing I did was run to her, put my arms around her, started thinking about that cancer thing she said her big sister had died from.

I asked, "What's wrong, Momma?"

"Happy tears this time, baby."

A voice startled me. "Happy tears. The only kind I don't mind seeing."

That was when I saw this bear-sized man on our old sofa. It was the same man I'd seen in momma's bed. He had a little nappy-headed girl in his lap. The little girl stayed close to him the same way I stayed close to my momma around strangers.

His voice boomed, "Frankie, Olivia, I want 'chall to meet Thomasina."

He spoke our names like he knew us. I remember that now, so Frankie was with me.

He went on, "We call her 'Sina. This my daughter. In a few months, soon as we get some thangs straightened out, 'chall gonna be sisters, so get to know each other. She's four, so both 'chall gonna be her big sisters, if that's all right with 'chall."

I remembered it being real quiet, except for Momma's happy tears.

I asked, "What's your name?"

Frankie scrunched her face. "That's Mr. McBroom. He's the janitor at my school."

Momma tightened her lips. "He's a plumber. Works part-time as a janitor at Woodsworth."

"He's still the janitor."

Momma gave Frankie the shut-the-hell-up look.

"Bernard McBroom." He smiled and looked at his baby, then at us. "When we get everything situated, 'chall can call me Bernard if you like."

Momma wagged a finger at him. "Children shouldn't address adults by their first name."

He laughed his big hearty laugh.

Frankie said, "Everybody else does."

Again, Momma gave Frankie a look. "Well, we ain't everybody else, are we, Frankie?"

Most of the time Momma and Frankie were too much alike. Momma was seventeen years older than Frankie and they would go at it more like two sisters than mother-daughter.

Frankie said, "Uh . . . well . . . you marry our momma . . . then can we call you . . . daddy?"

But she had her soft side. The side that wanted a real daddy, just like I did.

He smiled. "If you want, then that's what 'chall call me. Li'l 'Sina can call your momma Momma, if that's what they agree upon. I'll let 'chall women figure that out on your own."

Something inside me glowed. It lit up the room when I smiled back at him.

Momma went and got the decorations and all of us started decorating the tree. By the time we were done, it was like we were a real family, and Frankie and I were both crying.

Tommie's mother had died two years before. Car accident out in Moreno Valley. Our dad had died four years before that. Got sick all of a sudden and a month later he was gone.

When we were growing up, our neighborhood was a world of latchkey kids being raised by aunts, grandparents, and stepfathers. Then there were the drive-bys and the crack houses.

So in a city where there wasn't any moral fortitude, Momma found a man named Bernard. He looked you in the eye when he talked to you, walked with his head up and chest out. Bernard was as big as a bear, skin as thick as a football's, a brother from that generation of hardworking men who shaved their finger-nails with a pocketknife.

We had a daddy. Momma had a man in the house.

And in the deal, the two Wimberly girls became the three McBroom daughters.

Livvy

My consciousness came back like a good scream.

Something inside me was going off. A warning.

I jerked awake. It took my eyes a moment to focus on the digital clock. It was between three and three thirty in the morning. I had come back home. I was in my marriage bed, as naked as I was on my newlywed night. Our bed was waist-high, the right height to make love with him standing up. Mirrors. Pillows. An armless chair. Silk scarves. All the essentials. I came back to my husband because if I didn't come home to him, I know where I would've gone.

Tony wasn't in bed anymore. His side was warm. I pulled the covers back and the night air chilled my naked flesh, hardened my nipples. Tony's cologne was on my skin, traces of him on my arms, on my hands. Condoms were on the nightstand. A three-pack of Trojans, one used.

I sat up. The light wasn't on in the master bathroom.

Curtains were open so there was enough light for me to make out silhouettes of everything in the room: the unlit candles on the dresser, the French doors, and the armoire.

Something was wrong. Out of place. I stared at the dresser. Couldn't figure it out.

I was about to lie back down and try to get some sleep. Then it hit me.

Before I knew it, I was hurrying across the room, standing in front of the dresser.

My purse was missing. I had left it on the dresser. I always put it on the corner dresser closest to me. I looked on the floor, but I knew it wasn't there because Momma had told us to never put our purses on the floor. Bad luck to do that. I looked in the chair. Not there either.

My purse was missing. My cell phone was missing. My husband was missing.

I was about to scream, but Tony's name caught in my throat. Even though it was dark, I hurried to the bathroom door, turned the handle, pushed it opened. Empty. Same for the guest bedroom, guest bathroom, office, and laundry room. The carpet hid my rushing around while I eased down the stairs. Halfway down, I stopped on the landing and listened. It was quiet, but the glow from underneath the door to the downstairs bathroom betrayed my husband.

I stood in front of the bathroom door, heard him in there going through my belongings. I turned the doorknob. It was locked. Sounded like he jumped and dropped a few things.

My heart sped up and I shouted, "Tony, give me my purse."

I hit the door with my fist, then turned the handle again.

"Give me my damn purse, Tony."

I hit the door with my fist again.

The bathroom light went off. The door opened. In the darkness he handed me my purse.

I asked, "Where is my damn cell phone?"

His hand came out in the dark, handed me that too.

I didn't have to look at it to know he'd gone through my cellular phone, looking at phone numbers from missed calls, incoming calls, and outgoing calls. I'd cleared all of those before I came home. I'm not stupid. My phone was on and I know I'd turned it off.

I exploded. "I hope you found what you were looking for."

"You want me to answer that?"

I ignored his bluff, went into the living room, sat on the carpet facing the fireplace. It was off. The room was dark and cold. I heard him walk into the room behind me.

"Livvy . . . It's too cold to be on the floor naked."

I didn't turn around. "Tony, don't come near me."

"At least get a blanket."

"Keep away."

His voice was feet away. "Why was your phone vibrating at two in the morning?"

"My phone didn't vibrate because my phone was off."

"You just thought it was off."

"So you turned it back on?"

"I didn't turn—"

"Stop lying."

"Who sent the text—?"

"Why would you violate my privacy—?"

"Because your damn phone was blowing up like Baghdad. No friend would call—"

"For all you know, it could've been my sisters."

"They would've called the house. That's if they knew you were coming home."

A headache came on.

He asked, "If it's nothing, why are you scared?"

"I'm not scared. I'm pissed off."

Then came the tears.

He asked, "You seeing somebody?"

I didn't say anything, just wiped my eyes with the back of my hand. He asked again. Still no answer from me. I never argued the truth. Right now my home felt like my prison.

I said, "I shouldn't have let you fuck me."

"Why did we have to use a condom?"

"Why you think?"

"I got tested. You got tested. We were fine—"

"I still don't trust you, Tony."

"Trust? You've been gone for weeks, I can't find you, and you don't trust me?"

"If you would've used a condom with that bitch—"

"Livvy, I told you—fuck it."

"And you have a lot of nerve questioning whatever I do."

"Is that how you see it?"

"That's the way it is."

"You're pretty suspect yourself. We haven't used condoms since—"

"So, is that why you're going through my purse and my phone?"

"You've had a Depo shot, so why would I need to use—?"

"Because I made your hoing ass put on a damn condom?"

My eyes were closed. Cellular phone in my hand. Purse in my lap.

His voice remained behind me. "You know what?"

I didn't respond.

He said, "You didn't delete the text messages."

I pulled my lips in, then for some reason, I laughed and shook my head.

I asked, "Did you show your mother the pictures of your baby? It has eyes just like you, so that means the kid has eyes just like your mother."

Tony didn't think it was funny.

I said that to hurt him, but my words only made me feel barren.

"Who were you with in San Diego?"

"Will you give it a rest?"

"Were you alone?"

"Keep away from me, Tony."

In the movies, this was where the couple went insane, screamed, fought, and tried to kill each other, then the neighbors dialed nine-one-one and the police came, put chalk marks around the scene of a murder-suicide, and the end of your life became fodder for the morning news.

We did kill each other, only we did it with silence.

I opened my eyes and stared at the fireplace. There was no fire.

That was when I noticed a light blinking on and off. The oscillating luminance came from across the street. Colorful, happy lights letting people know Christmas was on the way.

I closed my eyes the way a child did when she was trying to make herself invisible.

Eventually I said, "She had you served at my dinner party. Then she sent pictures to my mailbox. To our house. To this goddamn address. This is our home and it's like she's moving in. She knows the baby is yours, Tony. She wouldn't do some shit like that if she didn't know."

My eyes stayed closed, my world black. Tony's breathing told me how bad he felt.

I said, "We've spent eight thousand on fucking legal fees. And on top of that, we'll have to pay back child support for damn near a year. Then there is going to be child support every fucking month and . . . visitation."

He whispered out his frustration, "What can I do to . . . What can I do, Livvy?"

Tony left the room, his footsteps going up the stairs. Then I heard him coming back, each step so heavy. He put a blanket around me, then there was a click. The fireplace came on.

He said, "I love you, but I'm not going to kid myself. I'll call my lawyer tomorrow."

He went back up the stairs.

Tommie

You need me to get Frankie and come over there?" I'm half-awake, rolling out of my bed, grabbing my jeans from the floor. My clothes are scattered all over the room, some in laundry baskets. I step on a bag of Doritos, bump into the wall, say forget the jeans, grab my purse, and make sure I have my keys, wondering if I'll need to use the Mace. "I'll call Frankie as soon as I hang up and I'll be there in five. Coming in my pajamas and slippers."

"Tommie, no. Calm down."

"Do I need to dial nine-one-one?"

"Tommie, *will you calm down?*"

Livvy sounds distraught and I need to see her. By the time I get to the back door, she convinces me to not come over there. She tells me that Tony is upstairs and she is okay.

"Okay, okay." I take a sharp breath. "He put his hands on you?"

"I'm okay."

"Yes or no."

"No."

Livvy needs to talk it out. She tells me what just happened between her and Tony, how she woke up and he was playing Eye Spy with her purse, and the argument.

I'm pacing, shaking my head. "Divorce?"

"He didn't say the D-word, but that's what he meant."

She's in her living room, sitting on the floor, talking to me on her cell phone, crying soft and easy. I'm walking from room to room, listening to her talk about her marital problems.

She says, "He's so in denial."

"Denial is a defense mechanism, all about self-preservation."

"Look, if I wanted a shrink, I would've called a shrink."

"Yes or no, you need me to come over there?"

She sighs. A moment goes by.

I head into my living room, turn on the light, walk around, then turn the light off.

She says, "Let me pack and come over there. Won't be able to sleep without dreaming he's going to kill me. And I can't stay awake because I'll start dreaming about killing him."

We hang up.

My place is bright and colorful, cheap Salvador Dalí prints tacked on textured red and orange and blue walls, colors and art that reflected my mood when I was painting, my furniture just as colorful. My world is a mess. Dirty dishes for days. Dust covers both my secondhand and IKEA-style furniture. I turn on a few lights, rush to start cleaning up before Livvy gets here.

I'm straightening up the pile of bootleg CDs on my living room floor when my phone rings. I rush and put the CDs on top of my small television and they all fall down. I get to the phone, see the name Jerry Mitchell on the ID, and answer in a distant tone, "Yeah, Blue?"

"Whaddup?"

I click my teeth, wish I hadn't answered, and say, "Whassup?"

"Catch you at a bad time?"

I want to say yes, that it's four in the morning, but instead I repeat, "Whassup?"

I let my word hang there, biting my lip and suppressing any emotion in my voice.

He asks, "Everything all right over there?"

"What you mean?"

"I saw you pacing back and forth."

"You're watching me?"

"No. I was up listening to Front Page and working on my screenplay, looked out my window, your lights were on, saw you pacing."

"You hide in the dark and watch me walk around my apartment?"

"I saw you. I don't watch you."

"You're watching me now."

"Okay, I look over there sometimes."

I tell him, "You're stalking me."

"No, isn't that what Neighborhood Watch is all about?"

"Put down the binoculars and watch the neighborhood, not me."

"Just making sure you're okay."

"Why would you care if I'm okay?"

I frown at my full garbage can when I go into the kitchen, frown because a brown rice box, cotton balls, and Crest toothpaste are about to spill out. I tie a knot in the plastic bag and rush to load the dishwasher. Blue is talking but I'm busy moving the garbage to the back door, then racing back and groaning at the sink filled with dishes. A couple of my orange plates have crusty, unidentifiable leftovers, so I have to rinse and scrub those first.

He says, "I haven't heard from you since . . . since you were over."

"I know. Saw you when I came in."

"I waved."

"I waved too."

He says, "And you kept going."

"Didn't want to . . . Look," I lose my thought when I start cleaning the chicken residue off my George Foreman grill. My place is a neglected messy, like a college dorm room, and I'm trying to rush it back to being a livable messy. "I . . . Look . . . whassup, Blue?"

"Any particular reason I haven't heard from you?"

"Whassup? Does Monica need me to hook up her do?"

"Rosa Lee braided her hair. What's that noise?"

He hears me spraying air freshener. "That's good. She got her six braids. Real good."

"Why are you sounding like . . . never mind."

I drop a glass in the sink. It breaks. I think I cut my finger, but there is no blood.

I grab paper towels, try to clean that up and say, "Glad you connected with Rosa Lee. They're good people. I'm probably going to be too busy to do her hair for a while anyway."

"She was over playing with Rosa Lee's daughter, and I didn't ask Rosa—"

"It's getting close to Christmas so I'll be working longer hours because I need the cheddar, so maybe you can ask Rosa to keep her hair tight. I'm sure she won't mind."

"Why do you sound like that?"

"Sound like what?"

It takes me a moment to find the Windex so I can squirt my glass kitchen table. The legs are uneven and the table wobbles as I wipe away the dust and scrub off the glass rings. My journal, notebook, and a few books are there too, things like *Prozac Nation, 203 Ways to Drive a Man Wild in Bed, Delicious Sex, Kama Sutra, Unleashing the Sex Goddess in Every Woman, How to Make Love to a Man, The Good Orgasm Guide.* I leave *Prozac Nation* and my notebook, but grab the rest of the books and hide them in the washing machine.

I ask, "Where's Monica?"

"Sleep. We're mad at each other. She wet the bed and we were up fighting."

"Bad dream or something?"

"She gets real funky like that after she spends time with her mom. A couple of hours with her mom and it seems like all the hard work I put in goes down the drain."

"Well, going to a trailer park can be traumatic, especially during tornado season."

I hurry into my bedroom and start throwing clothes into the laundry basket.

Blue asks, "Okay, what are we doing, Tommie?"

"Blue, I'm not stupid. I got your message."

"You're mad because Rosa Lee did Mo's hair?"

"You know this isn't about Rosa Lee or Monica."

He hesitates. "Okay."

"I'm not a child. I understood what you were saying."

Then I'm in the living room. Standing in my bay window, a bottle of Windex in one hand, a roll of paper towels under my arm, looking across the street at Blue's silhouette, talking to him like we're in the same room, face-to-face. I feel his energy. First it tickles the hair on my neck, then spreads like a morphine itch, makes me want to run my fingers through my braids.

"Blue, I'm twenty-three and you're . . . not. I work like a mule and make the paycheck of a Hebrew slave. I don't have my degree and I'm kinda scared to go back to school. I left town because of an abusive relationship, but I'm doing a lot better, and I'm still in therapy because of those past issues, so who would want to hang out with a pill-popping woman who gets depressed from time to time. I've been celibate for the last two years because . . . just because. I'm living in my oldest sister's duplex pretty much rent-free. And I'm sales associate of the month at Pier 1 because I help idiots who can't coordinate colors pick out a bunch of candles and knickknacks."

"I don't think you understood what I was saying, Tommie."

"My shit ain't together and your shit ain't together."

"That's not what I said, Tommie."

"I understood. There's no future in what . . . I can't even say what it is, don't know how to address it, because there is nothing to address, so you're right, it's nothing. I was tripping."

"Tommie—"

"You know what it's late or early and Livvy just called over here with episode fifty of her drama and that took a lot out of me and she's on the way over because her and her husband got into it and I'm irritated and I have to get up early because I'm opening and I'm working zone three tomorrow so that means I'll have to clean the toilets and I'll be on my feet all day so I better get my sleep and I'll talk to you some other time and make sure you give Monica a kiss for me and please say bye because I'm feeling really stupid and I don't know how to end this conversation without . . . without . . . Just don't ask any more questions and I'm fine so say bye."

I stand in my bay window, feeling like a fool.

"Okay, Tommie."

We hang up. Neither one of us moves from the window.

I count to ten, swallow, then close my blinds and start using Windex wherever I can.

I'm in the kitchen trying to sweep the crumbs on my floor when my phone rings again.

I answer, "Whassup, Blue?"

"Look . . . I need to give you something, so let me know when you have a moment—"

"You know what? Bring it over and drop it off now. And I can give you Monica's Christmas present and we can get that out of the way."

"Mo's sleep. Would be cool if you gave it to her."

"Well, I'm . . . I can . . . Look, right now, I'm busy, and I'm waiting for my sister."

"Let me check on Mo. I'll throw on some sweats and run over real quick."

I pause. "Sure."

As soon as I hang up, I grab the broom and get ready to sweep the hardwood floors.

Then I almost can't move.

My body tingles and an anchor holds me where I stand.

Numbness rises. Anxiety come in waves, tries to steal my breath.

At first I think the sudden stress is because I'm not sure if I want Livvy to meet Blue; I stop sweeping, drop my broom. But I know why I feel that way.

Blue's never been invited over here, has never been in my space.

We'd be alone.

I break free from that monster's grip, race to the phone, and call him back.

My voice wants to give away my anxiety, but I focus on my breathing, my words, then I talk in a controlled tone, tell him, "Look . . . if . . . since Monica's sleep, I'll run over there."

He says, "I'm dressed and I was on the way."

"No," I snap. Again, I focus on my breathing. "I mean . . . Blue . . . I'll . . . let . . . I was about to take the trash out and then . . . then . . . then I'll run over there."

Livvy is coming down Fairfax, on the other side of the stop sign at 62nd Street. I see her bright headlights zooming this way as I jog across the street. My front door is open so she can get in. I wave, not sure if she sees or can tell it's me, then rush up the stairs to Blue's building.

His door is open and I go in without knocking, wanting to rush inside before anyone sees me. I say his name, then walk to the kitchen. He has on jeans and a GARY COLEMAN FOR GOVERNOR T-shirt. Blue is putting a cup in the sink, as if he were cleaning up the kitchen before I came over.

We're face-to-face.

I say, "Hi."

He says, "Hi."

We say that as if we haven't seen or talked to each other in weeks.

He says, "Nice pajamas. Matching duck slippers. Cute."

"Thanks. From the Peabody in Memphis."

He walks by me. We don't touch. I stand in the doorway between the kitchen and the living room, watching him go to a table near his bay window. The table is small, has a candle-holder with seven candles: three red, three green, the center one black.

I say, "Nice Kinara."

"Thanks."

The wooden table is set up with fruits, vegetables, one ear of corn, and a straw place mat.

I say, "It's beautiful."

"Bought the table and place mat yesterday."

"You're getting geared up for Kwanzaa."

"Have to get to Leimert Park and find a better Unity cup."

I ask, "You getting a tree?"

"Not big on the commercialization of Jesus' birth, not the way it's become a selfish bogus holiday, would rather Mo learn about our heroes and the value of family. We need to celebrate Malcolm, Marcus Garvey, Nat Turner, Harriet Tubman, Fannie—"

"All I asked was if you were getting a tree."

Blue bites his top lip. "A small one. We don't have a lot of space."

"Monica should have a tree."

He looks at his feet and pulls at his hair. "Tommie . . ."

Forever goes by before I respond. "Whassup?"

He takes a deep breath, lets it out, and creates a smile. "Why is it easier for us to talk when we're on the phone, or standing in the window, than when we're face-to-face?"

I rock a bit, but offer no answer.

He goes to the corner. My eyes go to the mantel, to the picture of Blue, Monica, and Monica's mother. A family portrait. The way life should be. Blue moves some things around and comes back with a second candleholder, one nicer than his. He hands it to me.

He says, "This Kinara is from me and Mo."

"Wow."

"She picked it out."

"Wow. This is . . . wow."

"Giving it to you now so you can get what you need to make it complete in time."

"Well, I don't have children, so I won't need corn."

We laugh.

He says, "Hopefully you will need many ears of corn one day."

The way he says that adds to my clarity. There is no *we* for me in this world.

I smile. "When the time is right, two ears of corn will suit me fine. No more than three."

I put the Kinara down and hug him. He hugs me tight. In his arms, I feel secure. The anxiety that had crept up on me wanes. In that moment, I argue with myself in silence, frowning and chewing my lip. And it feels like he was right. We're platonic friends, and friends last longer than most lovers. He's older, has a child, and I have a lot of living to do.

And he's my neighbor.

I let him go, step away, resign myself from my romantic thoughts, move those to my mental hope chest, a place that holds fantasies unfulfilled.

I thank him again, then politely say, "I better go. My sister is—"

"I have something else for you."

"This is more than enough."

"It's from me. I need to give it to you now . . . in case we miss each other."

"What is it?"

"Its Latin name is *Viscum album*."

"What kind of herb is that?"

"The ancient Druids of northern Europe and other pagan groups celebrated the beginning of winter by hanging it in their homes."

I wait for him to go to the mantel over his fireplace. He picks up an evergreen shrub, one that has a cluster of white berries.

He brings it back and shows it to me.

He says, "It also represents sexuality and fertility."

"Do we roll it up and smoke it? Livvy's stressed and could use a good—"

"No."

"Just checking because I have some papers at home. A pipe too."

"Most people put it over their door this time of year."

"Druids and pagans." I shrug. "Okay. *Viscum* whatever. Sure they didn't smoke it?"

"You might know it better as mistletoe. With . . ." He clears his throat, shifts like he's a little nervous. "With each kiss . . . you kiss and you take away a berry. . . . When they're all gone, it loses its power. So, when . . . when it's over your head . . . that's when . . . you have to kiss."

He puts it over my head, then pulls me closer to him, his other hand up to my face.

My heart gallops. Again my palms become rivers and my throat a desert.

"We're supposed to kiss, Tommie."

"Oh, shit . . . Blue . . . oh, shit."

My palms turn into fists, and a pagan tradition anchors me where I stand.

"Blue . . ."

He touches my face with his hand and I feel him shaking too. I close my eyes, my body on the road to becoming the sun. His breath warms my skin.

"Blue . . . just woke up . . . ate onion Doritos before I fell asleep . . . need to brush . . ."

My breathing thickens when his lips touch mine. Then his tongue moves across my lips, not rushing, asking my mouth to open, to let him inside me, but only if that is what I want.

It is.

His tongue meets mine, and I shiver as my heart rushes and settles between my legs. A groan comes and I'm liquid fire. Breathing in shallow gasps, struggling to stay afloat. My knees betray my weakness and I hold him, dig my nails in his arms. We kiss, nibble lips, suck tongues. He pulls me closer to him. Firm chest presses against swollen breasts. He moans. My hand raises, touches his face, strokes his stubbly chin, then touches his strong mane.

Blue moans and drinks me. With the same passion, I drink Blue.

We never stop kissing. When I think we're about to end, we begin again.

I'm in the zone, floating with Blue, the kiss never-ending, tingling, every nerve alive.

"Daddy."

We jump away from each other, two children being caught by their parents.

Monica comes into the living room, her hair in six beautiful braids, a tablet and a crayon in one hand, a flexible brown-skinned Barbie doll in the other. She gets on the futon, oblivious.

Then she stretches and yawns before she sees me.

She says, "Good morning, Tommie."

I say, "It's not morning time—"

Blue says, "Sun's coming up."

He's right. The room isn't dark anymore. Our kisses have stirred the sun, made it envious. Seems like minutes have passed, but on the wings of our kisses, so much time has gone by. I have never kissed anyone that long, never with that intensity.

Monica says, "Daaa-ddy, I'm hungry."

"You're always hungry. What do you want?"

"Oatmeal and raisins and banana. And I gotta use it."

"You want orange juice?"

"Water. Can I have some bread with butter on it until I get my oatmeal?"

"Okay, Mo. Go potty."

"Okay, Dad."

"You gonna need help?"

"You stay right there, Daddy, and I'll call you when I need help, okay?"

"Okay."

"Make sure you stay right there."

Monica goes into the bathroom and pushes the door up.

She calls out, "Daaa-ddy."

"Yeah, Mo."

"I need toilet paper."

"Okay, Mo."

Blue and I look at each other. No words.

I take the mistletoe, put it over his head. He gives me another kiss, this one short.

I whisper, "How long is this Druid-pagan thing good for?"

He smiles. "You've used up two of the berries."

"Where can I get a mistletoe tree? Better yet, is there a mistletoe forest?"

We laugh, then hug each other. His hardness presses against me.

Our lips meet again; our tongues engage in another spiritual exchange.

Monica calls out, "I'm finished."

Again we jump, our breathing so thick, his eyes glazing, just like mine.

Blue's voice is soft. "Damn, Tommie."

I blush. "I don't want to use up all my berries in one day."

Monica calls out, "I'm fin—"

"Here I come, Mo."

"No, you stay in there, Daddy. I want Tommie to help me."

"Here I come, Monica."

Blue stares at me, gradually letting go, heads into the kitchen to start making oatmeal.

My world is light. I bump into things and fan myself, then go get a roll of toilet paper out of the hall closet. I straighten out my pajamas, but my erect nipples are too hard to hide.

I knock on the bathroom door and Monica tells me that it's okay to come in. Her nose scrunches up and her little hands are over her eyes. She does that whenever she does the number two. She holds Barbie in one hand, leans forward on my leg, and I clean her. Then she gives me Barbie. She wants to pull her panties and pajamas back up on her own. In some ways I'm imagining her daddy doing the opposite to me. I haven't imagined letting a man do that in years.

She laughs and tells me, "You look funny."

"Do I?" I touch my cheeks and feel pleasure that doesn't want to wane. My heartbeat is still thumping between my thighs, the cadence not as strong, but still steady. "I guess I do."

She educates me on the wonders of her flexible Barbie while I help her wash her hands.

Blue calls out, his tone sudden and urgent, "Tommie."

"What's wrong?"

"Two sheriff cars are in front of your duplex."

"Are they going to the downstairs neigh—?"

"They just went inside your place."

"Oh, damn. Livvy. I forgot about Livvy."

I leave Monica behind me, a paper towel in her hand, and rush to Blue's front door. I look first to verify what he said, and I see the cars, one blocking my narrow driveway.

Frankie's convertible is outside too, parked in front of Womack and Rosa Lee's building.

My heart moves to my throat. Something is wrong.

My first thought is that Tony has hurt Livvy. Maybe he followed her . . . maybe he . . . too many thoughts of being beaten and battered clutter my mind all at once, none of them pretty.

My movements become opaque as trepidation gives me wings. I'm down the stairs, flying across Fairfax, almost being hit by a car, then I'm at my door, breathing hard and upset.

I push the door open.

Two officers are in my living room. Livvy is on the sofa, but hops up the moment I come in. Her mouth is wide open. Everyone is looking at me like I've done something wrong.

Livvy says, "There she is. That's her."

The officers stare at me.

I get scared. "Oh shit. This isn't about the parking tickets, because I intend to pay—"

The officers laugh. I don't know if it's because of what I said, or the duck pajamas and duck house shoes that I've almost run off my feet.

Frankie is leaning against the red wall, no makeup on, dressed the same as Livvy, in old sweats and older running shoes. At first they look surprised, relieved, then pissed off.

My sisters' combined attitudes tell me what's going on long before their words come.

I'd run out the house, left it in shambles, broken glass in the sink, purse left behind, Jeep still here, keys and cellular phone on the table, front door wide open.

Two hours had gone by.

It didn't feel like it, but while I kissed Blue, time had no meaning.

Livvy thought somebody had broken in, trashed my place, and I had been kidnapped.

Nobody thought that was funny, except me.

Frankie

I stormed out of Tommie's crib before the sheriffs left, mad as hell.

Talk about two friggin' drama queens.

Since I was up, I drove my sleep-deprived butt to Kenneth Hahn Park, put on my hooded jacket and gloves, and got my run on. This morning running helped keep me from going nuclear and catching a case. Put in five miles. Needed to run ten, but I wasn't feeling it. Had to stay on my program. I have this picture of myself taped on my refrigerator. My before shot: cellulite in a bikini. Before my meals, I had to face the old me with the Halle Berry cut and the Fat Bastard butt. Let me tell you, just like Al "The Thin Man" Roker said, it ain't easy getting it off, and was a full-time *j-o-b* keeping it off, especially this time of year. Food was every-damn-where.

I had a lot of things on my To Do list. I was tired as hell, still pissed off, was craving the company of a man, but told myself that I was better off chilling and getting in some me time. Told myself that I had more glory than sadness in my life right now, yakking out all the Oprah bullshit a sister said to herself to make it seem like being alone was so damn cool.

Next thing I knew, I was firing up the laptop. I had a lot of junk cyber-mail, crap asking me if wanted to purchase a vibrator that played "O, Cum All Ye Faithful."

I ordered one.

Then I called Tommie's crib and woke Livvy up. She was still in a foul mood and I was doing what I could to get her spirits back on track without her dragging me down.

Livvy said, "Tony messed up the fantasy. I had this fantasy of a perfect life."

"Bitch, quit the Mother Teresa act. You fucked a nigga in Cancún."

"That was before we got married."

"So what?"

She yelled, "And you slept with two guys in Cancún."

"Twins count as one. And I didn't have a boyfriend at the time, so don't hate."

She cursed me out and hung up on me.

I laughed, plopped down in front of my PC, and logged on.

I was so tired of stupid-ass people forwarding me dumb shit like BLACK VOTING RIGHTS EXPIRE IN 2007. Me thinketh thou weave be a little too tight. ASBESTOS: SECRET INGREDIENT IN TAMPONS. Gimme a friggin' break. COCKROACH EGGS AT TACO BELL." Okay, I believed that one. Anytime a place of fine dining had a flea-ridden mutt as a spokesperson, anything was possible. But still, there should be some sort of a friggin' IQ test before you're allowed to log on, because too many candidates for the short yellow bus were dancing in the fields of cyberland.

After deleting all that crap I yawned and went through a ton of e-mail from that personal ad, deleting and laughing and cursing. When that many fugly men sent you e-mail, half of 'em butt naked, it made you wonder what the hell they saw when they looked at your picture.

Then one of them sounded pretty promising.

Okay, first, the picture he sent me was off the chains. Professional and hip. I e-mailed homie, and he was online, another cyber-junkie, and he hit me right back. Outside of a few misspelled words, his online conversation was nice. And he said that the picture he sent was him, and was taken in the last six months. And to prove it, I went out to his job's Web site and checked him out. Then to be sure, I had homeboy fire up his digital camera, take a mug shot, and e-mail it to me right then and there.

What really made me interested was the quote on his ad. *Love is friendship set on fire.*

Corny, but at least he knew how to fake the funk and not broadcast the vibes of a pervert.

I hopped my rooty tooty butter pecan booty up, jumped in my sweats, and zoomed down to Manhattan Beach. Needed to run up to Tommie's j-o-b at the overpriced candle factory. Wall to wall, the plaza was jam-packed with frantic, rude, and irritated shoppers—loved the way holiday sales, bad traffic, and jacked-up parking brought out the heathen in everybody.

Tommie was running around in those whacked green pants and red shirt under that blue apron, looking like a super-sized leprechaun. Reindeer socks and frosted makeup. She was making the McBroom name look as bad as it sounded. She was so busy working the cash register, fooling customers and making them think she could decorate, smiling and guiding their decisions as if they were children. That's why she didn't see me until I was right up in her face.

I tried not to laugh, but couldn't hold it in. "You're giving people decorating tips?"

"What do you want?"

"The Jeep."

"Going to get a tree?"

"Meeting a guy for drinks. Wanna roll low profile."

We traded keys, kissed cheeks, and I ran out of the store, still laughing.

I was almost at Tommie's Jeep when an Escalade passed by me, then slowed down. It was chromed out, had twenty-four inch-wheels and rims that kept spinning when the tires stopped moving. That was what I called SUGS—Straight Up Ghetto Shit. I used to call it SUNS, but I've been trying to cut back on using the N-word. His eyes were on me, already slowing down to get his mack on. Damn. I pretended I didn't hear him toot his horn or see his window roll down.

He yelled, "Nigga, I know you see me. You ain't that damn pretty."

"Who the—" I looked and saw a dark-skinned brother wearing a bright yellow velour FUBU sweatsuit, his Raiders hat turned sideways. "Do I know you?"

"Ray Ray, fool."

"Ray Ray? Man, when you get out?"

He double-parked and pissed a few people off, then hopped his slim butt out of his ride and hurried to me, sweatpants sagging so low it looked like his crotch was below his knees.

He said, "Damn, Cousin. Fat Frankie done lost a lot of weight."

"Dag, Ray Ray. How many more muscles and tattoos you plan on getting?"

We laughed and I asked him about the rest of the Wimberly side of our family, people who lived on the other side of the 110. I hadn't been down that way in years.

I asked, "What happened to your girl Shellei?"

"We divorced."

"Didn't know you two jumped the broom."

"Did my time with her." He chewed a toothpick. "She was worse than my parole officer, so I gave her the boot. Sent her back up on Pico to her crazy-ass momma's three-room crib."

"Where the kids?"

"Hennessy and Alize are staying with me. They getting big."

"I hear you. What about Paula?"

"Man, I love my sister, but Paula got so many kids, have to call 'em by their last names to keep 'em straight. That's why she lost her job at the gas company. Had to keep trying to find somebody to take care of those bad-ass kids. Day care put 'em out because they kept fighting and tearing up the classroom and trying to burn the place down."

"What happened to Rashonda?"

"She got caught up in some mess with a gangbanger." He

made a motion toward his nose, sniffed, and I understood. "Police caught her in one of those high-speed chases. It was on television. Her big butt tried to run, big-ass titties just flopping up and down and side to side, hitting her all upside the head and shit. Got it on tape if you want to see it."

"Maybe you can show it at the next family reunion."

"Damn, you look like Grandma Willie Mae every time I see you."

Somebody blew their horn at us. One look at Ray Ray and they sped away.

"Look, playa—" I checked my watch. "Traffic is a bear and I gotta get across town."

"We need to exchange digits before you bi-zounce."

We did and I hugged him again. There was nothing like family, no matter how ghetto they were. Had to remind myself there was a lot of love for us on the other side of the 110.

I said, "Holla at Tommie. She's working in Pier 1."

"Will do as soon as I hit Old Navy. Y'all got any kids?"

"Nah. We still . . . still don't have any."

For a moment I felt like the Fat Frankie he remembered, and as barren as the Mojave.

He said, "We gotta hook up. Come by Christmas, or Super Bowl, or something."

"Might do that." I held on to my smile. "Kiss Hennessey and Alize for me. Holla."

He took my parking space and I left so I could battle the traffic on Rosecrans.

By 8 p.m. I had on my black leather skirt, sexy peasant top with a plunging neckline, long leather coat, locks hanging free, and had driven across town to Westwood. I chug-a-lugged Tommie's filthy Jeep up to valet parking and before I could get out, a guy walked over.

"Frankie?"

"John?"

Brotherman looked better in person, had serious curb appeal. Nice chocolate skin, short hair, teeth so white and straight I thought I had sashayed into a Colgate commercial. He was my height, and if that didn't bother him, it didn't bother me. When you're a little on the tall side, you have to be prepared for emergencies. That was why I had plenty of flat shoes in my closet as backup. He was nicely dressed: wool pants, mock turtleneck, Italian loafers, three-button jacket, and a five-o'clock shadow that said he had a little bad boy in him.

I said, "Lot of people up in here."

"Laker game."

"My kinda crowd."

Lots of men were here. Around the bar, women were lined up like lonesome queens. With the different styles and complexions, they looked like thirty-one flavors at Baskin-Robbins.

We grabbed a seat at the bar so we could catch some of the Laker game, and he dropped his keys on the bar in between us. Guess he did that high school move to impress me. Maybe he thought that I'd start *oooing* and *ahhhing* when I saw the big golden *L* on his car key. And you know I had to hold in a groan because if that's what he was doing, it was played out.

"What you drinking, Frankie?"

"Riesling."

"Bartender . . . Riesling for the lady, Heineken on this side."

"Daaaamn." Like the rest of the room who were die-hard purple and gold fans, I exploded, pumped my fist and applauded a bad-ass play. "You see Kobe take it to the hoop?"

"Brother brought his A-game tonight."

"He has his A-game every night."

In between us getting all into the game, talking about Kobe's drama, high-fiving plays, just having a damn good time, I did the yada yada, told him the standard résumé: divorced, no kids, played it down and told homie that I lived in a duplex near LAX; then flipped the script and asked for his verbal résumé.

John worked in radio, so I kept the conversation flowing in his direction.

He told me, "All the major companies are buying up the urban market."

"Big fish eats little fish."

"Big companies are about the bling. Why pay ten crews to do ten shows, when they can prerecord or simulcast? Simulcasts send a lot of talent to the unemployment line."

"Technology is a beast."

He had another beer. I was still nursing my Riesling. Late in the third quarter, Lakers had a good lead.

John said, "This game is in the refrigerator. The lights are off—"

"Jell-O is jiggling, eggs are cooling, and the butter is getting hard."

We did another serious high five, toasted to the late Chick Hearn. This guy wasn't too bad. Laker fan. Didn't get turned off by the dirty Jeep. Hadn't tried to grab my breasts yet. Nothing in his nose. Breath didn't stank. Wasn't bald in the mouth.

He sipped. "Strange meeting a woman as smart and beautiful as you on the Internet."

Smart before *beautiful*, mos def my kinda guy.

I confessed, "Well, I haven't had the best of luck."

"So, you're not seeing anybody?"

That was when I was tempted to say, *Nobody who isn't deniable or unforgettable.*

But I kept it smooth and said, "Nope. You?"

"Nope." He shook his head. "Curious. Why the Internet?"

I sipped to give me some thinking time. "Frustrating trying to date in a city that has no character, just a beautiful body with no heart. That's how a lot of men are around here."

"Sounds like you've been going out with the Tin Man."

"Most of them do need to see the Wizard."

"Can't be that bad."

"C'mon now." I took another sip. "Hard to meet people when everybody is either looking at themselves in the mirror or doing eighty on the freeway."

"Yup. It's hard."

"And we have you brothers outnumbered something like twelve to one."

He shrugged. "Quantity doesn't mean quality."

"Oh, please. The flip side of that, a sister ain't got those kind of options. Hard to meet a man who ain't a piranha in that feeding frenzy. Hell, just hard to meet a decent brother in L.A."

"I think it's the other way. The shortage of men has made women turn into piranhas. Men have buffet after buffet to choose from. Women are starving. Hungry and desperate."

"Good point." I hated that truth. "There is no equilibrium in the dating world."

"C'mon, I know you've met at least one decent man."

"The brothers who come up to me are either fugly and smart, or handsome and dumb as a brick . . . or handsome and broke . . . or fugly and rich . . . or fugly and—"

"Fugly?"

"Oh. Never mind."

The conversation stayed smooth and we ordered another round of drinks, this one on me.

"Damn. First time a sister ever bought me a drink."

"You're welcome."

Then he said, "Wanna catch a Laker game with me day after tomorrow?"

"That might work."

"Your call. Let me know. I've got floor seats."

"That will most definitely work. Popcorn and parking will be on me."

I usually gave out a business card that had the e-mail address and the number to the fax machine; the fax line had a message center that I checked every blue moon. It was a long and hard climb up Kilimanjaro to get to the A-list and earn the digits to the phone next to my bed.

But I was feeling . . . well . . . sentimental. And since Dick Clark was warming up to sing "Auld Lang Syne," reflective too. I needed to plant some seeds if I didn't want to keep running up and down my B- and C-lists from now until Valentine's Day.

Anybody below the A-list wasn't obligated to buy flowers, presents, or cards. Yep, all they had to do was throw the morning paper on the porch on the way out.

Right about then this brother to end all brothers stepped into the room. Man was so fine he made Denzel look like Pee Wee Herman. Four-button black suit, yellow Italian shirt and no tie, caramel skin, looked like the centerfold out of every woman's fantasy book. All of those lonesome queens around the bar, they all did some quick tit adjustments and positioned their bodies so homeboy would know they were volunteering to become flavor of the night.

But his eyes were all over me.

Then the guy headed my way, and I was thinking, damn, talk about being bold. I was thinking more along the lines of me slipping away to the ladies' room and sliding him my digits on the way. He moved around the crowd, glass of wine in hand, like Bogart going to Ingrid Bergman in *Casablanca*.

That made me lose my place in the conversation I was having with . . . uh . . . with John. Good angel and bad angel started having a tug of war inside my head. John was cool, but hell, there was no commitment. Hell, I didn't even know his last name.

The brother stared like he was offering me a chance to upgrade from coach to first class.

I smiled back. Then his smile changed. His eyes looked a little weird, off-center. That busted my buzz and all sorts of burglar alarms started clanging inside my head.

I'd seen that expression before. I'd had that expression a few times myself.

I patted John's arm, then pointed. "I think you might have a fan."

John saw the guy and his body jerked. "Ramón? Oh, shit."

The brother got right up on John. "Aren't you supposed to be home with the flu?"

The moment John opened his mouth, Ramón tossed his drink in John's face. Ramón must've done that a thousand times before because his aim was awesome, damn near as good as squirting water in those plastic clown faces at the L.A. County Fair. Half of the wine went down John's throat. He started coughing and gagging with fluids coming out both his mouth and nose, choking like he was drowning in the Pacific Ocean.

The crowd parted and Ramón marched away, adjusting his suit, shaking his head.

Talk about sucking the zippity right out of my friggin' doo dah.

John gagged, was flustered. "I'm sorry . . . but that's my . . . an old associate."

"Whatever." Strange that he picked a word that started with *ass* and ended with *ate* to describe their . . . relationship. "Knew you were too pretty . . . dressed too damn nice . . . damn basketball throws a sister off every friggin' time."

"You're leaving?"

"The refrigerator light is off and the game is over."

"Here's my card. Call me."

"Nigga, please." I shook my head. "I'll call you when Dr. Laura becomes grand marshal at the Hollywood Gay Parade."

$\mathcal{F}$rankie

I snapped, "I don't have any cash."

Livvy yawned and checked her watch. "They have about twenty ATMs in the lobby."

Tommie asked, "Is the concession stand open?"

It was after seven in the morning and at least ten thousand people were here, more coming in every second. CP-time was in full effect.

Somebody's phone vibrated. Like cellular gunslingers, Tommie, Livvy, and I reached into our purses and yanked out phones at the same time. Livvy's was humming and glowing. She'd been getting text messages all morning. She turned away from us, read the message, blushed like she was in high school, then typed something back.

Tommie said, "There go the spotlights."

"Reminds me of UniverSoul Circus. They need a contortionist under the Christmas tree."

"Damn, Frankie. Let me get this straight."

"Shut up, Tommie."

"You were out on a date with John . . . then this guy named Ramón—"

"Didn't I just tell you to shut up?"

"And you saw Ramón out on the curb crying like a three-year-old?"

I snapped, "I don't want to talk about that ever again."

Livvy didn't look up; too busy sending and receiving text messages.

The band started playing. The Solid Gold for the Glory of Jesus dancers came from everywhere, spinning and twirling their way down the aisles, followed by the Gaudy for God choir members who Crip-walked in dressed in gold lamé, being led by a midget choir director who was a wannabe Kirk Franklin.

I said, "Laker flashback time, people."

Tommie and I started doing the wave.

Livvy cut her eyes at us. "Y'all going to hell in gasoline thongs."

The sanctuary still had a scoreboard letting people see the score: SAINTS 100 SINNERS 0. Left-behind championship banners from the Lakers and the Kings were high up on the walls. We were in the nosebleed section, under Kareem, Worthy, and Magic's retired jerseys.

Tommie said, "This is better than the All-Star Game."

I added, "Much better."

"Y'all going to hell."

L.A. was a city where preachers bragged about the size of their congregations, and no matter how large the congregation, it was never big enough. They all wanted a congregational-enlargement. But if you asked me, their congregations were never as large as they claimed it to be from the get-go. Not that I've seen that many congregations. I was just saying.

"Damn," Livvy said. "You see what that heifer has on?"

I groaned. "I have on a thong bigger than that dress."

Livvy retorted, "Surprised you have drawers on at all."

"Who is that?" That was Tommie. "Those are stripper shoes."

"I think that's the preacher's wife."

"No, that's his mistress. The wife sits on the other side."

I shook my head. "Viagra has kept these old-school players in the game too long."

Livvy bumped us both. "Smile. One of the cameramen is pointing the camera at us."

"No! I have on what I'm wearing to Pier 1."

"Act like you're a praying leprechaun, start shouting that people are always after your Lucky Charms or something."

The camera shot changed from us doing our Hallelujah dances with the other people in the nosebleed section, and switched to all the women down on the front row, the true season-ticket holders. Short skirts, super-cleavage, three-inch heels, and leather pants.

I said, "Bet them sisters had the same clothes on last night at Bistro 880."

Tommie shook her head. "Reverend has more groupies than the Lakers."

We were up so high that everybody on stage looked like hand-clapping ants, so we had to watch the Greatest Spiritual Show on Earth on one of the five sixty-foot-tall monitors.

Right after that, all of our cell phones rang. People we know in church had seen us on the monitors and started calling. I had calls coming in on top of calls: two from old B-list lovers sitting in the choir, one from a C-list deacon I had long forgotten about. Everybody was trying to hook up later on tonight. Everybody was getting turned down. Tommie was smiling hard, the way a woman did when she was talking to a man. Whoever it was, she told him to tell Monica hi before she hung up. She was floating after that. And Livvy, well her call put her in a bad mood.

Livvy had her arms folded, leg bouncing, staring off into space.

I stopped clapping and asked Livvy, "You okay?"

"That was Tony. He's here. With his family."

"You want to leave . . . or go down there . . . or—?"

She shook her head as an answer to all my questions.

I asked, "What did he say? Did the DNA—?"

She exhaled. "I'm gonna need a divorce lawyer."

"You're going to try and serve him before he serves you?"

I waited. Tony's call had rocked her. I put my hand on Livvy's right hand. Tommie was on her other side, holding Livvy's left hand. Livvy closed her eyes. I understood what she was feeling. Been there, done that. Divorce was like losing your past. Your future . . . after going through that trauma, you didn't know what your future was.

We sat like that the rest of the service.

The minister hit the stage and asked everybody for an extra thousand dollars to help the needy in the community, said that message came straight from the man above.

Tommie laughed that I-know-you-ain't-asking-me-for-no-mo'-money laugh.

I reached over and slapped her arm. She slapped me back.

Tommie said, "What did he do with the chunk of money he asked everybody for last year? The community looks jacked up the same way it did after the L.A. Riot."

Livvy said, "Well, he just put new twenty-four-carat-gold fixtures throughout his estate in Palos Verdes. Heated marble floors. Don't know what he has at his home in the Hamptons. So, yeah, his communities are looking better every year. And his mistress is hooked up big time."

I mumbled, "Both of y'all going to hell in gasoline . . ."

I was about to feel guilty and write a check for extra money I didn't have. Then I looked at the man on the sixty-foot-tall monitor, stared and remembered that the minister rode through the hood in a limo, wore tailored suits, and, when he had to walk with the masses, did a special announcement and let everybody know he had on two-hundred-dollar tennis shoes.

Now that I thought about it, the last time I saw him in public, he didn't have any idea who I was. I've been coming here for ten years. When I ran into him at Aunt Kizzy's all I wanted to do was say hello and move on and get my Sunday dinner, but I couldn't get in two words to my spiritual leader before his gorilla-sized bodyguards whisked him away.

I put my checkbook back and told the McBrooms, "Time for us to shake this spot."

As we were leaving, they were doing the announcements, "Today's first service was brought to you by Coca-Cola . . . it's the real thing . . . just like Jesus."

* * *

Livvy said she didn't want to get her grub on, that she had more shopping to do. She told Tommie that she'd be at her place tonight, then hurried to her SUV and drove away.

Tommie and I stood out in the sunshine and watched her blend into traffic, then vanish.

I said, "She's stressed."

"I know. It's like she's pushing us away and holding on at the same time."

"Watch out for that broken forty-ounce."

She stepped around the broken glass. "They must've had a concert here last night."

We were parked in the back forty of the parking lot. Tommie didn't have to be at Pier 1 for a hot minute, and I didn't have anything on my plate for a while, so we headed over to 'Bucks, grabbed a cup of java, found an empty table outside, chilled out and talked about what we needed to do on Christmas morning. We had our own little McBroom tradition.

She said, "I don't want to end this year holding on to old issues."

"What are you saying?"

"Think . . . Think I'm going to . . . maybe not be celibate."

"The nappy-headed creamy-vanilla guy with the LL thang? . . ."

She blushed. "That's who just called me at church. He invited me to go pick out a Christmas tree with him and . . . with him. After I get off work."

"You make that sound like a date."

She shrugged. "Have to start somewhere. It's about time, not money."

I felt small when she said that. Like maybe I expected too much because I had so much. But I had a lot to lose. I shook it off and said, "You're two years into being a nun, right?"

"It ain't easy."

"You haven't—?"

"We kissed. That's where I was when the sheriff came . . . kissing him."

What she was bringing to me, well the conversation surprised me because she hadn't talked about hooking up with anyone, not on that level, not the two years she was gone to Galveston, hadn't brought anybody around us since she came back almost nine months ago.

"He's older . . ." She swallowed and shifted around. ". . . and has a child."

"How much older is—?"

"Real old. Your age."

"Be serious. His child?"

"Four."

I was bothered by it, maybe even envious because she'd been floating around like she was IV'd to helium, but I could tell she expected me to give her grief over the age difference, twice as much grief over the guy having a kid, but I saw how she was glowing, and I smiled.

"I talked to my therapist about him. And the explicit dreams." She laughed her cute little shy laugh again. "And I think the *vitamins* I take, damn; the side effect is a high sex drive."

"They're not *vitamins*."

"Whatever. The meds have me so . . . excited. I think I almost have orgasms in my sleep."

"Can you get me a prescription? I promise not to OD."

"Hush. But I don't quite get there."

"You're telling me that you haven't—?"

She shook her head. "Never had an orgasm. I don't feel complete."

"You don't know what you're missing, Boo."

"Oh, I have an idea. When I first came back and crashed at Livvy's, I'd wake up in the middle of the night and hear them going at it . . . whooping and hollering . . . and—"

"Damn. Sounds like Momma and Daddy."

"Tony would growl, and she'd whine like a cat. Thought he was killing her butt. *What's my name? What's my name?* He asked her his name so much, I thought he had amnesia."

I laughed.

She laughed too. "Livvy is way louder than Momma used to be. And Livvy . . . she gets vulgar. *Fuck that pussy eat that pussy slap dat ass dat dick is soooo good.*"

"Tommie, lower your voice. It's Sunday. We just left church."

"Oops." She moved a loose braid from her face, looked to the skies. "Sorry."

"Well, when you get it good, trust me, you'll say and do some vulgar things too."

I laughed because I'd done some freaky things and let a man make love to me in ways I never thought I would, and loved every minute of it. Trusting and loving a man made a woman ready and willing to try almost anything, if only one time.

Tommie was in question-asking mode, almost like a woman climbing a mountain in search of answers from the master. It was hard to explain to Tommie what good sex was when she didn't really know her own body, not the way a woman should be familiar with herself.

I told her, "Explore your own body."

"I'm not into paddling the pink canoe."

"Stop acting silly. Swing by the Hustler Store and get a vibrator."

She shook her head. "That's why God made men."

"After you've had a few men, you'll understand why we buy so many vibrators."

She smiled, got a little giddy, then checked her watch. It was time for her to get to Manhattan Beach so she could clean bathrooms and sell candles.

Before she could get away I asked, "Who is Livvy having an affair with?"

"You know that she's—?"

I made the get-real face. "I'm not stupid."

She shrugged. "If you find out, tell me."

We hugged, kissed cheeks, and I watched my sister as she pulled her braids back into a ponytail and headed toward her Jeep. Saw how the brothers in the area stopped doing what they were doing and broke their necks staring at that Amazon queen.

Hell, maybe I should give up the locks and get me some braids the color of Epsom salt, put a silver earring in my nose, belly button, and left eyebrow, too.

I chuckled because, damn, she was just as sneaky as Livvy.

Hell, guess it ran in the family because Momma and Bernard were sneaky too.

When Momma and Bernard married, the crib over on 110th was kinda cramped, and with the thin walls, they didn't have the kind of privacy a newlywed couple needed. Bernard would help us with our homework the best he could, then Momma would make sure we'd eaten and bathed, then made us go to bed, which was anywhere we were comfortable. After that, they'd creep out to the car and drive up the street. We'd kick the covers off us, line up and look out the window. They never went far. The muffler on Bernard's car told us where they were, two houses over, in the driveway of an empty house. We could see the car from the front window. It would get dark in that car. Then the silhouettes would vanish. Awhile later, we'd see the flame from a match. All of us would start giggling and laughing. Bernard didn't smoke. So we knew Momma was putting the match to her cigarette, taking that first pull that made her face light up.

Momma and Bernard would tiptoe back in the house glowing like fireflies.

As soon as I had that memory, I had an epiphany.

I was about to kick back and savor the business and real estate sections of the Sunday *Times*, but I chilled out and started people-watching instead, wondering how many of these sisters got hooked up in a special way this morning. I think it was my girl-sex-talk with Tommie, especially when she mocked Livvy's *Fuck that pussy eat that pussy slap dat ass dat dick is soooo good.* Have to admit, that imagery made me tingle, had me in that sensual frame of mind.

I figured it out, who got the hookup this morning.

The sisters who ordered tall cappuccinos got no dick.

The sisters who ordered a Venti vanilla latte got some lame

dick, because lame dick was worse than getting no dick at all. Their folded arms and frowns said it all. Lame dick was the dick that got a woman in orgasm escrow, but couldn't close the deal.

The women who ordered bottled water had Kool-Aid smiles and skin glowing like Chernobyl. They woke up in a sexual hurricane and dragged themselves in here out of habit. Looked like they wanted to break out singing, "The hills are alive with the sound of music."

Just like Momma did when she came floating back in the house.

Yep, the ones who didn't get no satisfaction were wolfing down the hard stuff.

I figured all that out while I guzzled my second Venti quadruple espresso cappuccino.

Just like I figured out Tommie was seeing one of my tenants.

I'm not Einstein, but I'm not Algernon either.

Livvy

I left church and met Carpe in Manhattan Beach at Sand Dune Park. It was midmorning and all the weekend warriors were out doing repeats on the steep hill. He had on black shorts and a white T-shirt with red letters advertising a good time at Daytona Beach. I had cleansed my face and changed out of my all-black outfit at Tommie's pigpen before I came here. Now I was wearing a yellow sports bra under a white tank top, gray sweatpants, and a yellow bandana.

I'd spent some time with him almost every evening this week.

We met at Baja Grill in Manhattan Village one night, did some Christmas shopping, ate, caught a movie at the small theater next door, then sat in my SUV, talking, kissing, then got in the back seat, pleasing each other, sweating, and fogging up my windows, while cars and people passed by, Christmas goods in hand. It was almost like being an . . . exhibitionist. I came so hard.

Late the other night, we were in the deserted parking lot at Coco's in Compton. Standing outside our cars, in the dark, him behind me, making me come and moan into the cool wind. Cars were feet away from us, zooming down Central. All people had to do was look our way.

Last night we sexed in the shower and bathtub in a rented room at the LAX Hilton. He left me there, went home close to midnight, and I stayed there, hugging a pillow.

That was why when he saw me parking we smiled. No words were needed.

One look at him, everything that was wrong went away. Livvy didn't exist anymore.

Just Bird.

And he was just Carpe, my escape, the lover I needed to seize every day.

He said, "Hotter than I thought it was gonna be."

"Not as hot as you were getting me in church. You and those messages . . ."

He gave me that smile and winked at me. I tossed him a small tube of sunblock.

He shook his head. "I don't need sunblock."

"Just because we have more melanin in our skin doesn't mean we won't burn. Eighty percent of aging is caused by the sun. That's why black women age better than white women."

"Is that right. So, you must work in dermatology, or the medical field."

I laughed. "Put on the sunblock, dammit."

He smoothed the cream on his face.

I nodded. "Thought it was gonna be in the seventies today."

"It's supposed to rain."

"Doesn't look like it."

It was a California winter day. Seventy-five at the beaches, over eighty inland.

We took our shoes off and hiked up and down that monster mountain of sand. Pain had become my friend. Plenty of people, track clubs and firefighters carrying hoses, football players, all were out doing the same. We were very competitive. At least I was. Each time up, I looked at the timer on my watch. The first time up took close to three minutes. Then it took a minute and a half to make my way back down. Each time up took a little longer, but I kept pushing myself. I had to do that hill at least one more time than he did. Ten times had me aching. After ninety minutes of agony, we rested a little while, got hydrated, and jogged the steps twice.

After that we drove up Highland and found street parking. We walked two blocks in our socks and Rollerbladed. First we went toward Redondo Beach, then came back and bladed down near the power plants in El Segundo. Blading was easy and I would've kept going until I made it to Venice, but I looked out at the ocean. It was so beautiful.

We sat on the rocks and watched the waves. The sky was clear. Lines of surfers were out in the water, waiting for a nice-sized wave to bring them back in.

He kissed me a few times.

We bladed back and stopped at a little workout section right in front of the lifeguard's building, did push-ups on the ground and pull-ups on a metal bar while a group of women below played volleyball in the sand. I was burned out. Sat and watched him workout the muscles in his arms. Did that with a smile.

He asked, "Hungry?"

"I'm always hungry."

He laughed.

I slapped him on his ass. "Not funny."

"I know this place that has great lobster burritos."

We hiked up the hills, T-shirts soaked with sweat, dirty socks on our feet, Rollerblades over our shoulders. After doing the sand dunes and blading, it was a hellified walk. I pretended I wasn't aching from my ankles up to my ass. Every muscle was on fire.

He said, "Do curls with your blades."

"You are really getting on my nerves."

"Curls. Work your biceps."

"Okay, okay. Geesh."

We slowed down and looked at a sign for a large studio apartment. A rental going at $1,120 a month—typical beach prices, especially two minutes from the ocean.

I said, "I could buy a three-level house in Atlanta for that much."

"Atlanta doesn't have a beach outside the front door."

Both of us stared at that sign, just shaking our heads at the outrageous cost of beach property. We went back to doing curls and hiking up that hill.

The eating place called Sharkeez was right on Highland, not too far from where we had parked. We changed into our sandy workout shoes and walked into a place that had red and blue tiled floors, everything else a combination surfer and Mexican motif.

He said, "You worked out hard, so give yourself a break on the points."

"When you get a butt like this—"

"Maybe I can get you a job at Stroker's and we can become millionaires overnight."

"What's Stroker's?"

"Strip club."

"Pervert."

"Put the menu down. I'm ordering for both of us."

"Oooo. A take-charge kinda guy. Me likey, me likey."

Two lemonades and two lobster burritos were right at thirty bucks. We sat at a booth facing the street, sat on the same side of the table, leg touching leg, his hand on my thigh, moving up and down. Sanyo televisions all over the place showing surfer videos.

He took out his cellular phone and I went to the ladies' room to wash my hands. When I got back, he was still on the phone. His wife called him a lot. He always answered. I never said anything. We knew the rules of this game.

He told whoever he was talking to, "Thirty minutes will be fine. Call me back at this number when you get close and I'll meet you there."

Then he hung up, leaned over, and kissed me.

I didn't ask him any questions. Just knew that he had to go back to his real world.

I asked, "You go to strip clubs?"

"Haven't been to one in a while."

"Sounds like fun."

We ate, enjoyed each other's company.

Outside on the beach, the surfers were surfing and hundreds of people were Rollerblading, playing beach volleyball, and tanning. Life was one big episode of *Baywatch*.

His cell phone rang right as we were finishing up our meals.

Outside, he turned right. I told him we were parked the other way.

He said, "Come with me."

"Awww, man. I know we're not working out again."

He took my hand. "Come on and stop complaining."

"My legs are dead."

"Come on, Bird."

We went back down the asphalt and concrete hill toward the beach, holding hands, my legs aching with every step, but we didn't make it that far. We stopped at the next block, right in front of the studio apartment that was renting for $1,120 a month.

A middle-aged woman, slender with golden skin and huge, perfectly round, gravity-defying breasts was standing in front of the sign, looking toward the beach. She wore frayed jeans shorts, red sandals, big orange glasses, and a floppy pink and yellow hat. I imagined she was fantasizing about living there, a stone's throw from the waters and sands of the Pacific, waking up to that marine layer and falling asleep under the ocean's breeze.

Carpe went to her and said, "Mrs. Klein?"

"That would be me."

"I just called you about renting the property."

"Well come in." She had a narrow nose. When she smiled, her lips moved, but not the rest of her face. Like Joan Rivers, she'd overdone the Botox. She went on, "As you can see on the sign, I just reduced the price from eleven-ninety."

"Good timing."

"Your timing was great. I had just come by to make sure the

apartment was cleaned properly and was just about to leave the area. You and your wife from around here?"

"We're not married."

"Oh."

"We're having an affair."

Mrs. Klein was stunned. So was I.

He went on, "I want to rent your studio so we can have a place to make love."

I was about ready to hit the floor. Mrs. Klein and I stood there with our mouths wide open. She looked at me, a non-blinking stare, and I didn't know what to say.

Then Mrs. Klein's lips curved up. She laughed. "Well, this is the perfect love nest."

"How firm are you on your price?"

She took her shades off, her face now serious. "What did you have in mind?"

"Maybe a discount for paying six months in advance."

"Uh huh. Of course we're talking cash."

He smiled. "Of course. And to sweeten the deal in your favor, you can still pretend your property is vacant and write the note off as a loss with the IRS."

I stood there, rubbing my neck, my face so red, looking away from her scrutiny. My skin burned by the sun. Sweat drying on my face. Both hands were underneath my sweaty tank top, pulling, twisting, unable to be still, rocking from one foot to the other. That was all I could do.

Mrs. Klein took my hands in hers. She sang, "My, my, my."

I blushed.

Her smile was devilish. "How I envy you."

Carpe went with Mrs. Klein to talk over the business.

They laughed a lot.

He asked, "How soon can I get the keys?"

"How soon can you get me the money?"

They weren't whispering, but I could hardly hear. I was day-dreaming, looking at white walls, thinking about decorating, about a small bed and candles, moving to a place of ecstasy.

I heard her say, "I can go as low as . . . say . . . hmmm . . . sixty-six hundred for six months."

"Cash?"

"Cash."

There was another long pause.

"Wish I had a lover so generous."

"She's a good woman," he told her.

I walked to the window, looked out at the ocean, inhaled the ocean's breath, and I smiled.

I waited inside the studio until Carpe returned. When he came back I was lingering in the bathroom doorway, a hand on each side of the doorframe, heat rising from between my legs.

I asked, "Where is Mrs. Klein?"

"Gone."

He came in, closing the blinds. We never took our eyes off each other.

I whispered, "You did it?"

"It's done."

"Geesh."

His voice had become a husky whisper. "This is yours."

Mine was velvety. "Ours."

"Ours."

He inched my way, came over and kissed me, put his mouth on my face, licked my collarbone, then kissed me again, gave me my own salty taste.

Still I needed more than that to salve what I was feeling.

I whispered, "Rental car sex."

He turned me around, yanked my pants down.

I moaned, almost suffocated.

He did the same with his workout shorts and jock strap, both ending up somewhere around his knees. His penis bobbed against my ass, hard and thick. My toes curled in my tennis shoes and I braced myself against the doorframe. He teased me like that.

He dipped, the head of his penis finding its way to my vagina. My ass curved upward, welcomed him. He entered me a little at a time, pulled back to the tip, then sank inside me, gave me all his length, stretching me with his sensual strokes, then pulled out to the tip, played with me, then rushed into me all at once. My face heated, turned three more shades of red.

He fit inside me so good. From tip to root, his size was so perfect.

I held the doorframe and moved back against him, pushed him in me as deep as I could. Wanted him to crush all of my pain. First we danced slowly, then our own ebb and flow changed, our soft moans became the growls of greedy lovers, the pornographic sounds of two tigers devouring each other. His strong hands were on my waist, pulling me back into him.

"*Yessss*," I hissed over and over. "That's it, baby."

He snarled and spanked me like I was a very bad girl, then yanked me back into him, hit my spot so good and I screamed until he put his hand over my mouth.

"This. How. You. Want. It. Bird?"

"Harder . . . harder . . . hard . . . harder."

With each thrust, the world became distorted by pleasure.

My lips tightened; breathing turned hard and fast. "That's. It. Baby. Ooo. That's. It."

He spread my cheeks and tried to crawl inside me. Insanity took over and all sorts of dirty talk came out of me, came from nowhere, sounded like some erotic whore was in the room with us. The pornographic things I moaned surprised me. I cursed over and over when I felt him growing, swelling, making sounds that told me he was thirsty for me. Like he'd never had me before. And it felt like I'd never had him before. There was no barrier between us, our first time skin to skin. I tried to look back at him, wanted to see his face when he came, see that tight-eyed expression that looked like hot wax was being dripped on his body, but he held my waist with one hand, pushed my bandana away, and pulled my hair with the other hand.

The sounds of the ocean had faded, its salty aroma replaced with the perfume of sweat and suntan lotion and sand . . . and sex. Wall to wall, the room smelled like us.

Spasms ran through me. Eyes squeezed shut. Legs trembled. He had to hold me up.

While I gripped the doorframe and came, all I could hear was skin slapping against skin.

"Harder baby . . . do me harder . . . like . . . that . . . yeah."

I came again.

He groaned deep, was about to come, and pulled out. I turned and held his swollen penis. He seemed so powerful and so weak all at once. He closed his eyes and gave his control to me. Since high school, these hands made a few men orgasm. They all felt different, yet they all felt the same. But one thing was constant, how they always submitted to their pleasure. Seeing a man from that perspective showed me how weak they were, how supremacy belonged to women.

He squeezed my breast while I kissed him, sucked his tongue, swallowed his sounds and stroked him toward orgasm; let his pleasure spill to the floor, both of us marking our territory.

In the middle of the night, I left my love nest. Left Bird behind and gradually became Livvy again. Out of instinct, or maybe intentionally, I drove from crisp ocean air in Manhattan Beach to the hills of Ladera and without thought, my life on autopilot, slowed down in front of my home before I realized what I had done. Colorful lights adorned both levels of the house, the front lawn covered in faux snow and a nativity scene. I almost laughed at the fake snow scattered on the grass and palm trees. Best decorations on the block. The curtains were open. He had put up a frosted tree. The kind he hated, the kind I loved. It was beautiful.

I grinned at that winter wonderland, swallowed my emotions, bit my lips, and moved on.

Tommie wasn't home. Her Jeep was in the driveway, her purse in her bedroom, her heater on low, place still looking like it had been burglarized.

Her place was an oven. I turned the heater off, washed her dishes, showered again, moisturized my skin, tied my hair up in a silk scarf, put on pajamas, grabbed covers, moved a stack of books from her sofa, and made myself comfortable. I stared at the silver key in my hand. The key Carpe had given me to our love nest. Shiny and new, like all things should be.

I stared at the key. Felt Carpe throbbing deep inside me, crumbling all the pain.

Restless, I got up, made a cup of peppermint tea, walked in circles.

I called Frankie. She'd just got in from another Internet date.

I asked, "How'd it go?"

"He stuttered."

"Bad?"

"Took him five minutes to say my name. F-F-F-F-Frankie, you are so f-f-f-f-fine."

"Really?"

"Spitting everywhere. I needed a damn umbrella."

"Gross."

"I had on a denim dress that clings to my ass, this funky necklace, locks were down, sexy chocolate strappies, and I end up with Porky Pig spitting pork juice all in my damn face."

I said, "Some cute guys at the gym. Especially in Evelyn's and Taj's class."

"You don't date people at your gym because that's too much like dating somebody at your job. You break up, who gets Evelyn's aerobics class? Who gets to keep Taj and Tae Bo? Who gets Pilates? Would I have to give up my 24 Hour membership and join Crunch?"

"What about at church?"

"Break up at church, then date somebody else, they think you're the church ho."

"You are the church ho."

She hung up on me.

I smiled and chuckled.

I was in the living room, in the dark, lounging on Tommie's beanbag, almost in fetal position, looking out the bay window. Across the street, in another bay window, I saw a couple standing, talking, then kissing. At first I thought they were movie stars because he was as smooth as Billy Dee and she was as statuesque as Pam Grier.

Then I realized it was . . . her height . . . those braids . . . that was Tommie and her friend.

"Oh, my God."

Their kissing, whenever it stopped, it started right back, went on forever.

My cellular phone rang, startled me away from my voyeurism. My home phone number popped up on my caller ID. I didn't answer. After that, it beeped. My husband had left a message this time. Something in me hollowed. It had to be about the results to his paternity test.

Hello, Olivia. Saw you drive by the house. I was up . . . staring out the window . . . wishing that I knew where you were . . . and just like that you drove up. Then you left.

I rubbed my eyes, smelled another man's intoxicating scent rising from my pores.

I need you in my life right now. I miss you. Miss you a lot. Hope things are okay for you. I mean, it's rough on me not talking to you. I know I fucked up. I know I did. You know you were my closest friend. And not being able to talk to you . . . Guess I took that for granted.

I licked around my mouth, tasted an invigorating flavor.

I'm trying to be strong. Trying to get through this holiday . . . It's hard, you know? Anyway, I'm not going to beg or anything like that. Just letting you know how I feel.

I was about to hang up, but he took a sharp breath, and his message continued.

One of our friends called, told me they saw you in Manhattan Beach this afternoon.

I listened to his ragged breath as he struggled with the next part of the message.

It's not until you've been betrayed that you understand the pain of betrayal.

My eyes closed.

Things are in motion. You should be getting served soon.

Numbness covered me.

If I don't talk to you . . . Merry Christmas.

Then his message ended.

For a while, I sat on the sofa, bouncing the phone against my head.

I dialed my home number.

I let it ring once, then pushed the red button and ended the call. My number showed up on the caller ID, my way of telling him *I got your message, Tony. I got your fucking message.*

I went back to the bay window. It was dark across the street. Darkness was a lover's light. I held the silver key tight in my hand, got back on the couch and pulled the covers up to my nose, closed my eyes.

Three hours later, keys jingled and the front door opened. I was still awake, tossing and turning. I sat up. Tommie was stumbling home in her pajamas, housecoat, and duck slippers.

I said, "Hey."

She yawned and closed the door. "Why didn't you get in the bed?"

"Too much shit on your bed."

"You could've thrown it on the floor."

"Too much shit on your floor."

"C'mon. You'll wake up with your back out of alignment."

"Is that a menorah in your hand?"

"A Kinara. For Kwanzaa."

"Oh. Where are you coming from?"

"I know you don't want to start a question party."

I followed her to her bedroom. The temperature had dropped and the room was cold. She moved everything from the bed and we got under the blankets and comforter. Her warmth made it easier for me to get closer to sleeping. I became a child snuggling up to her mother.

I found sleep, but Tony's voice was there waiting for me, that last message playing over and over. Somewhere in the darkness, a baby wouldn't stop howling.

I jerked awake. The neighbor's dogs were barking at the moon.

Like we did when we were kids, I whispered, "Tommie?"

"Huh?"

"You using condoms?"

"We don't go there. Just kiss and cuddle."

"I'm going to leave some condoms in your nightstand."

"Why do you have condoms?"

I yawned. "G'night."

"Whatever you're doing—"

"—is none of your business."

She kicked me. "Don't think I won't put you out."

I started to drift, my mind bobbing and weaving, dodging all bad dreams.

"Livvy?"

I jerked awake. "Huh?"

"Help me take my braids down."

"Now?"

"Today."

"That'll take all day."

"Help me clean up too."

"You're pushing it."

I looked in my hand, made sure the silver key was still there, that that part of my life wasn't a dream, then closed my hand tight, gripped it like I was a slave holding on to freedom.

By the middle of the morning, rain was coming down hard. Roads were slick and winds were high. Every freeway and most of the surface streets were backed up. By then Frankie was over and we were taking down Tommie's braids.

Tommie asked Frankie, "When you want me to wash and tighten your locks?"

"Tomorrow or the next day."

She asked, "When you want me to hook you up, Livvy?"

"Mmmmm. Whenever."

Tommie's hair was the thickest of the lot. Frankie was on her right side and I was on her left, all of us talking and watching DVDs. Tommie had a bootleg copy of *The Matrix: Revolutions*. After our lunch break, we popped in *The Preacher's Wife*.

By late evening, the storm over Old Ladera was a steady drizzle. Tommie cooked dinner and Frankie ran and got a bottle of wine from the trunk of her car. We turned on the television, ate dinner, and saw that rain was still coming down hard from Oxnard to the mountains.

Frankie sipped her wine, pulled her sweatpants up above her calves, then retied her black bandana. She said, "Snowing big time at Big Bear. Anybody feeling spontaneous?"

Tommie frowned. "Awww, y'all know I'm working."

I told them, "Hush. I can't hear the news."

Frankie sipped her wine. "Livvy, if we bounce out of here by five in the morning, we can be there by eight, ski half a day, then be back home before traffic gets too crazy."

I didn't want to go skiing. I wanted to slip away and become Bird again.

I shook my head. "None of my ski pants fit anymore."

Tommie said, "Your feet didn't blow up like your ass, so get your skis and rent a bib."

"Tommie." I pretended I had a phone in my hand and slammed it down. "Click."

She pretended she had a phone in her hand and clicked me too.

I told my sisters that I was going to the store, but went back to Manhattan Beach. Lied to them so they wouldn't question my missing hours. Wanted to sit in that empty space, feel that energy, maybe make a list of things to buy to make it more comfortable, maybe pick up an inflatable bed from Costco, towels, things like that.

I opened the door, turned on the light and thought . . . I don't know what I thought.

There was a refrigerator. Mangoes. Kiwis. A five-foot palm

tree and a small fountain. Eight colorful throw pillows. A pastel radio/CD player. Sarah Vaughan and Norah Jones CDs.

And there was an armless chair. Beautiful, made of cherry wood, with red padding.

I would've thought I was in the wrong place, but there were two presents in the middle of the bed. FOR MY BIRD, OPEN BEFORE XMAS IF YOU WISH, THERE WILL BE MORE was written on a card in blue ink. I hadn't seen it two days ago, but there was a bed built into the wall. A bed that closed up like a closet. Full-size. New pillows, a pillow-top mattress and sheets with an enormous thread count were waiting to be soiled with sin.

There was no phone, so there wouldn't be any calls, no getting online. No television. Simple dishes and silverware. Lots of tea candles and an oil burner. Erotic books. An arrangement of exotic flowers from Accent on Design in Westwood.

I traced my fingers over his handwriting, felt like I was touching him.

I sat in the chair, opened one of my presents. Lingerie from Victoria's Secret. I opened another. Thongs and bras. Then another. It was a vibrator, girthy and long, but not too long.

It wiggled when I clicked it on. My laughter filled the room.

I opened his note. It had one word written inside: CLOSET.

I went to the closet. The door was swollen, a little hard to open.

There were clothes. Pretty clothes from Macy's, Banana Republic, and Kenneth Cole. All in size eight. As if he were telling me he desired me as I am now, without change.

Boxes of shoes were on the floor. All size eight.

I wondered how he knew my sizes; then I remembered he had asked me in San Diego, I had moaned out my sizes when he was sucking my toes.

The shoes had me going crazy.

Bebe. Enzo. Nine West. But the ones that made me scream and prance around were the Lucite and leather T-strap Manolo Blahniks.

I'm not a materialistic woman, but the shoe whore in me sparked to life. I jumped up and down, wanted to call Tommie, call Frankie, but I knew I couldn't.

They don't know Bird. They only know Livvy.

I took off all my clothes, put on the Manolo Blahniks, modeled naked for a while. Had to, because nothing in that closet did these shoes any justice. Shoes like these were an aphrodisiac, made something inside me burn, tingle, and ache for Carpe to come to me.

I pulled the covers back on the bed, held the card in one hand, close to my heart, and the vibrator was in the other. I pretended he was here, humming deep inside me.

I crashed at Frankie's, then we yawned our way to my truck at the crack of dawn. Our skis and gear stuffed in the back, trying to beat traffic and heading toward the mountains.

Four Christmas presents were on the backseat. So was my mail.

It was cold. Down to fifty degrees. A lot colder in the mountains.

My cellular vibrated over and over. Carpe was sending short text messages offering oral pleasures and the chance for us to fall into another mating dance. We'd been sending messages since I left the studio last night.

Frankie sipped her coffee. "Could you not type and drive in the rain?"

"I got it under control."

I messaged him back, told him that I was going skiing with my sister today, but I'd rather be with him at our nest right now, sent that message, then put the phone down.

Frankie told me, "Be careful."

"I'm not driving that fast."

"You know what I'm talking about. People get killed behind that kinda shit."

"What am I doing?"

"Livvy, I get tired of that what-did-I-do game with niggas, I don't need it from you."

A moment goes by before I tell her, "I'm being careful."

She downed more coffee. "Who is he?"

"Guy I met."

"You fucking him?"

"What do you think?"

"Geesh. I think you need to stop living like a refugee on the run."

I told her, "You know, if it's gonna be like this all day, we don't have to go skiing."

She let her seat back, closed her eyes. "When I went in your house and got your skis—"

"Uh huh."

"Tony told me to tell you that he loved you, no matter what."

My headache returned. My insides were being pulled in too many directions.

I tell her, "That was the same message he had left me yesterday."

"Your house is decorated big time. You have a ton of Christmas and Kwanzaa and Happy Holiday cards from everybody. But it felt . . . empty. Strange. Anyway, he told me to tell you he had presents for you under the tree, if you want yours. He has presents for all of us."

"Did you hug him?"

"Why?"

"Did you hug him?"

"Yeah, I hugged Tony."

"How could you hug him?"

"I don't like what he did, because it was jacked and disrespectful, but, no matter how much I want to, no, I don't hate him. I told him that."

"You kiss him on the cheek or on the lips?"

"Yeah, I kissed him on the lips, like we always do."

Again I'm popping my jaw, sucking my tongue, riding with Judas.

Frankie went on, "When Momma was sick, Tony was there. When that fool beat up Tommie and . . . damn, the nigga burned her face, Tony was ready to go to jail for all of us."

"Well, since you have so much love for the man, you might be able to dust off your old wedding dress and marry him in about six months."

"Don't go there."

"I'll be your maid of honor, cool?"

"Shut up."

"And to save money on a photographer, you can cut my face out of our wedding pictures and put yours in."

"You know what, *Olivia*, we don't have to go skiing."

"We're going, *Frankie*. And I hope you fall and tear your friggin' ACL."

"A'ight. Fuck around and get pushed into a tree."

My eyes went to the rearview. I adjusted it, looked at the Christmas presents Tony had given her this morning. Two small boxes wrapped beautifully in reds, greens, and gold.

I asked, "The gifts Tony gave you . . . whose are those?"

"They go with us Christmas morning."

I pulled my lips in, swallowed another emotional feeling.

She asked, "You okay?"

"Damn Depo shot . . . friggin' side effects . . . that's all."

We talked about Tony's love child, and I vented, shed a couple of tears. That's what I hated. Livvy cried; Bird owned no tears; Livvy only had pain; Bird only had pleasure.

"I hate this shit." I sipped bottled water. "Marriage was supposed to protect me, and now it's another damn game. Why do I have to play the game?"

"That's just how it is, Livvy. It's about game. Even when you get married, you still have to play games. The game never stops. So either you get good at the game, or you get out. And the sad thing about the game is nobody ever wins."

I pulled my lips in, started popping my jaw, swallowed and held the tears at bay.

I said, "In that case, maybe people shouldn't get married. Hell, damn near everybody ends up divorced any-damn-way, so what's the point? Hell, men probably invented this marriage bull-shit as another way of turning us into . . . into . . . into property."

"No, women invented marriage. That way, when it doesn't work out, we can take half their property. That's called Affirmative Reaction."

"Not in the mood for jokes, Frankie."

She rubbed my hand, softened her tone, and asked, "Why did you marry Tony?"

"Loved him. Wanted to have his babies. Cook his every meal."

She laughed. "You couldn't cook worth a shit."

I laughed too. "I learned. I took classes, and learned."

"You sure did. Surprised me."

"Wanted to be with him, get old and be looking at each other the way Momma and Bernard used to look at each other every day and every night."

"And now you don't love him, right?"

"Humiliated at my own dinner party. Eight thousand dollars in legal bills. A bastard child who will have to spend weekends and holidays at our home. How would you feel?"

"It's not the baby's fault."

"So, am I supposed to accept the situation and—?"

My phone vibrated again. Frankie shifted. I left the phone where it was.

My thoughts took me farther down the 60, then up the 15 to the 10.

"Maybe I'm searching for an antidote, Frankie. I guess I thought that marriage was supposed to edify, kill all primal urges, make us safe from the outside world, shit like that."

She shook her head and turned the radio onto KJLH. Cliff and Janine were on.

"Frankie?"

"Whassup?"

"Remember when I told you I asked Momma what marriage was all about? . . ."

"Uh huh."

I clacked my teeth. "And she said it was about the end."

"Uh huh. She told me when I was about to get married to G.I. Asshole."

"What did she mean?"

She didn't say anything for a moment. "You'll figure it out."

"So, you know what she meant?"

That was all she said about it.

Frankie told me, "I want you to stop seeing that guy."

I never answered.

Tommie

The doorbell rings.

Without looking through the peephole, I know it's Blue. I stand there, working on my breathing, my smile, trying not to answer too fast. I've been waiting, spying out of my bay window, watching him come down the walkway, then hearing the stairs rattle under his weight.

I open the door. "You're on time."

"Wow . . . your hair . . ."

My hair is five inches high, an uncontrollable Afro. My mane owns a new color, the hue of a brown penny. My dark skirt is new, and so is my wide-sleeved blouse. My blouse is tied at the bottom, showing off my navel ring. Silver bracelets jingle every time my left arm moves.

Blue looks at me like he's never seen me before. "You look nice, Tommie."

My face hurts from blushing. "Thanks."

"Never seen you in a dress before."

"Haven't worn one in . . . years."

"Just getting off work?"

"Nah. I wear dull pants and reindeer socks to work."

"About to go out to a Christmas party or—?"

"Not tonight. I'm in for the evening."

"Your hair . . . You look like you should be in a magazine . . . like a model."

"People at work complimented me all day. Half of 'em didn't recognize me."

"You look . . . wow. You're stunning."

"C'mon in before I call an ambulance. You're gonna compliment me to death."

"That skirt is kinda . . . like . . . bam. You walk into a bar, you'll start a fight."

"Be quiet. You bring your screenplay?"

"Right here."

"Can't wait to read over it."

I don't know whether to hug him, kiss him on the cheek, kiss him like we did before, so I wait, decide to follow his lead. He closes the door, puts his screenplay down, hugs me a long time, then kisses me, first lip to lip, then nibbling, then his tongue moves with mine for a while.

"Hey, Blue, I didn't see any mistletoe."

"My bad."

"It's on the mantel if you . . . How many berries do we have left?"

He kisses me again.

When we finish our hello, he smiles. "Nice place."

"Thanks."

"Colorful. Lots of pillows and candles. It smells like . . ."

"Pier 1." I laugh. "I have a tendency to over . . . Sometimes I get a li'l bit too creative."

"You're cooking?"

"I was putting a little somethin'-somethin' together."

"Smells off the chains." Blue checks his watch. "Expecting company?"

"Well, yeah."

"Then I won't keep you too long."

"You, Blue. You're the company I'm expecting. My sisters decided to stay in the mountains another day. They went skiing. And I . . . I thought you might break bread with me . . . if you have time. Thought it would be nice for us to share some literature and supper."

He smiles. "Supper?"

"Yeah. Nothing extravagant. Rosemary chicken, brown rice and vegetables. Hungry?"

"Sure. Single men shouldn't turn down free meals."

"I made enough for Monica too."

"Thanks. She loves your cooking."

"Make yourself at home." I rub damp hand over damp hand, swallow and clear my throat, touch my face and hair. "You can see everything I own worth seeing from the door."

"Lots of candles."

"Got them from Pier 1. Employee discount."

"How much you get off?"

"If I go in at the right time and since I know where the cameras are, one hundred percent off."

He laughs and shakes his head, his hand in his pocket, shaking loose change.

I shrug. "I can't afford any of that stuff, so I do like the rest of the employees."

"Your place . . . very nice."

Thanks to my plethora of candles, my rooms smell like heaven, but I'm still hoping the blissful aroma from the candles cover the fading scent of Clorox and Pine-Sol.

I tell him, "Let me show you something."

He follows me into the living room, the room I spent the most time decorating.

Once again he says, "Wow. This is . . . wow . . . awesome."

Black, red, and green streamers, flowers, and cloths decorate my front room, the one with the bay windows facing Fairfax. My Kinara, Unity cup, a straw bowl with a cornucopia of crops are in a straw basket, all of the symbols neatly arranged on a second-hand table I borrowed from my next-door neighbors, the Womacks. A gorgeous cloth with an African print covers the table.

I beam. "I have almost everything I need."

In the far corner stands a small, undecorated Charlie Brown Christmas tree and a growing stack of presents, most of them small items from Pier 1.

He nudges me. "You're making me look pretty bad."

Then I go to the presents, hand him one of the two extra Unity cups I bought.

He says, "This is beautiful."

"For you and Monica." I want to impress him with all the things I do. "And guess what?"

"What?"

"I can decorate with corn. I was talking to Womack and Rosa Lee, and they said that I didn't have to have children to have corn. If you don't have any kids, then the corn symbolizes the African concept of social parenthood."

He nods as if he's learning something new. "It takes a village."

"Right. The concept Hillary Clinton plagiarized and ran with."

"Cool. I have extra corn if you . . . I can't get over how . . . You're stunning."

My smile remains perpetual.

We walk back toward the kitchen. On the way I compliment Blue on his clothes too, his wool slacks and white shirt. His beard is coming in, making him look hip and distinguished.

"You look purty handsome yourself. Going somewhere tonight?"

"Just . . . over here. Mo's with her grandparents until the morning."

He stands in the door while I check on the food, and when I'm done, I focus on his face, hoping he doesn't see the nervousness I'm trying to hide by staying in motion. The moment I quit moving, I feel the anxiety settling in the corner of my lip. I tremble for a brief second.

I have a new hairstyle, new clothes, new perfume. I remind myself everything is fine, that my apartment is spotless, that every CD, every magazine, every little thing is in its place. It took hours of work to get my home in order.

He comes into the kitchen.

Blue asks, "What're you listening to?"

"Bonnie Raitt."

"Never heard of him."

"He's a she and she's a white woman."

"Oh."

"Meant to change that before you got here. I can put on a CD, or the radio—"

"No. It's fine. Just wondered who it was."

"It's no problem to change it."

"It's fine."

He says that kind of strong. My posture changes from calm to defensive. The energy in the room shifts and first my breathing cuts off, then speeds up. He had said that like he was at work telling one of the children the same thing he'd told the entire class two minutes before.

I wipe my hands on the front of my skirt.

I say, "It's programmed to play the mellow songs."

"Sounds smooth."

"I like her lyrics. That's the only one that sounds so 'white,' I guess you could say."

Uncomfortable silence.

I go back to the food, my back to him, my thoughts everywhere, wondering what I'm doing, wishing I wasn't doing this, asking questions, doubting myself, wishing I could call Livvy or Frankie and get some advice, maybe have them walk me through this, maybe I can call—

He interrupts my thoughts, asks, "Need some help?"

"Uh . . . well . . . mind taking the trash out for me?"

"No problem."

He moves by me to get to the white trash can. The space is tight and his crotch rubs across my backside as he passes. I flinch. Then I feel warm. I tingle.

He says, "Sorry about that."

"That's okay."

Blue puts a hand on my shoulder.

I pretend I'm too busy to look up.

He asks, "Nervous?"

I turn around, put my head on his chest, take a few breaths, and nod.

He asks, "Something I did?"

I shake my head. "It's . . . It's been a while, that's all."

"What's been a while?"

"Since I had somebody over in my space. A man, I mean. Since I cooked for a man. I don't usually cook for anybody . . . don't try to make myself attractive. Not like this. I haven't had on mascara for over a year. Well, that frosted makeup, but that's not like real makeup."

"Sure that's it?"

"Feels like it's everything. Being alone with you in my apartment is a big thing for me."

He rubs my back. "What happened?"

I don't answer. Heavy memories make my voice uneven.

Blue kisses my forehead. "Where are they?"

"Who?"

"Your trash cans."

"Oh. Bottom of the stairs on the left. Thanks."

"No problem."

Blue picks up the two garbage bags, both with his right hand. One of the bags smells sour. He stops at the back door and looks at another collage of pictures I have on that wall. Pictures of me and my family, most taken back when my hair was in flips, French roll, and spirals. Back when my look was conservative and conforming. Each photo has a real smile.

He says, "You've always been beautiful."

My smile comes back as the art of speech continues to abandon me.

He walks out the back door, goes down the wooden stairs, then vanishes. I stand there, stirring food and wondering if he'll come back, or take the walkway and go back home.

I take the lid off the brown rice, check the vegetables and vegetarian beans, look in the oven and test the tenderness of the chicken. On the counter are white plates with rose patterns, sil-

verware, cloth napkins, two wine glasses, a bottle of Spumante.
A packet of Kool-Aid too.

I'm making our plates when I hear him coming back up the
stairs.

He comes in and takes my hands, pulls me to him, kisses me.

He whispers, "You okay?"

"Truth be told . . ."

"Uh huh."

"I'm scared."

"Of what?"

"The unknown."

Tommie

After dinner, one long kiss leads us down the hallway to my bedroom.

I blow out the candles. I turn my back to Blue before I take off my skirt and blouse. I fold them. Place them on the floor. Slip underneath the covers before he can see my nakedness.

Bonnie Raitt sings the reflective and lingering song about "all at once."

Blue follows my lead, undresses in the dark.

He says, "You blew out the candles."

"I like it dark."

"Mind if I crack the shade and let some moonlight in?"

"I'd rather not."

Blue gets underneath the covers, puts his warm skin next to mine.

We kiss.

I whisper, "Blue?"

"Yeah."

"I'm on the pill. Helps with my cramps. So if you don't wanna use a condom . . ."

"You have any?"

"Got a couple from my sister."

"I'd be more comfortable with one on."

Blue runs his hand over my body, then I open the nightstand and hand him a condom.

He touches my back, feathers his fingers down to my butt.

He whispers, "You're so soft. Beautiful. Awesome shape."

"I could stand to do a few squats."

"Watching you walk is like watching a gentle breeze. Your voice . . . love it."

He traces his fingers down my back, then up, like he's riding the curve of my butt.

He whispers, "You still have your bra and panties on."

Damp palms refuse to dry. "Didn't want to steal all of your fun."

He unhooks my bra with one hand. I shift, jump a little.

I say, "Wow. You're . . . you're good at that."

"Luck of the draw."

"That wasn't luck."

My bra is made of a rich material. Silky with nice support, like Frankie and Livvy wear. I take it from his hands, fold it, put it under my pillow. He kisses me again, touches my breasts, and his hands wander down to my panties. He starts pulling them down. I wiggle out of them.

He asks, "You okay?"

"Yeah."

"Open your eyes."

I do.

He says, "You have a hurry-up look on your face."

My mouth feels dry. "Sorry."

"Looks like you're in the doctor's office about to get vaccinated."

Blue kisses my breasts. Nipples rise. He eases his kisses down my stomach to the ring in my belly button, goes lower, but I gently pull him away from his journey south, pull him toward me, kiss him, and try to hide my being uncomfortable.

I say, "Put the condom on."

"Okay."

I lie back, wait. Blue crawls on top of me, kisses me again.

My legs open.

I close my eyes and feel him.

He says, "Something's not working."

I pant. "Hurts a little."

"Relax and let me—"

"I'm trying. That's it right . . . Ouch."

"What?"

"That's not it."

A moment later, Blue asks, "Why are your eyes scrunched like that?"

"I'm concentrating."

"You're tense. We can't do much with your legs that tight."

"Blue . . . I'm not ready for this."

"Why did you go through all of this if—?"

"I didn't mean to upset you."

"I'm not upset. I'm just saying."

"Wait . . . don't get up."

"What do you want me to do?"

"Why don't you go ahead and please yourself?"

"Jack off?"

"No, I mean . . . just don't wait for me. Get it over with."

His voice owns frustration and confusion. "Get it over with?"

"I mean, you know, go ahead and, you know."

"It doesn't work like that, Tommie."

I pause. "I'm sorry."

Silence magnifies the awkwardness.

"Blue . . . I'm trying to relax."

"Why won't you let me see you naked?"

"I'm sensitive about that."

"It's just me and you."

"I know." My voice is a deep whisper. "I'm not comfortable with my body right now."

"Don't sweat it."

"You slipped out."

"Don't think I was really in."

"I felt something."

"The tip."

"I felt it."

"Your thighs are tight. Look, you want to put it back in?"

"You mean touch it?"

"Yeah, touch it. Guide it home."

"You do it."

"Never mind."

He rolls to the other side of the bed. The sound of him pulling latex off his flesh rings like the period at the end of a sentence.

My brain wants to go liquid. The picture I have in my mind, the way I imagine this will be, how everything works like clockwork, from dinner to here, fades like warmth against ice.

I sit up, leg bouncing, running my fingers through my hair. "Blue, it's not you. I really wanted this with you."

His silence disturbs me even more.

My voice remains uneven. "I'm not real good at this to begin with. Haven't done this that much to start with. Only been with two guys . . . and it's been . . . been years . . ."

He sighs.

"Say something, Blue."

"I . . . I don't know what to say . . . just . . . dunno."

I lower my head. "You can leave if you want to."

"You want me to leave?"

"I'm saying it'll be all right if you do."

Blue sits on the edge of the bed, his back to me, his hands gripping his thick hair.

I wiggle back into my panties, sit in profile, my hand in my hair, inhaling the wonderful scent of stolen candles.

Blue turns and makes a quick move in my direction; my eyes widen and I shriek, cower away from him. My expression rattles him as awkwardness blankets us.

He raises his palms, waits a moment, then asks, "You okay?"

I own no words right now. Hands shaking. Again, embarrassed.

He waits, watches me, then asks, "What was . . . What just happened?"

"Thought you were gonna hit me or something."

Blue pauses, sadness in his every move.

"Who hurt you, Tommie?"

My eyes close. "My ex."

"What'd he do?"

"He used to beat me and stuff, that's all."

"That's all?"

My fingers come up to my face and again I trace my history. My head shakes; my vision darkens. I didn't mean to say *that's all*, didn't mean to minimize the damage. Shame did that.

I raise my head and look Blue in the eyes. "He'd beat me over nothing."

"That's why you left L.A.?"

"Yeah."

Silence again.

I say, "This is really hard for me, but I'm trying. I've been in group . . ."

"Therapy."

"Yeah. He messed my head up so bad. The last time he beat me, he kicked me . . . burned me right here . . . I ended up in the hospital. That was when my sisters found out . . . Livvy came with her husband . . . Tony beat him up real bad . . . They took me to the emergency room . . . and . . . after that . . . had to . . . told them what had been going on for the whole year . . . Frankie was ready to kill him. Stupid me lied and defended his butt. It was a big mess. A real big mess. My family was mad at me a long time. Then . . . I came back out here to finish school."

"You came back to be with him?"

"Heck, no. Came back for me. Had to prove I could do this by myself."

Blue pauses. "Where is he?"

"Somebody said he was in Seattle or Oregon or something."

"Wanna talk about it?"

I shake my head. "One day. Not now."

He says, "I don't know what to do right now."

"Me either."

"You want me to go?"

"No, just talk to me."

"Don't know what to say."

We both lie back on the bed, on our backs, eyes to the ceiling.

I ask, "How many women have you been with?"

He shrugs. "Don't know."

"More than ten?"

"Yeah."

"Twenty?"

"Yeah."

I ask, "How old were you when you first did it?"

"Fourteen."

"Wow. Did you have an orgasm, or just put it in?"

"Had an orgasm."

"How was that?"

"Scared the shit out of me."

I laugh. "You were getting your freak on before I was born."

He chuckles. "You?"

"I was a sophomore in college."

"I think that gets a *wow* too."

A dog barks out in the neighborhood. A car passes down a side street, music playing loud. I hear the kids next door, Womack's family, outside. They run out of their house. A basketball starts bouncing. Their kids start screaming like heathens.

I get up, reach under the curtains, and close my window, then get back in the bed.

Blue asks, "Are you crying?"

I shake my head. "Sinuses are draining."

I get up again, walk down the hallway to the bathroom.

I talk louder, "I know you're disappointed. So I won't feel bad if you leave, Blue."

He moves around. I hear him and imagine him reaching for his clothes. His footsteps move from the bedroom to the living room, going toward my front door, knowing that it's time for the erotic shades of Blue to fade from my mind.

My voice catches in my throat as I call out, "Don't forget your Unity cup."

I blow my nose soft and gentle. His footsteps move back toward the bedroom.

He calls out, "Maybe you should take an allergy pill."

I open my cabinet and pop two red pills, go to the kitchen, and get a glass of water.

Blue is on my bed, still sitting up, still undressed. Even in the dark, he's awesome.

As I pass by, he touches my arm. First I tremble, then relax. He invites me down next to him. I put my head on his chest. He massages my neck and shoulders with a gentle touch.

Bonnie Raitt is still in the air.

I join in, singing about an old house falling down at the dimming of the day.

He asks, "Why do you like Bonnie Raitt?"

"White girl I was in group with liked it. She was a twenty-six-year-old battered wife. Three kids." I laugh like it was a good memory. "I hated that music at first, but she made me sit down and listen to the lyrics. Go beyond the music. You have to do that sometimes. Get below what you think is on the surface. That's what you have to do with people. Go beyond the surface. Get beyond the music they're dancing to. She taught me that."

"She's in Texas?"

"Gloria died last year. Her husband gave her AIDS."

"Wow."

"He plays pro football in Florida. He had sexual hang-ups and took it out on her to make himself feel like a man."

"So, he's—?"

"From what I hear, he's still walking around spreading the disease."

His fingers make smooth circles on my back. My moans rise in jazzlike riffs.

He said, "You're beautiful. Smart. Why stay in an abusive relationship?"

"Stupid me thought I could change him by loving him. I

used to get on my knees and pray to God that he would change. My friend Gloria said that trying to change a man was like trying to cure cancer; we knew we were gonna fail, but we tried anyway."

My fingers make circles in the hair on his chest.

He whispers, "Sorry if I came off too, I dunno, wrong."

"You didn't know. I think I told you too much."

"No you didn't."

"You okay with it?"

"I don't have a problem with it. My mood isn't the best."

"What's wrong?"

"Baby-momma drama. Same old."

"Wanna talk about it?"

"Nah."

We keep feather-touching each other. I'm calm and tingling. Fear is gone.

"I like you, Tommie. Like you a lot. Mo loves you."

"But?"

"I don't bring women around Mo. I'm very protective of her."

"You're supposed to be. My daddy was the same way."

Some thinking time goes by before Blue speaks again. "I've got a lot going on."

"We all do."

"Guess so."

I say, "If you can accept my baggage, I'll accept yours."

We laugh, but I laugh harder and longer.

I start back singing my duet with Bonnie.

Blue listens.

When I'm done, I rest in my thoughts and desires. I say, "I've never had an orgasm."

"You're joking."

"Why does everybody think that's a damn joke?"

"That's another wow."

"I want to have one with you."

"Whenever you think you're ready, we'll try again."

"Thanks."

"I more than 'like' you, Tommie."

"I know."

Silence.

I tease my fingers through my wild mane. "I've been reading stuff like *203 Ways to Drive a Man Wild in Bed, Kama Sutra, Unleashing the Sex Goddess in Every Woman*—"

He repeats, "*Unleashing the Sex Goddess in Every Woman*?"

We laugh.

Laughs change to light chuckles. Chuckles evolve into erotic stares. To light touches.

We kiss. The fire returns and we drink each other. I float away.

I inhale his heat, kiss him, and whisper, "Guess I've been studying for the big moment."

"Some things a book can't teach you."

Another blistering kiss and everything becomes . . . ethereal. Haunting. Heavy breathing creates evocative sounds. Intoxication quilts me. My fingers play in his wooly hair, move down his back. All that is cold turns warm, and all that is warm catches fire. In this moment, I have no scars, no old wounds. And I feel it, like in my dreams. My heartbeat moves from my chest, down my stomach, and settles between my thighs, blends with fire and wetness.

I'm wet. God, I'm so wet.

I feel him against me. He's firm.

Erotic desires decorate my rising moans. He kisses me like I'm delicious.

I take his hand, move it between my thighs.

I whisper, "I'm not scared anymore."

PLEASURE PRINCIPLE

The theory, not the song.

Livvy

My photo smiled at everyone the moment they came into the lobby. There I was, Miss Happy to Work Here, in my gray-and-white uniform advertising Dermalogica products, my image on a white wall decorated with purple blocks. The quote under my picture jumped out at me. THE FACE IS A MIRROR OF THE SOUL. Employees were in the poster-sized ads up and down the hallway. We always joked that this place looked like either a clinic or an asylum.

"What are you doing here, Livvy?"

"Hey, Jenny." I took my sunglasses off. "Came to buy products. Making baskets."

"Want to help with a European skincare class while you're here?"

"Shorthanded?"

"Need someone to work as a student. I mean . . . no pressure . . . up to you."

I smiled. She had read my face the way some specialists examined organs to diagnose patients. Didn't matter. Everyone knew. Coworkers had been at the dinner party, witnessed my humiliation. My business echoed in these halls, another reason I kept working on the road.

I ended up being at work half the day, first helping out with the class, then sitting in the break room, reviewing articles on aromatherapy treatments and Chinese diagnosis on the skin.

I finally broke free and made it to the cashier, paid for all of my goodies, everything from cleansing gels to daily microfoliants to skin renewal boosters. A group of us were jaw-jacking near the window that faced the parking lot, talking and laughing with a couple of the other instructors, when I looked out and saw a red-haired woman jogging away from the building. Could've been one of the students. We trained several hundred women a week.

If I hadn't turned my back, I would've seen her speed away in a red Miata. I would've seen that the back window of her car had been torn, then repaired with duct tape. If I had seen her face, I would've remembered her from that club in San Diego.

Frankie

"Frankie! Come back, Frankie!"

I was so livid that as soon as I saw his ass, I turned around and stormed out of the friggin' restaurant, pushing people out of the way and kicking down doors. The only reason his ass caught me was because I had to wait for damn valet parking to bring me my damn car.

"Frankie! Frankie!"

"What the hell do you want?"

"What did I do?"

"Besides looking under my damn dress?"

"I didn't look—"

"Then you started cracking jokes. 'I didn't know Bush had a Hitler mustache on his lips.' That was . . . I should kick your ass."

"It was a joke."

"Pervert."

"It wasn't intentional, besides . . . one look at me and you got an attitude—thought a little humor would make it—"

"Damn right I have a fucking attitude."

"What did I do?"

I snapped, "Your profile said you were six-two and your picture looked like Taye Diggs."

"That *was* Taye Diggs."

"You sent me a friggin' picture of Taye Diggs?"

"Can we just finish the date?"

"Tell ya what, I'll e-mail you. We can meet and get a Happy Meal. Booster seats on me."

"You're racist."

"You're fugly."

"Discriminating against short people."

"Oh . . . grow the fuck up. You ain't tall enough to get on this ride, baby."

Valet pulled up in my car. I pushed Mini Me out of the way.

I got in my car, revved the engine, and fought the urge to make his little ass roadkill.

He yelled, "Whoooo hoooo! Bush does have a Hitler mustache!"

I sped away, top down, heater on full blast, my middle finger saluting him in the wind.

"That was a short date."

"Tommie, you just don't know how short it was."

An hour later I was at Tommie's crib. She was in her living room with a little girl. The girl was pretty, had on Old Navy sweats, her hair in braids, she had on glasses. She looked like a genius in training. The little girl was a straight-up type A, bouncing all over the place, doing cartwheels in between laughing and watching Tommie wrap presents.

I looked around and asked, "Somebody break in and steal everything?"

"Ha ha."

After I got over how clean her space was, how beautiful her living room looked with the Kwanzaa setup, I went to the bathroom, walked into her bedroom, saw three empty condom wrappers in her trash can, then came back into the front room feeling like a space invader.

I smiled, asked the little girl, "What's your name?"

She smiled. "My name is Monica Mitchell."

"My name is Frankie. I'm Tommie's big sister."

"Tommie, I didn't know you had a big sister."

"I have two big sisters."

"You're really, really, really tall, Frankie."

I smiled. "You're pretty tall too. You're taller than my date was."

"Wow. I want a sister one day. I want her name to be Nia."

"Really?"

"Uh huh. Nia means purpose. I used to want my sister to be named Keisha, but I like Nia better now, because Nia means purpose and I don't think Keisha means anything."

She went back to running and flipping.

I asked Tommie, "Where's Livvy?"

"Called her. Got her voicemail."

I nodded. "Soooo . . . you're babysitting?"

"Not really. Just hanging out, e-mailing Santa, stuff like that."

"Uh huh."

"Her daddy needed to go *s-h-o-p-p-i-n-g* for a *B-a-r-b-i-e* and other stuff."

I raised a brow. "Creamy Vanilla with the LL thang? . . ."

She blushed. "Yeah."

"Something going on I need to know about?"

"Why you all up in my grill, Frankie?"

I sucked on my bottom lip, arms folded, foot tapping, the image of what I'd seen in her trash can in my mind. All of a sudden I felt like . . . geesh . . . like . . . like her friggin' mother.

I asked, "His name wouldn't happen to be Blue, would it?"

"Please don't tell me he's on your B-list or C-list or whatever."

"I don't mix biz with my personal life."

"Thank God."

"And why are you *d-a-t-i-n-g* your *n-e-i-g-h-b-o-r*?"

"Not now, Frankie. Please, not now."

"Are you having . . . Are you . . . you know."

"I know you don't want to start a question-asking party up in here."

I went to the bay window and looked out on the streets. A red Miata was parked across the street. A white woman got out and stood there for a moment.

I said, "Looks like we're in the midst of gentrification."

Tommie came to the window. "I saw her out there yesterday."

"Looking at properties, a place to squat, or trying to get some coffee in her milk?"

She shrugged. "She was just sitting there like she was waiting on somebody."

"Looks like she's coming over here. Is that Monica's mother?"

Monica was between us, holding Tommie's hand. "My mother's hair is yellow, not red."

Right about then, an SUV slowed down in front of her. It was Womack and his family. They said a few words, and then the woman hopped back in her sporty little car and sped away.

I sat on the floor, grabbed some wrapping paper, and started helping Tommie wrap a few gifts. Most of the stuff she had was from either Old Navy or Pier 1.

She said, "Pick which one of those sweat suits you want and put your name on it."

"I'll take the gray one because it looks like Blue is your color."

"Don't hate."

"How did you meet him?"

"Sometimes you have to open the curtains and look out the window."

Not long after that I kicked my shoes off, changed into a pair of Tommie's sweats. We cranked up Radio Disney and danced like we were losing our minds, Monica leading the way. Then she sat at the kitchen table and talked me to death while she bounced and ate a peanut butter sandwich. When I was tired of the preschool jaw-jacking, I went back into the front room and watched them interact. I'd never seen Tommie like that, playing the mother role.

Monica told me, "I'm practicing my spoken word for Daddy's present."

"Really?"

"I'm going to be a poem writer when I get bigger. Want to hear it?"

"Sure."

She jumped up, did a cartwheel, then ran to the middle of the room. "I *love* my daddy when he works so long it makes me saddy call him on the phone—"

"Whoa, whoa. Slow down, Monica."

"Now I'll have to start *allll* over again." She took a deep breath. "Call him on the phone. When he's gone too long. Always wish he were near. Wish he were here. I *love* my daddy."

Tommie and I applauded. Monica smiled and went back to doing her cartwheels.

Tommie's phone rang. She was busy doing cartwheels and backbends with the kid, so I answered. It was Womack calling.

He said that the woman out front was looking for Livvy.

A hand went to my hip and I raised a brow. "Looking for Livvy?"

"She was asking questions."

"Like?"

"If that was where she lived, then wanted to know if I knew who lived in your building."

"Was it somebody from Dermalogica?"

"I backed down with the talking. Something about her . . . Her ass was being too friendly, smiling too much, you know? Didn't wanna say too much, know what I mean?"

"What did she say?"

"After I started asking her a question or two, she got uncomfortable, kinda freaked out, just ran to her car and took off. Frankie, that woman burned rubber like she'd seen a ghost."

"Thanks, Womack."

I hung up and told Tommie what that call was all about. Her expression was the same as mine, hoping Tony didn't have a string of paternity suits heading this way.

She took the phone from me and called Livvy's cell phone.

Livvy

Tommie's number showed up on my caller ID.

I didn't answer, just turned my phone off and put my hand back in Carpe's lap.

Carpe drove me down Rosecrans, away from the beaches, past the 405, across Hawthorne, down under the dim lights on Western, an urban area that was black and Hispanic. Second-rate businesses, used car shops. Nothing sparkled on this strip.

He turned right on Western, slowed, then pulled over in the parking lot of a strip club.

He asked, "This okay?"

The building was stucco, small, nothing special. But the small parking lot was full.

I said, "Never been to one."

"Never?"

Vibrations ran through me. The bass line from the music they were playing inside.

"Been to a bachelorette party," I said. "Never a strip club."

"How was the bachelorette party?"

"Wild."

"How wild?"

"Women were on the guy jacking him off."

"Pretending?"

"No, for real."

"They make him come?"

"I think so."

"You touch him?"

I laughed. "No comment."

We sat in the car and looked out at the front of the building. Watched the people walking inside. My hand was on his leg, moving up and down, then making circles on his crotch.

He asked, "You want to?"

"I'm with you."

Security patted Carpe down. We walked into a room filled with either topless or naked women in glittery thongs, trashy pleather lingerie, and six-inch stilettos. We were dressed in blacks, him in a leather jacket, and me in a new leather skirt. So many different types of perfumes mixed with the smell of so many different brands of alcohol. Weaves were all over the place, some looked good, some atrocious. The women were mostly black, but quite a few were white, Asian, or Hispanic, doubt if many were over thirty, and the ones who were over thirty, doubt if they got as much attention as the girls who were barely legal. Some of them were slim with the bodies of aerobics instructors. One had fresh stretch marks. Another had more tattoos than I could count. Some had on the wrong makeup. Hair in every primary color. Fake boobs. Hot pants. Thigh-high boots. I watched men watch the women. The dancers with the junk in the trunk and the women with the real curves got the most attention.

Carpe asked, "Where you wanna sit?"

"I'm with you."

We moved past the pool tables, by men transfixed with their lap dancers. A few looked at me, eyes lingering on an ass they'd never get to feel, taste, touch, or smell.

I made a face. "I can dance better than that."

"There's an empty spot."

I felt uneasy, but the place had a big neon sign: WOMEN FRIENDLY. There were groups of women here, sitting on the front row, getting lap dances, that look of lust in their eyes. Some were here with their dates, men who were getting off on letting their woman get a lap dance, or their woman was getting off by watching another woman arouse her dick for the night.

The dancers performed for men, made their asses shake one cheek at a time, rubbed their breasts on the men's faces, touched themselves without shame.

After twenty minutes of looking at naked women, I had adjusted. I was about ready to leave and go back to my nest in Manhattan Beach, make love, shower, then head back to Frankie's so we could finish wrapping presents and start making pies.

Then this dancer named Panther took the stage.

Panther was dark, sensuous, exotic eyes, and full lips. She had perfect mocha skin and was very curvaceous. Nipples like ripe raspberries. Hair was like spun silk, a top-shelf weave. She danced like the ocean, movements that hardened men and softened women.

He asked, "What do you think about her?"

"She's beautiful." She was thicker than most of the other women, didn't have that L.A.-ness about her. "Want her to dance for you?"

We watched her dance her way out of her silver boy shorts and bra. She danced like she was born in stilettos. She was nice up top, a B-cup at the most, full and curvy on the bottom.

Carpe rubbed his finger across my palm. "What do you think?"

I nodded and smiled. "She's hot."

"She's sexy. Classy. Not a hood-rat ghetto stripper."

"She's like a . . . goddess."

We held hands and watched her for a while. I reached over and touched Carpe between his legs. He was swelling. I traced the outline of his penis.

I said, "I'll be back."

I took a few dollars and went over to the edge of the stage. Panther saw me and came toward me. She was naked, a woman sculpted from the sweetest mound of chocolate. The closer she came, the prettier she looked. Beautiful skin moistened by some sort of cream blended with sparkle dust. She had an ethereal, luminescent appearance.

I put three dollars down. "My . . . the guy I'm with . . ."

"Over there?"

"Yeah, him. He thinks you're hot."

She smiled. "Wow. Thanks."

Her voice was soft, made her sound so innocent, as if she had never heard that before, as if she had no idea how beautiful she was, as if she had no idea how the men and women in this room were eye-sexing her the moment she walked out on the stage.

I said, "He . . . We . . . The guy I'm with . . . he . . . wants you to dance for him."

She reached down and took my hand, but she never stopped dancing. "Sure."

My heart was about to burst from my breasts.

Palms became a river; throat a desert. I managed to say, "Okay."

"I'll come see you as soon as I finish."

She let my hand go and I felt lost, had the same expression a lot of the men in the room had while women sold them fantasies at ten dollars a dance. The expression of seduction.

When I turned around to go back to my table, I felt wobbly, like the whole room was watching my clumsy, uneven steps. Carpe didn't say anything when I sat down, just put his hand on my thigh, traced his fingers up and down my leg. I sipped half of my wine, cleared my throat, and wondered if my desire was raining from my pores.

Panther did a pole dance that had dollars raining at her feet.

He nudged me and asked, "Can you do that?"

"If I could move like that," I laughed, "I'd be a millionaire ten times over."

Song after song, Panther moved with seduction and invitation. She had great showmanship, shimmying up and down that pole, twisting and writhing, so damn limber, doing isolations like she'd had a lot of African dance classes, maybe even a class or two in public relations because she knew how to make everyone she touched feel special.

She kept looking at me, smiling in a way that told me she'd be coming to visit our table soon. She stood on the edge of the stage, made her butt bounce to the beat, then made it go round and round. While she did that she took her breasts in her hands, ran her tongue across her nipples, sucked on her black pearls. Her eyes came back to me.

The stares she gave me made me think she wanted me too.

I imagined my hands cupping her breasts.

Then I put my drink to my lips and swallowed, tried to wash that image out of my brain.

Panther came to our table wearing a different outfit, a goddess in a yellow thong and bra.

She asked me, "Have you been here before?"

"No."

Her voice was music. "You look familiar."

She rubbed my hair in a way that made me feel exotic. Electricity ran through me and just like that I was giddy. It scared me that a woman could touch me and excite me that way.

I struggled to maintain my coolness, said, "First time here."

"Nice to meet you." She smiled at Carpe, then looked back and forth between both of us. "Who am I dancing for?"

I told her, "Him."

She pulled her thong off, stood in front of me, naked and beautiful, and told me, "Pull your chair up so people can get by."

"Okay."

I moved and Panther was sandwiched between us. She faced my lover, but her ass was touching my legs, moving up against me.

They were laughing, saying things I couldn't hear, openly flirting. He whispered something in her ear and her smile broadened. Then she whispered something back. And she moved. God, I'd never be able to move like that, so liquid and sexy and vulgar all at once.

Carpe, the look on his face, the glaze in his eyes, I didn't exist anymore.

Panther was a goddess, and goddesses turn men into slaves.

She looked back and touched my legs, put her hands inside my thighs, had me open my legs so she could have more room to work her body up against mine at the same time.

The record was over and I gave her the ten dollars. My hand was shaky.

He said, "Dance for Bird."

I shook my head. "No."

He said, "Fine. Dance for me again."

She winked at me and laughed, danced facing him. Then she turned around and faced me, touched my hair again, put her hand on my legs when she leaned over and started rubbing her backside against him. Her eyes stayed on mine. Her eyes; she had lover's eyes, the kind that hypnotized and made me drift to a place where there was no pain or thought.

She asked me, "Are you a virgin?"

"A virgin?"

She licked her lips. I did the same. Her eyes stayed with me. Panther's beauty filled my vision, and I inhaled her scent. Her hands touched me, a very light pressure that went so deep. I wanted to pull back, but I didn't. She had me anchored.

She asked, "Ever had a lap dance?"

"No."

"You're a virgin."

"Oh."

"Sure you don't want to give me your cherry?"

I asked, "Would that be my Christmas present to you?"

"Could be my present to you."

Her smile remained sweet and confident. Mine became nervous.

She asked, "Where you from?"

"Here. You?"

"Atlanta."

"Never been there."

Her fingers traced my clothes. "I love your outfit."

"Thanks."

Heat and tingles made me shift. She leaned forward, gave Carpe her backside, her breasts grazing me, our position looking like were having a ménage à trois.

She said, "Your shoes are off the chains."

"Thanks."

"Manolo?"

"Manolo." I beamed. "How do you like L.A.?"

"Love the beaches. But I might move back to Atlanta."

She came closer to me; spread my legs, stood closer, her perfume a wonderful sweetness, her hair moving against my face, her breasts pressing up on me. She raised one breast, rubbed it across my face. One touch and I was floating. Everything around me disappeared. She bent over again, her backside rubbing against Carpe's crotch, her face and breath between my thighs. She touched me, but I wasn't supposed to touch her. That didn't seem fair. Not at all.

"Goddamn."

"Dey get'n dey freak on up in here tonight."

That came from a group of guys at the next table. Voyeurs wearing Lugz boots, baggy FUBU jeans, and Raiders baseball caps. Whenever the record ended, we told Panther to keep dancing. We lost count. My hips moved with her. My body came to life and danced with her. We were setting the room on fire, becoming the show. Most of the room watching us, so many men with one hand on their beers, the other on their crotches, so many women with rock-hard nipples the size of raisins, mouths wide open, looks of desire painted on all of their faces.

Carpe paid her, gave her a nice tip. Panther put her money in her garter, held my hand, smiled like we were the best of friends. Or maybe we had been lovers in another lifetime.

I told her, "Thanks . . . thanks. Nice meeting you."

"Come back and see me."

Call me foolish, but I felt like we had bonded, wanted to ask

Panther what her real name was. But I knew this was her gig, that her sweet voice and excellent presentation, her looks of adoration, the attention she gave, was all false, bought and paid for by the record, by the dance.

Then she was gone. Within minutes she was across the room, naked, dancing for another man, offering him her breasts and ass and smiles and laughs.

Carpe asked, "How did Panther make you feel?"

"She made me really want her."

"Would you?"

"I wouldn't want to do anything that I might regret afterward."

"Damn. She is working that guy out."

Panther was heating up her customer. I chuckled because I felt betrayed, like she was cheating on me. Our religious experience had passed and I'd been reduced to being the voyeur. Watching her tease him with her tongue and breasts, rubbing her warmth all over him, spreading her legs, showing him her pussy lips, letting him imagine her excitement going down his throat.

Carpe went to the men's room. On the way back, he stopped and talked to Panther. She was finished with her customer, first tucking her money in her garter, then easing back into her thong. More smiles and laughs and nods. He touched her shoulder and a different kind of heat consumed me. My hands became fists when I imagined him fucking her. Taking the keys to the studio away from me, giving them to her, loving her twice a day until the ocean went dry.

Carpe came back, rubbed my hand, asked, "Ready?"

"Yeah." I swallowed, rubbed my hands on my legs. "It's getting late."

He checked his watch.

When you were having an affair, you were always aware of the time, of every unaccountable minute. Always watching the clock and working on your next lie.

I staggered a bit when I got up. Still flustered. Tingling. Wet. Every nerve roaring.

On the way out, men looked at me with that one-sided smile. But the women, I mean damn. With Carpe in front of me he couldn't see how the women were watching me, a couple of them even winking and making bold motions for me to leave my lover and party with them.

I'd walked into this world a pauper and left feeling like Venus.

We had started this party around ten. Now it was after midnight.

Before I went out the door, I took one last look back at Panther.

The radio was on; car windows were cracked, cool air riding across my skin. Couldn't cool down, couldn't stop wiggling or tingling, and couldn't get this fire to die down.

I said, "You know what?"

"What?"

"Pull over and hook me up."

"No."

"I want you to thug me."

He laughed.

I moaned. "Please?"

"No."

Sirens punctured the night air as we rode under the streetlights and into the blackness of the urban track, riding pothole after pothole, passing by motel after motel, passing by women who have their merchandise on display. The true whores of the Southland. My breathing was strong, fists moving up and down my thighs, legs opening and closing.

He took my left hand, put my fingers in his mouth, and sucked each finger.

I doubled over and moaned from that feeling. "God, I need to come."

"No."

"Pull over."

"No."

Couldn't stop shifting side to side, trying to fan myself back to sanity.

"Right now or I'll do myself."

"Wait."

"Can't."

"Wait."

He touched between my legs, held my heat in his hands.

"Why are you torturing me?"

I squeezed his fingers with my legs; beat my thigh with my fist. He massaged, stirred, traced the outlines of my dampness and heat. I touched his erection; he moved my hand away.

Carpe undressed me, took away everything except for my shoes, carried me to the bed, lay me down, took my vibrator out, left it next to me, told me not to touch it; then he went to the armless chair, sat down. I knew what I needed, but I didn't know what he wanted.

Aching, desperate to have an orgasm, I reached for the vibrator.

He told me to leave it alone.

My hands came to life, fingernails raking up my legs, reaching to touch myself.

He came to the bed, moved my hands away, sat next to me, sucked my wetness from my fingers, my breasts, my toes, kept my fire on high, but never allowed me to cross that threshold.

I hated him.

For a long while he fed me kiwis and mangoes, rubbed juices on me, licked the sweetness away. Fed me, tongued my breasts, put three fingers in me, but never let me come.

I loved him.

There were two soft knocks at the door.

I jumped the way an adulteress jumped when a new fear gripped her heart.

He rubbed my leg, said, "It's okay."

I lay back down, adjusting my legs and hands so my breasts and sex were covered.

The door opened and I saw the silhouette of a goddess.

Panther.

She came into our light, her face sending me a slow smile, one that made my back arch, made my legs want to move away from each other.

That familiar liquid sensation crept down my neck. My breath caught in my nostrils as the air turned electric.

In the sweetest voice Carpe asked me, "Yes or no, baby?"

Fourth Week in December

For every reaction, there is an overreaction.

Read dat somewhere

ℒivvy

I rub you, I rub you, baby, I rub you!"

Frankie slapped the table and doubled over laughing. "Lawd . . . somebody hep that child."

Days had gone by and Christmas was staring us in our faces. We were drinking wine and laughing. Me and Frankie had done some last-minute shopping at the Camarillo outlets, about an hour north of Los Angeles proper. Today I drove. I fought the 405 from the city and battled the madness on the 101 to get north of the valley because I wanted to get Carpe a special gift. On the way back we got off the freeway because traffic was a brick, then ended up at The Brass Monkey, a karaoke bar off Wilshire in the heart of Korea Town. Huge crowd. Mostly white.

"Baby, I rub you."

We had gotten up and turned the house out McBroom style, jumped super dramatic and acted like we were the Supreme Destiny En Vogue and performed Aretha's *R-e-s-p-e-c-t*. Then this Korean girl started howling YMCA. She was dressed like Britney Spears, had on over-the-top Cleopatra makeup and when she started doing the letters . . . she was so small and perky . . . she was so hilarious. I didn't mean to laugh at her, but I couldn't help it. We were red in the face and dying. The poor girl couldn't say the letter *L*, so all of her *L*s sounded like *R*s.

"I rub you, baby, I rub you." The song ended and Miss Perky

threw on a wide grin and took a bow fit for Broadway. "Now I will sing a Ricky Martin song . . . Riving Ra Vida Roca."

"Riving Ra Vida Roca!" Frankie cackled. "God, I wish Tommie could see this."

I laughed so hard I thought I was going to pee on myself. We couldn't take any more, so we headed out to the parking lot, then I drove up Wilshire and cruised the Crenshaw Strip.

Frankie said, "You're in a much better mood."

"Am I?"

"Considering."

"You'd rather see me depressed?"

"No. You're glowing."

"Am I?"

"Like something . . . dunno . . . you're different."

My cellular vibrated and I smiled.

After we crossed the 10, there were miles of sidewalk vendors and bean pie hustlers on every corner. Frankie asked me to stop down near Slauson. She wanted to go to a makeshift booth that had everything from bootleg Laker gear to Disney movies to XXX movies.

Frankie bought a couple XXX flicks.

I bought a Lakers jersey with Kobe's number.

When I drove us away, Frankie said, "Every time you get a message from your friend, you look like you're intoxicated."

I laughed. "What's the wildest thing you've done?"

"What do you mean?"

"You know what I mean. With a guy."

"What did you do?"

"I think I had the sexual experience of my life."

"I don't want to know."

I laughed and left it at that.

She asked, "Is that who the present is for?"

"What present?"

"Rolex Oyster Perpetual Datejust watch. The one you just drove about one hundred and fifty miles to buy. The one with the diamond hour markers. Your memory coming back?"

"Why?"

"You just spent over five thousand dollars, that's why."

"Back down, Frankie. Don't spoil our day."

"Answer the question. Is that a present for Tony?"

"Tony already busted a nut and made his present."

"So, are you leaving Tony for this new guy or what?"

I paused. "He's married."

"What?"

"Now, let it rest."

She was quiet for a moment. "You're dealing with a married man?"

I didn't answer.

"Fucking insane." Frankie shook her head and sighed. "Five thousand dollars. If you're going to end your marriage, the last thing you need to do is spend that kind of money."

"He spent more than that on me."

"I don't give a shit if he bought you the twenty-three bridges in Paris."

She kept shaking her head.

My cell phone vibrated and a fever came over me.

She said, "Guess somebody's looking for his concubine."

"You know what . . . fuck you."

"Don't disrespect me."

"Don't disrespect me."

"Livvy, I don't have to disrespect you because you're disrespecting yourself."

"Oh, please. I've *only* been with two men the last six years."

"Cancún."

"Cancún doesn't count."

"Oh, please."

"You know the rule. Vacation sex doesn't count."

"Whatever."

I snap, "And even if it did, the dick count is still below the national average. Mine is anyway. You want to comment on that?"

"Whatever, whatever, what-the-fuck-ever."

Then we were silent. Pissed off and silent.

When I pulled up in front of her place I said, "I'm not a concubine. A man doesn't spend six thousand dollars on you and—"

The car door slammed. She went inside without saying good-bye.

I drove away, thinking about Tony. Missing him more than I would admit. Six years were about to end and that was fucked up. On the way back to Tommie's I was remembering how we used to wake up in the morning and either he'd give me that look, or I'd give him that look, and we'd fall into each other and become husband and wife.

I was still awake when I heard Tommie's Jeep pulling down the driveway. She put her truck in the garage. Then she came up the stairs, came in the back door, rushing. The light in her bedroom came on, then she came in the living room, saw me sitting on her sofa in the dark.

She said, "You scared me."

"Hey."

"Thought you were staying at Frankie's tonight."

"We got into it."

"Figures."

"I can leave."

"It's cool. Uh." She twisted her lips. "Livvy?"

"Yeah."

"You . . . uh . . ."

"Have any more condoms?"

"Yeah."

I handed her my last two.

She said, "I want you to meet Blue."

"Not tonight."

"I don't mean tonight."

I winked at her, hoped my jealousy didn't show. "Have fun."

"Livvy?"

"Yeah?"

"What's the longest you've—?"

"Had sex?"

"No, no. Kissed."

"Kissed?"

"Yeah. What's the longest?"

"Oh. Dunno."

"He mistletoed me for over an hour."

I smiled and remembered when me and Tony were like that. When it was still new.

I asked, "You coming?"

"Coming where?"

"Not coming like that coming. I mean, you know, coming."

"Oh, God. Yes. Three times. The first time, I thought—"

"You had died and gone to heaven."

"*Yes*. I was like . . . my, God . . . like an epileptic with Tourette's syndrome."

"Welcome to the club. You were in heaven."

"Are you feeling me on that? Lord, I am so . . . so . . . so sprung."

"Sprung? Not good."

"It's cool because he's sprung too."

Tommie took a shower, put on her flannel pajamas, then came back into the living room.

She said, "One more question."

I sat up. "What?"

"How do you know when you're having too much sex?"

I told her, "No such thing."

"Good. I was getting worried. Thought I might be a freak or something."

She pulled on her housecoat, put on her duck slippers, and headed out the front door. I was in the living room, staring out her bay windows. She jogged across Fairfax and hurried up the stairs that led to her friend's apartment. I sat in her beanbag. His lights came on. I saw them laughing. Talking. Kissing like Billy Dee and Pam Grier. Then the lights went out.

I sent Carpe a text message.

He didn't respond.

First I was angry, wondering where he was, what he was doing.

Those were foolish thoughts.

I was having an affair.

An affair was a false world made of perceptions.

This wasn't the kind of shit I want to think about, but I couldn't escape my thoughts. I was awake and wanted sleep to be my friend, but not even sleep would come to comfort me.

Then it felt like I wanted to cry. I sat there in the dark trying to figure out my life. Twenty-nine years old. Thirty in four months. Sleeping on my sister's sofa. Starting over wasn't easy at thirty, not when you thought you had it all, but realized you had nothing at all.

And it was almost Christmas.

I couldn't remember the last time I felt so empty and alone.

Damn Depo. Had to be the fucking Depo.

I went back to the sofa. Picked up my cellular. Dialed.

He answered, "Hello?"

"It's Livvy."

"I know. Surprised you didn't hang up."

"I am too."

I held the phone, breathing. He did the same.

I said, "Tony?"

"Yeah, baby."

"Why did it happen?"

"I don't know."

"Why did you go to her?"

"We've had this conversation, Livvy."

"And we're having it again. I really need to have it again. I really need this."

"I don't have an answer."

"There is always a reason. Were you lonely?"

"No."

"Was sex with me that bad?"

"No, it's . . . It was wonderful. Every time we made love it was wonderful."

"What happened?"

"I was tempted. I was weak. I was evil."

I said, "Evil is a theological term, Tony."

He knows the issues I have with the black and whiteness of religion. Always good versus evil and so absolute. I think humanity lives in that gray area where it all overlaps.

He cleared his throat. "But still, we reap what we sow."

"That we do."

"I got caught up in the moment and . . . fell short of the man I was trying to be."

"Caught up in the moment." I repeated and rubbed my temples. "Was it the excitement?"

He breathed heavily.

"Was it?"

"Livvy . . . this is giving me such a goddamn headache."

"Welcome to the club. Now, was it exciting?"

"No, it wasn't exciting, dammit. Shit, Livvy—"

"Don't lie. All I'm asking for is honesty. Maybe I have unrealistic expectations."

He took another hard breath. "Not like it is . . . was . . . like it was with you."

"It was just sex."

"Yes, with her, that's all it was."

"How many times?"

"I saw her twice. Then I never saw her again, until . . . until I got served."

"Were you expecting to get served?"

"Livvy, I had no idea."

Silence.

I softened my tone, asked, "Was it exciting?"

He paused. "It was . . . new. So, in some ways, it was exciting."

Silence.

I bit my bottom lip. "Thanks for being honest."

"In the big picture, it was nothing. It was an illusion. Not even real."

"It's real, Tony. Take the red pill, unplug yourself, wake up from the dream, it's real."

A moment passed.

I asked, "How's Roomba?"

He laughed.

I laughed too.

Tony said, "Roomba misses you."

I imagined my husband smiling a little. Not much, just a little.

I said, "We've been together a long time."

"Yeah. I can still see you in that devil outfit. The most beautiful thing I'd ever seen."

Again we paused.

I said, "The decorations, the Christmas tree, it all looks good, Tony."

"I have ornaments with the faces of your parents and sisters and my parents and siblings up on the tree."

"Bet it looks nice. The fake snow, all of it looks . . . It's beautiful, Tony."

"Well, I have surgery tomorrow. If you want to come see it while I'm gone . . ."

His words lingered, like he didn't know how to finish his sentence, or maybe he wanted me to finish his thoughts.

"Tony, I want this to be civil. I want it to end with a little dignity, if possible. I don't want it to get ugly. Don't want all of our money going to attorneys. I want it to be fair. I'm devastated, but I don't want to destroy you. I'm not greedy, don't want all of what we have, just to be fair, then we can go on with our separate lives."

"I've always been fair with you, Livvy."

"Since we're being honest, were there others? Anyone else?"

"No."

I went back into the living room, sat down on the beanbag. It was dark across the street. On that side of the street a relationship was beginning. On this side, the sun had already set.

"Have you . . . ," I started, then the pain slowed me down. I pushed my lips up into a smile, struggled through that barrier with a soft voice. "Have you talked to Miesha's mother?"

"Attorney said not to contact her."

"Is that the best strategy?"

"Shit . . . I don't know."

"Maybe you should nice up to her. Get in some visitation so the courts will look at you in a positive light. Buy the kid a ton of Christmas presents. It'll only help."

"Too late for that."

"Tony, not facing it won't make it go away."

He took a hard breath. "When this shit first went down . . . I was so angry . . . and . . . and I had thought about getting somebody to hurt her."

"What are you saying, Tony?"

"You know what I'm saying."

I paused. "That's not like you, not with a woman."

"I wouldn't do anything like that. I'm just saying I thought about it. That's how I feel about her. My love for you . . . I wouldn't do anything that could cause me to not be with you."

"You already did, Tony. You already did."

For a moment I wished that baby was mine. Was ours. But it wasn't. Then I wished that he'd had it before we met. But he hadn't.

His lover had a part in this crime too. An equal part. I hated her for bringing hate into my world. Women destroyed each other just as much as men destroyed women. She knew Tony was married. I closed my eyes and saw her face, a face blinded by desperation and selfishness.

And I remembered how I felt that night he was served. The night *we* were served. Wanted to stab him while he slept. Wipe the fingerprints down. I know a girl who pretended to set her husband on fire. That night I wasn't in a make-believe mood. Wanted to set the house on fire with him in it. Or take him out Lorena Bobbitt–style. Then when I was done with him, I wanted to find her. Hurt her. Turn green. Go on a rampage. And if I got caught, plead insanity.

That hurt came back in waves, the headache became more intense.

"Tony, let me say this, because this might get ugly. No matter how ugly it gets, I want to thank you for how good you were to Momma. And what you did for Tommie."

"I did it out of love."

"I know. I'll never forget that. Thanks for being there."

"I'll never forget you, Livvy."

We both held the phone for a while.

Without saying good-bye, I hung up.

POETIC JUSTICE

The theory, not the movie

Livvy

Carpe's car was down at the end of the block, closer to the beach.

It was brisk, too windy to Rollerblade or play volleyball. Too chilly to even think about walking on the boardwalk. But plenty of people were in the bars and restaurants on both Highland and Manhattan Beach Boulevard. Parking was a mess. After I wrapped a scarf around my hair, I buttoned up my leather coat, put my hands in my pockets and hurried toward our nest, my lover's present under my arm.

Carpe wasn't inside. I put his present by the small porcelain Christmas tree, adjusted the heat, then opened the shutters and let some light in.

That was when I saw some of my clothes had been taken out of the closet and put on the bed. Again I smiled. He had been here, waiting for me, picking out something for me to wear. I looked out the window and didn't see him coming from either direction. More Christmas lights were up, the last-minute people giving in to peer pressure. Only saw a few people on the side streets. When it dropped below seventy degrees, Southern California went into hibernation.

I tossed my coat and purse on the bed and rushed to use the bathroom.

Once again I was Bird. Once again I smiled. No problems existed in my world.

A key was put in the front door. The door opened. Cold air flooded the room.

My voice was bright and cheery as I called out, "Carpe."

The door closed. No answer. Keys jingled. Then silence.

I listened. "Hello?"

There was the click clop of shoes moving.

My heart sped up. "Hello? Can I help you?"

"I'm waiting by the door."

Fear jolted me off the toilet, back to my feet. I yanked my panties and pants up. It was a female voice, her tone cold and hostile. My purse and my keys were on the bed.

I yelled, "Who are you?"

"I think you know. You should know."

Her voice sounded vacant. And she had an accent, one that I couldn't figure out, not from the few words she said, not while my heartbeat was speeding up.

She said, "And I'm alone."

She was standing near the front door. She was taller than me, thicker, full breasts, arched eyebrows, her brown hair pulled back into a bun, wearing jeans and a sweatshirt, her long leather coat across her arm. She stood as still as a mannequin. Motionless, until her eye twitched.

She came to life, evaluated me head to toe, said, "Hello."

I paused. "Can I help you?"

Her delicate perfume came to me as her heels clacked across the floor. She took four slow steps to the bed and dropped a silver key. It landed next to my silver key, its twin.

She cleared her throat. "You thought I was Michael."

Our eyes met. In a blink I evaluated her. Diamond earrings. Tennis bracelet. Her jewelry was expensive. Well put together. But her skin was dehydrated, like she drank too much coffee and not enough water. She had post inflammatory pigmentation, a mild case, her face was breaking out and she had been picking at her pimples.

She said, "You always fuck married men?"

I tried to not be scared, but I was. My trembling was rising and it was a struggle to keep my composure. This had happened too quickly for me to think.

She asked, "Are you a whore?"

"I'm not a whore."

Her eyes left my face and went to the clothes, the shoes, and all the gifts that Carpe had given me. Then I knew she'd already been here, had gone through my things.

She became fidgety, started opening and closing her hands, and that had me on edge, wondering if she was going to attack me.

Once again she nodded. "You're a whore."

"I'm not a whore."

"Then why do you . . . why do you keep fucking my husband?"

I shook my head. "You don't know me."

"Whore."

I snapped, "Leave."

She pushed her lips up into a smile. "You are right. From what I see, this is serious. Maybe you started out as his whore, or he as yours, but now . . . this is serious."

"I want you out of here."

She shook her head.

It felt like I was clinging to the hood of a speeding car, trying to figure out how to survive before it crashed. I moved to the bed, grabbed my purse.

She took a quick step to the front door, stood there blocking my way out of this . . . this room that had become a cage.

I stood firm. "Move."

She didn't.

There wasn't a back door. Her eyes told me that she wasn't going to let me leave without a struggle, that she'd come to slaughter the sheep. I reached into my purse, and pulled my phone out, didn't know who I was going to call, but I only had two choices, either nine-one-one, or text message Carpe. By the time I did either of those, she could be all over me.

She said, "Your name is Olivia Barrera."

Her words were a noose around my neck.

"You work at Dermalogica in Torrance."

That second surprise tightened the noose, made me lower my phone, made me stop and face her, my mouth wide open.

"Barrera. Spanish surname, but no accent." She paused, evaluated me from my complexion to the texture of my hair. "I expected a Latin woman. Are you Latin?"

"Move out of my way, please."

She pursed her lips and stepped away from the door. "Go ahead. Leave. Run. I'll find you. I can go to your home in Ladera. Or to Dermalogica. It doesn't matter to me. We can finish this now, finish it later; either way, we'll finish it."

One hand trembled through my hair; the other hand reached out to the wall, my damp palm pressing into the barrier and holding me up. A moment ago I wanted to knock her out of the way and race out the door. I'd been ambushed, now trapped. I was terrified. Once again I'd become a lioness trapped, moving back and forth in her cage.

Seemed like forever went by before I was able to look at her again.

Her face was dull, wore pain and suffering, bags under her eyes as she stood rocking side to side. That desperate look in her eyes, I knew it because it was reflected in my own. A painful reminder of what had driven me here. The feeling that I had been damned. She looked the way I did the moment I found out about Tony's indiscretion, maybe the morning after I had been given my humiliation on a platter and I had been numbed by the truth.

"How do—?" My tongue had become lead. "How do you know my name?"

"Mrs. Barrera, I'm Mrs. Davidson. I'm Michael's wife."

All I could do was swallow. I tried not to choke. All I could think was I was standing in this room with the wife of the man I'd been sleeping with; all I could say was, "Oh, God."

"And I'm hurting. I'm trying to . . . I just want some answers, that's all."

She opened her purse and I jumped, took a distrustful stance. She jumped too.

We stared at each other, very primal wide-eyed stares, both of us very defensive, bodies positioned to fight or flee, both of us breathing heavily and waiting to see what was about to happen next, who was about to do what to whom.

Her hand shook. "I'm not . . . I wasn't . . . I wanted to show you . . ."

With nervous movements, she took out a stack of photos. She looked them over, then tossed a few on top of the clothing. She moved away. I went to the pictures. My insides became hollow. They were photos taken in San Diego, the same night I met Carpe, both of us dancing and sweating at the hip-hop club in the Gaslamp District. A photo of my arms wrapped around his neck, us kissing while we danced and sweated in the heat of that club.

In a flash I remembered the drunken red-haired white woman taking our picture.

The woman who *pretended* she was drunk and photographed us all night.

In disbelief I asked, "You had him followed?"

She motioned at the images in a way that told me to draw my own conclusions. There were pictures of us shopping, working out, everything we had done in public.

She nodded. "We can be evil, or we can be civil. It's your choice."

Suddenly, tears fell from her eyes. She lowered her head. Carpe's wife started to cry. She cried quietly with her head down, her hands over her face, the way a small child cries when it tries to hide itself from a world of pain and suffering. She cried the way I should be crying now. The tall woman moved to the bed, the one I had sinned on with her husband.

Her legs wobbled. She sat down.

Her eyes went to the exotic fruits, candles, the romantic CDs. She pulled her lips in and cried.

I stood where I was, doing the same.

Her red-rimmed eyes looked at the bed, saw the colorful pillows and realized where she was sitting. Then her damaged expression came to mine, the eyes of a woman betrayed.

She glared at me like I was some selfish, low-life, evil woman, not a victim of any kind. In her eyes I had no history, and this moment would define how she regarded me from now until eternity. Just another bitch on the prowl and waiting to screw up another happy family.

"How long—" She started, fidgeted as she shook her head, cleared her throat, and softened her voice. "How long have you been . . . how long have you and Michael—?"

I owned no lies. Once again I had become that teenage child who had been caught stealing at Home Depot, the one who had stolen in order to decorate her life.

Eyes closed, living inside my own darkness, my leg bounced as I told her how I met her husband, that it was a chance meeting on the Internet.

"The Internet?"

"Yes."

My words were few.

"How did you meet him on the Internet?"

I told her about his ad, about him being a man betrayed in search of a woman betrayed.

She shook her head. "Why . . . why my husband?"

That was a universal question, the same one I had asked about my own husband. I've heard so many women ask that question, or variations of that question. *Why my husband? Why my man? What did I ever do to you to cause you to do this to me?* Those were the screams and the tears I had cried months ago when my world shifted from underneath me.

I shrugged. "It was just a pop-up ad . . . and . . . and I responded."

"Why? Why would anyone—? Why?"

I had no answer, none that rationalized what I had done, and nothing that could make what was wrong sound right. None that could soften this moment for either of us. I'd thrown myself into my work. That helped at first. But it didn't help anymore. So I threw myself to another man who could relate to my trials and tribulations. The poison became the cure.

She said, "This box . . . your Christmas present to him?"

"Yes."

She picked up the present and my heart galloped. I wanted to run and snatch it from her. But I was frozen. Gingerly, she pulled the wrapping paper away, her breathing so hoarse.

Her lips didn't move. "A Rolex."

"Look, I think it would be best if you left and . . . and . . . talked to your husband."

"This is serious."

I pulled my lips in, leaned forward in sprinter's position.

"Tell me how . . ." Her voice splintered a thousand ways. "What made this possible?"

She sounded so small, so helpless, so unraveled.

I lost something when Tony had his affair. Lost the feeling of being significant. Carpe made me feel significant. He came into my life the same way I had imagined I'd come into his, like a bolt of lightning, gave me so much passion, and now, tear by tear, the storm was ending.

She wiped her eyes and put the present to the side. "All lies."

"I'm not lying."

"No, what he told you . . . all lies. We're . . . we're . . . we have no problems. And even if we did . . . you have no right . . . not even if those lies were the truth . . . you have no right."

"I'm sorry. I know you don't believe it, but I'm sorry."

Her name was Selina. She was from the small Caribbean island of Antigua. Educated at Baruch. Just like Carpe had said. She was upset, venting to me the way I did to strangers.

Listening to her problems only reminded me of my own.

We both jumped when someone knocked on the door. Then we looked at each other.

She said, "Let him in."

I went to the door, held the handle a moment, then eased the door open.

At least twenty people were outside. As soon as the door opened, they all started singing "Joy to the World." Some stood on the porch, some on the sidewalk underneath the streetlights. A couple held surfboards. Wearing Dockers, hiking boots, sweaters, leather jackets, gloves, and red Santa Claus hats. Some had on Rudolph the Red-Nosed Reindeer noses. At least three wore fake white beards. The aroma of Coronas, daiquiris, and apple martinis on their breaths.

I stood there, fidgeting, wiping my eyes, crying, breathing heavily until they were done.

"Whoo hoooo!" Their spirited breaths fogged the air. "Happy holidays."

I nodded. "Merry . . . I mean . . . Happy holidays."

They staggered away singing a cheerful and off-key "Jingle Bells."

Then I closed the door, got ready to face my lover's wife again.

She was behind me, right up on me, her red-rimmed eyes, her scorned glare cutting deep into me. While I was being sere-naded with a yuletide melody, Carpe's wife had been staring at the clothes, touching the bed, taking in all the things her money had bought, with each thick breath inhaling the scent of im-moral lovers, struggling with herself, her anger rising, cresting.

And now she was about to snap.

She grabbed my throat, started choking me before I could . . . my nails dug into her hands . . . she kept . . . banging my head into the door . . . I was choking . . . her eyes wide . . . nails deep in my neck . . . her lips moving . . . words I couldn't make out . . . cursing me . . . then I was falling back into the wall . . . hitting her face . . . kicking her . . . trying to pull her hair . . . stumbling over the bed . . . my head being pushed into the wall . . . each step, each stumble she followed me . . . never letting go . . . choking me . . . light-headed . . . couldn't fight her anymore . . . numbness covered me . . . then . . . then she let me go.

I collapsed to the floor, wheezing, struggling to breathe, like a drowning woman finally given a teaspoon of air, legs moving like a runner trying to get away.

I tried to scamper away. Wiped the sweat from my eyes. My vision came back.

She stared down at me, hair loose and disarrayed, sweat all over her face, her chest rising and falling faster than mine, a new fear in her eyes, as if she were afraid because of what she'd almost done. She picked up her purse, her coat, stepped over me, her heels click clacking at a fast pace as she walked out the door, left the cold air blowing across my body, the sound of carolers singing "The Twelve Days of Christmas" coming in on the ocean's frigid breath.

I made it to my SUV. Sat in my truck for a long while, thinking, trembling back to life one heavy breath at a time, wiping my sweat away on my clothes, on napkins, anything I could find. Drove away from my nest. The present I brought for Carpe rested in my lap. My phone vibrated, danced, lit up. A text message. Carpe was looking for Bird.

I typed him a message back. *My name is Olivia.* Bird didn't exist anymore.

Then I broke the phone in half. I let my window down and let the pieces fall into speeding traffic, let his words scatter at sixty miles an hour.

Flashing red lights and a siren wailed behind me. I changed lanes. The police car did the same. I cursed and pulled over in a well-lit area. Didn't move. Had a brief thought about a young girl in Riverside who was gunned down in a parking lot and kept my hands on the wheel.

Brighter lights came on. Blinded me. A female officer came to my window. Asian. Round face. Dimples. Hair in a bun. She motioned and I let my window all the way down.

She said, "Do you know how fast you were going?"

I shook my head. "Wasn't paying attention."

Her flashlight lit up my face. "Your blouse is ripped."

"I know."

"Neck is scratched up. You're bleeding."

Again, there were tears. "I know."

"Were you in an altercation?"

I wiped my hair away from my face and my fingers throbbed. Three nails were broken. Some blood was caked under the others. I put my hands in my lap, shook my head.

Our eyes met. There were certain things a woman knew. Whether she had on high heels or a badge and a bulletproof vest, there were things a woman knew.

She took my license. My registration. Speeding. Doing over sixty in a residential area. Littering. She asked me to get out of my SUV. The officer had me stand to the side, in the cold, on the damp grass, away from the flow of traffic, while she went back to the police car.

His last message was in my head. He wanted to eat my pussy.

His wife's angst, her tears, all of that damage was in my eyes.

This changed the perception of who I was, made me the perpetrator, not the victim. I didn't like being the victim, but I was less comfortable being the perpetrator.

She came back to me, handed me my paperwork.

She said, "I can write you up, but I'm leaning toward giving you a warning."

"I'll take a warning. I just . . . I . . . Am I free to go home now?"

"But I'm not going to let you drive, not in your condition."

I nodded. "Can I just sit in my truck, please?"

"Anyone you can call?"

"Yeah. My husband. No. My sisters."

"Ma'am?"

"One of my sisters. I can call . . . wait . . . shit . . . I don't have a phone."

"Pay phone is over in the mini-mall. Sit here a few minutes. Get yourself together."

"Okay."

"Then I'll follow you."

"Okay."

*   *   *

Frankie and Tommie showed up twenty minutes later. Both worried. I wanted to ride with Tommie, but Frankie made me get into her car. Tommie drove my SUV.

Frankie asked, "Do we need to go East Side and kick somebody's ass?"

Right or wrong, I was her sister. She was my protector.

I shook my head.

Maybe one day I'd tell her and Tommie all of what I had done.

Maybe they already knew enough.

Tommie

Sunrise. Christmas morning.

Frankie is the most outspoken of us all. That's why she and Momma always went at it like two hardheaded, headstrong women. Livvy told me that it had been that way from the moment Frankie was born. When Momma was first diagnosed, Frankie was the one who held us all together. When Momma died, Frankie cried the hardest because she was the last one to cry. We'd been crying all along, but Frankie had refused to break down. She came unraveled when the dirt hit Momma's coffin. Frankie needed us to be her bookends, and we held her up.

"Tommie, where are your presents?"

I say, "Right here, Frankie."

"Livvy, get to moving."

Livvy snaps, "Out my face, Frankie."

That's the way we start our Christmas morning, packing up gifts and going to see Momma and Daddy. We always take them their presents first, always honor them the way children should honor their parents, the way we should honor our ancestors.

But we're still sisters. The morning always starts out with us fighting each other, somebody mad because somebody did this, somebody didn't do that.

"Tommie . . . dammit . . . get in the damn car or I will leave you."

"Whatever, Frankie. I'll drive my-damn-self."

"You know what," Livvy explodes. "And I'm talking to both of you, I don't need no drama."

In stereo Frankie and I shout, "Shut up, Livvy."

All of our madness is love and nervous energy. It's like that because we were going to see our folks. Something about going to see Momma and Daddy always makes us revert back to being their children; gives us the right to throw adulthood and its problems to the wind, to become four, ten, and fourteen again.

And like every year, Frankie is the first one to go off on somebody, then the first one to cry. Her tears fall while we're driving up Prairie toward Inglewood Cemetery.

I blow my nose, wipe my eyes, and look around at the city. Christmas morning is just like any other morning in the desert, the only difference being less traffic and more tolerance for the next twenty-four hours. No one rushing to work. No one brushing their teeth while they sit in traffic. No one whipping from lane to lane, reading the morning paper, or shaving, or yelling at their kids, or doing their hair and makeup while they cut you off. Even the smog is gentle. It's a different world this morning. An abandoned town with no real trees. Most of the people who are out are sleep-deprived parents who forgot to buy batteries for the toys. People are polite, respecting signal lights and doing the speed limit. It's a safe day, maybe the only day that everyone pretends they respect each other. It's like a twenty-four-hour virus, because tomorrow morning, L.A. will go back to being L.A.: smog, relentless traffic, and the middle finger being an extension of inner feelings.

By the time we park, Frankie has a big box of tissue in her lap, half of the tissues used and on the floor.

I ask, "You okay?"

Frankie nods. Her sunglasses can't hide the redness in her eyes.

Livvy wipes her eyes with the back of her hands. Frankie hands her a few tissues. Then she hands me a few. We have an eye-drying, nose-blowing moment.

I sniffle. "McBrooms?"

They both nod and speak in chorus, "We're ready."

We walk shoulder to shoulder, smile to smile to where our parents are laid to rest.

Frankie says, "Somebody's been here."

Flowers are already at the base of our parents' tombstone. Fresh-cut roses.

We're all surprised.

Frankie picks them up, reads the card. "They're from Tony."

Livvy takes the card from her. Then I take the card from her. Tony has sent our parents his eternal love and his apologies.

Livvy frowns, shakes her head, looks around, but doesn't see him.

I wipe my eyes and tell her. "He came out yesterday."

She snatches a tissue. "So, you've been in contact with him."

I nod. "He called me."

"Uh huh. Where was I?"

"Nobody ever knows where you are, Livvy."

"And you didn't tell me?"

"Olivia, guess what?" I snap back at her. "Antonio called me. Happy? Geesh."

We stand in front of the headstone, wiping our eyes, presents and flowers in our hands.

BERNARD LEE McBROOM   BETTY JEAN McBROOM

Frankie whispers, "Livvy, you been getting your breasts checked?"

"I go back in January. Tommie?"

"I'm self-checking all the time. Frankie?"

"I have an appointment."

I put the green blanket down. We always come comfortable, most of the time in jeans and sweats and sweaters and jackets, sometimes gloves. A couple of times we came and stood underneath an umbrella while heaven cried soft tears. This year heaven smiles. The clouds are gray. A marine layer covers us. But we live in nothing but sunshine.

I ask, "Okay, who's going first this year?"

Frankie's gift for Momma is a bottle of Red, the perfume she used to wear all the time. Frankie used to steal Momma's perfume when she was in high school, and they fought over it all the time. Frankie bought Daddy another silk tie and a bottle of Riesling.

As a symbol of gratitude for bringing her into the world and keeping all of us out of harm's way, Livvy bought those lovebirds a basket of their favorite fruits.

My present is a beautiful Unity cup and candles, giving them the spirit of Kwanzaa. I have so much love for Daddy and the only mother I ever remembered.

I blow my nose. "Bet they're in heaven looking down on us right now."

Frankie shakes her head. "Nobody's in heaven until Judgment Day."

"You're wrong, Frankie."

She tisks. "I am not wrong, Tommie."

"Then why does the preacher say people are gone to heaven to meet God and Jesus?"

"Don't make me slap you with a Bible."

"Heathen. You do and I'll throw holy water on you and watch you burn."

Livvy snaps, "Can we, for once, not argue or have that conversation?"

I look around; see other families at several gravesites, honoring their loved ones. Sort of feel an emptiness for the resting souls no one comes to visit anymore. The people who have ceased to exist in the minds and hearts of others. Then I notice a few more tombstones around ours, the final dates on those markers anywhere between last Christmas and only a few days ago.

Livvy massages her hand. She has three broken nails. And she's wearing a scarf around her neck, hiding her scars. We know all of her injuries have something to do with her indiscretion. We don't question her. She'll tell us when she's ready.

We sit down awhile and talk to our people, make it similar to the Day of the Dead celebration in Latin America. Our party isn't out of place, because all around us are people having conversations with their loved ones, some alone and talking out loud, some in groups, some a capella and standing in silence, but the expressions on their silent faces let me know that they're transmitting and receiving memories and affections. We live in a city where patriotism lasts about as long as the X cap and baggy M.C. Hammer pants, but love is eternal.

Frankie pulls her Polaroid camera out of her bag and gives it to me because my arms are the longest. We huddle up close to each other, cheek to cheek, all smiles, and I take our photo.

"My eyes were closed, Tommie."

"Then open them, Livvy."

We take a few more pictures, wait for them to develop.

Nothing is promised.

Livvy asks, "Tommie, Frankie . . . What did Momma mean when she said that marriage was about the end?"

"She meant eternity." I said that, my voice so tender. To me it's so simple to understand, so straightforward. "Marriage should be about who you're gonna spend eternity with. It's about who will be by your side until Judgment Day. I guess, if you look at these people out here buried alone and . . . dunno . . . it's kinda sad to not have anybody to be buried next to. I think it's because . . . a man buried next to his wife, or a tombstone with a woman waiting for her husband to finish his journey so he can come and be by her side, or vice versa . . . that makes me . . . I dunno . . . when I see that I guess that makes me smile or something."

I show them the Polaroid. It's perfect. We all sign our names on the back of that indelible image of this moment. Then, like we do every year, we leave the picture and presents with our parents, their gifts resting in the middle of their headstone.

Frankie rolls up our blanket. By then, Livvy is standing in front of the headstone, her expression telling us that so many thoughts and decisions are going on in her mind.

I stand next to Livvy, put my arm around her. She sniffles. "Daddy was nineteen years older than Momma."

"Yep. Seems like we were all together yesterday."

She nods, whispers. "It's about who you wanted to be with at the end, when it's all said and done, all about who you want to be buried next to."

We stand there for a moment.

Frankie blows her nose again. "Okay, who is leading the prayer?"

I tell her, "Anybody but you."

I give the prayer this time, keep it short and sweet.

Like children who believed in Santa, we believe that when we leave, Momma and Daddy will sneak out and get their seasonal blessings, the same way we imagine they did on their birthdays, open them, stand side by side, hand in hand, and blow us kisses of protection. They will be loving each other until Judgment Day. Looking out for us until the end.

Livvy's tears came on strong. "I love both of you. Love both of you so much."

We become her bookends. I tell Livvy and Frankie the same thing, that I love them unconditionally and eternally. Frankie hugs us tight and gives us the same love.

Livvy

We had left our parents' resting place and were driving down Manchester, radio on KJLH. They played Christmas songs from midnight to midnight today. By noon we'd be ready to scream. But for now, we sang along with the Temptations. The song ended and five or six announcements for New Year's Eve parties came on back-to-back. This year was ending. My thoughts and emotions wafted in so many directions, asking me who I wanted to be at the end of this holiday season. If not this year, then by this time next year. No matter what I asked myself about my future, it always came back to the same answer.

I rubbed my hands on my jeans, stared at my broken nails, the pink elephant that my sisters hadn't mentioned. I said, "I'm going to work things out with Tony."

They looked at me. To them, my announcement had come out of nowhere, in the middle of them jamming with Donnie Hathaway, with no segue, other than a conclusion to the thoughts that were spinning inside my head.

We said a few things, nothing new, went back and forth on that issue.

Tommie asked, "What about the kid?"

My sigh was heavy; my tongue made of lead. "Her name is Miesha."

Frankie stared at me, testing my reaction, gauging my emotional level.

I told them that the kid's mom had sent pictures to our home, that I had kept one.

Tommie asked, "Where is it?"

"In my purse."

Frankie snapped her fingers in a give-it-to-me motion, and I went through my handbag, took the picture out of my wallet, gazed at that child's image, then passed it on. Frankie stared at my humiliation with her mouth wide open, shook her head, then passed it to Tommie.

Tommie had the same flabbergasted reaction. She held my reality, the picture that represented my dishonor and Tony's indiscretion, the catalyst to our coming apart. That made everything concrete for them, the same thing it did for me the moment I first saw that image.

Tommie's voice softened with concern. "Can you handle that?"

I imitated Momma, "Fuck 'im or leave 'im. Don't matter. Same problems you got with this one you gonna have with the next one. Only thing is since this one in the doghouse, you got the upper hand. He know he done done wrong so he ain't gonna ride down that street no more."

Frankie made an oh-please sound. "It'll be an eighteen-year situation."

"At least that long. Longer if she goes to college."

Frankie tisked. "That's a hellified commitment."

My lips went up into a slow and steady smile, like sunshine moving clouds away. "Tommie, your daddy took care of two girls that wasn't his, loved them like they were his own."

Tommie wiped her eyes. "Your momma took care of a nappy-headed little girl like she was her own daughter."

We passed the picture back and forth again.

I cleared my throat, swallowed, then struggled with it, but accepted my own reality. "It'll be rough . . . maybe . . . for a while . . . maybe it'll always be rough . . . but I don't want to be buried by myself, you know. I want to see if I can be with him until the end. Until it's all said and done."

Frankie nodded. "What about the guy you're seeing?"

I didn't answer.

Everything was starting to feel wonderful when we got back to Tommie's place. Sun was breaking through the clouds. Marine layer was burning off. No rain in the forecast, so it was going to be a wonderful day. Out in Palos Verdes and Beverly Hills people were probably doing laps in their heated pools. Joggers were out and about, burning up calories before they threw down at the dinner table. And barbecue. As we pulled up South Fairfax, I smelled some of the best Q I'd ever smelled. The aroma was so good I could inhale and gain ten pounds. Next door Womack had fired up the grill and was making the neighborhood smell like it was the Fourth of July. His boys were out shooting basketball. Rosa Lee yelled out the back door for her boys to stop playing in their new Christmas clothes. Such a loud and happy family.

We went inside Tommie's, sat in the living room, and swapped presents like we did when we were little girls. Jewelry and sweatsuits and candles and baskets filled with Dermalogica products.

I screamed. "Okay, which one of you sacrilegious bitches gave me this vibrator?"

Frankie laughed so hard she almost wet her pants.

I snapped. "I'm not putting nothing pink in me."

"You know you want to let Willie Wonka into that chocolate factory."

"It's big. And it feels so real." Tommie shrieked. "Oh, my god. It plays a Christmas song. That's so cute."

I took it away from her, then bopped her upside the head with that carnal toy.

Blue came over an hour after we finished our gift exchange. He had on faded jeans, black sandals, and a gray baseball Jersey, JETER on the back. His daughter was with him, dressed in sweats and Little Mermaid tennis shoes, her hair in braids. They exchanged presents with Tommie, then Tommie made us all breakfast. This year was her year to make breakfast.

Blue's little girl gravitated toward me. "What's your name?"

"Livvy. I'm Tommie's big sister."

"No you're not. Tommie is bigger than you."

"Good point."

"My name is Monica. Want to hear the poem I wrote for my daddy?"

We sat in Tommie's living room, not too far from the table set up with a Kinara, a Unity cup, and colorful corn. Monica performed her spoken word for me. I applauded and laughed.

She changed my disposition, made me happier than I had been in days. I told her, "You are so smart."

"I'm smart because I go to Escuela."

I told her, "*Escuela* is Spanish and it means 'school.' "

"So I go to a school named school."

"You sure do."

She said, "Tomorrow is Kwanzaa. And I can tell you *allllll* about Kwanzaa. And the parts I don't know, my daddy can tell you *allllll* the rest. And we're going to have a Kwanzaa party and we have red, black, and green candles, and a Kinara, and I get lots of presents from Santa Claus, but I get more presents from my daddy on the very last day of Kwanzaa and—"

Her conversation was never-ending.

While I sat on the floor with her and talked and played with her new brown-skinned Barbie dolls, pretended Barbie was a doctor and the doll I had was the patient, that sensation came back. The one that warmed my stomach and heart.

I wanted to have a baby.

Wanted a little girl just like her.

I smiled at Tommie and Blue. Pam Grier and Billy Dee. Then Tommie came in and had fun with Monica. I sat in the beanbag and watched her, so comfortable in her role. Not quite the stepmother role, but a role she loved. Blue sat down on the floor and they all played hospital together. Then they started putting together a puzzle. Played and laughed with a pure, unbridled, unrestrained laughter that could only be produced by happiness.

New hairstyle. Glowing. Tommie was blooming again, coming back to life. The mark on her face didn't seem as large. I touched my neck. There wasn't any pain, but my own marks were there. We all had marks that reminded us about things we wanted to forget.

Tommie had surpassed both Frankie and me in so many ways. My smile showed my love for her and hid my envy all at once. The way Frankie had her arms folded and was chewing her lip, her envy was on the rise as well.

I still wished Tony had fathered that child before we met. That could be us.

I was in the kitchen with Frankie, talking about nothing when Blue came in.

He said, "I'm glad I have a moment to see both of you at the same time."

We looked at him.

He told us that he knew he was a bit older than our sister, older than both of us, that he had a child, and sometimes things were rough between him and his child's mother.

He said, "I'm not a rich man. Don't think I'll ever be. But I'm an honest man. And I wouldn't want to do anything that would create any strain in your family. So I would like to ask your permission to pursue a deeper relationship with your sister."

We looked each other, both of us stunned.

Then our lips were quivering.

Again, two McBrooms were crying happy tears.

Not long after that Tommie walked across the street with Blue. He had Monica sitting high on his shoulders. Frankie stood in the bay window and watched them, then I went and stood next to her. By then Monica's mother was out in front of Blue's place. He brought his daughter down and strapped her in the car. Monica and her mother drove away.

Blue hurried back upstairs. Then they closed the curtains in the front room.

We cleaned up Tommie's kitchen, then Frankie packed up her gifts. I did the same. We were going to get together later on at Frankie's place for Christmas dinner.

She grabbed her presents, kissed me, said, "Three o'clock. Don't show up CP time."

Frankie told me she had to run an errand.

I said, "Stores are closed. What errand do you have to run?"

"I have . . . I . . . I need to . . . There is something I need to re-solve."

I nodded. "Yeah. Me too."

Neither one of us tried to start a question-asking party.

On the way out, we waved at the Womack's little boys. They were heading down the driveway in their new Rollerblades.

Frankie was in a strange mood, I saw the tension in her face. I asked, "You okay, big sister?"

"Was just thinking . . . I'm taking down my Internet ad."

I asked, "Why?"

"Midget Man, Michelin Man, Confused Man, Stutter Man."

"That's not nice."

"A legion of chromosomal mutations."

"Fugly men need love too."

"Oh, hell no. Dating a fugly man is like . . . like . . . like doing community service. And who wants a fugly man? Fugly people are trying to find somebody who looks better than them."

"True. Nobody wants fugly children."

"Trust me, when a sister has become a fugly magnet, it's time to unplug the PC."

"Be patient. Mr. Right'll come."

"You just walked into a Halloween party looking to have fun and *bam*."

"I was a lot thinner then."

"And you met a damn doctor."

"Don't hate because I was in shape."

"Not hating, just stating."

"And I met a *man*. I don't date occupations. That's the problem. Women chase occupations, never the man. I met a man who happened to be a doctor."

"Nigga, please. If he was a garbage man, you'd've kept on stepping."

"Would not."

"Oh, please."

"If that's the way you see it, then maybe your standards are too high."

"Not."

"Driving a luxury car, living in a big house, finding a man on your level is harder than finding an alibi for Scott Peterson."

"No, that's not it. People don't talk anymore. You see a brother out at 'Bucks and he's too busy yakking on his cell phone to say hi. They stare at you all evening, but not a word. You have to go out into cyberspace to meet a man because that's where they all are, lying to you from the comfort of their own home, hands in their laps . . . you get the picture."

"A cute brother works with Tommie."

"The manager at Pier 1? Last thing I need is a cockeyed brother in reindeer socks."

"But you'd get a discount."

"I'd rather send postcards to brothers in prison."

"They need love too. And they do have conjugal visits."

"You know what? You're about to get cursed out in a major way."

I laughed. "Can't be that bad."

"Liars, cheaters, womanizers, fugly men, and just a general collection of losers. If I wanted to meet those kind of men, I could just go back to the bar scene, pull up a seat at Club Ladera and sip Riesling until The Hunchback of Baldwin Hills hobbled in the joint."

We laughed together, in chorus.

Frankie looked over at Blue's apartment and sighed. I did

the same and shook my head. We both made naughty faces and fanned ourselves.

I said, "We're gonna have to get her off of those vitamins."

"For real."

"Or she's gonna kill Blue on the downstroke."

More laughter.

"But you know what?" My big sister pushed her lips up into a big smile. "Tommie gave us the best present anybody can give us."

"What?"

"Hope."

Frankie

It was what Tommie said about carrying her old issues into the New Year. That had been bothering me ever since she said that she was letting her old issues go and moving on. Not bothering me in a bad way. Just making me realize how old issues kept you from being able to move on.

That's why I called him a couple of days ago. Why I asked him to meet me. Why I sat in the parking lot at 'Bucks sipping on bottled water and thinking. The coffeehouse was deserted, just like the rest of the parking lot, but the traffic out on La Cienega and Centinela and La Tijera was starting to pick up. Everybody was out doing what we'd be doing later on, visiting family and dropping off presents.

A silver convertible Benz pulled up and parked on the side of the lot by TGIF. It was an older model, classic. Nicolas Coleman got out. He had on dark gray sweats.

I got out of my car, went and stood near the trunk.

It was awkward at first, him coming to meet with me after the way I'd tripped out the night I'd seen him at Reign. I know it might sound trivial to others, but it was important to me.

He said, "Sorry it took me so long."

"It's cool. Just chilling before we do dinner."

"Saw you on the monitor at church a few days ago."

"You were there?"

"I was there. Was visiting with some frat brothers."

I opened my trunk, tossed him a bottle of water.

I said, "First, I really want to apologize again for the way I acted at Reign."

"It's cool. I told you that when we talked that night."

"We didn't really talk. I was a mess."

"I know."

The night he called he'd woken me up from a too real dream, the one where Momma told me that she . . . that she was sick. Have to admit that I was pretty jacked up when the brother called, but he talked to me, brought me from tears to laughter.

I said, "Sometimes it hits me that my folks are gone. Hit me hard today."

He nodded. "You okay?"

"Went to the cemetery this morning."

"Sure you're okay?"

"Yeah. I'm okay. Just hard being strong all the time."

We talked and sipped on bottled water.

I said, "I just wanted to say a few things. Think I have a few unresolved issues when it comes to you."

"Okay."

I told him how I had felt about him back then, that residuals of that still lived with me now.

He said, "Frankie, I'm serious. Didn't know you felt that way."

"Guess I assumed you did."

"We were pretty . . . There was a lot of alcohol involved."

"I know. But that was because . . . Guess you were special."

"Well, to be honest, you told me about the other brothers you'd gone out with, always talked about them like they were no big deal, how you had them on a list. While we're talking about assumptions, I assumed that after we crossed that line, that I'd become one of them."

"What do you mean?"

"I didn't want to be just another one of the guys on your lists. Didn't want to become one of the guys you kicked out before the morning newspaper hit your front porch."

"Shit. Guess, I told you too much, huh?"

He chuckled. "I'm not saying that."

"I did."

"You didn't tell me any more than I told you about Nicole."

I ran my fingers through my locks. "I know, but men and women are judged by different standards."

"Hell, you made it sound like men were no big deal. A dime for a baker's dozen."

"Nick, a woman tells a man the truth because she's feeling him, she wants him to accept her as she is with no secrets and no bullshit, not because she wants him to think of her as a ho."

"That's not the way I see you, Frankie."

"I was just saying."

"It wasn't just that." Nick sipped his water. "But the other things you told me about, how you had a hard time being attached because of what your mother had gone through, that made it . . . hard to even think that you could operate at the same level I was willing to operate at."

I nodded. "Momma lost two husbands. That was . . . that was hard. Until Bernard came along I had to keep Livvy in line because Momma was so damn tired from working so much."

"She didn't have an easy life."

"But she had a lot of love at the end."

Momma lost both husbands, our natural father and the man who stepped in and raised us like we were his flesh and blood, and I think that was why I always had a rough ride. Hell, I know it pissed me off that my ex-hubby was a ho, but if the truth be told, I don't think I was the best wife either. I mean, I did the best I could with the tools I had, but still . . . I had a lot of fears. Fear of being as broke as we were when we grew up in Inglewood, fear of being alone and going off to glory a capella, and fear of spiders.

I think I allowed men to get only so close, then most of the time I backed away.

I told Nick, "You were different."

He smiled. "Was I?"

He came from a great family, ministers and doctors and all kinds of professional people, the kind of family I wished I had, the kind where the little kids had names I could pronounce. And he was brilliant in his own way. And the brother was packing pleasure, was a straight-up superfreak. In the one night we were together, he had me doing shit I never thought I'd do.

"Nigga, you know I was feenin' for you. Bringing you chicken soup when you had the flu, breaking my neck to read your stuff, writing to impress you, and I don't even like writing."

"You don't like writing?"

"Hell no. I was doing . . . hell . . . being the kind of woman I thought you liked. I did all that then . . . then . . . I thought we had connected and you . . . you . . . you vanished."

"Serious? Is that how you see what happened between us?"

"Yup. And so far as writing and finishing a friggin' book, hell, that shit is too . . . tedious. And I don't care too much for commercial fiction from jump street."

"Damn. So you hate my books?"

"I liked yours. And since we're talking about things I like, I liked you better with locks."

"Wait, wait." He was laughing so hard. "Forget the locks. Thought you liked writing."

"Not the way you do. Ain't got that kinda passion. I don't see how you sit by yourself all day long and do that shit. Write and rewrite and rewrite and . . . I don't have that kind of discipline, not the kind that makes a sister want to sit in one spot until she got hemorrhoids."

"And let me guess . . . you hated running too?"

"Oh, I love running. I'll run until I get down to a size six or my legs fall off."

We were laughing like . . . like friends. We talked, light and easy.

I said, "One question."

"Okay."

"And be honest. If you can remember . . ."

"Sure."

"How was it with me? The sex."

"You haven't changed a bit, Frankie."

"Well?"

He laughed, blushed. "I was an emotional wreck, buzzed . . . and I was attracted to you."

"Oh, really."

"I haven't forgotten. It was good. I just didn't . . . at the time there was nowhere it could go. I had too much . . . clutter. Too much unresolved shit."

"Nicole."

"Yeah."

"You're not over her, are you?"

"To be honest . . ." He paused and pushed his lips up into a soft smile, the kind that held old memories, then spoke in a soft tone. "Some things you never recover from, not fully."

I nodded because I understood how he felt, how complicated life and loving could be.

I asked, "Your wife? . . ."

"We're fine."

"Big celebration today?"

"Yeah. You know how large my family is."

"You snuck away?"

"She knows where I am. We don't have a marriage based on lies."

"Good."

"And she knows about you. Told her we had something unresolved."

He was a great guy, maybe that was why I had tripped so hard. I patted his hand, gave him my empathy. "Well, my timing has always been bad when it came to the good brothers."

"I'm not the best at relationships. But I'm trying."

"Good. And stay that way."

The conversation, despite the laughing and whatever, never moved too far from feeling awkward. Maybe because it was the kind of dialogue you had when you needed closure, and when it ended, you moved on with your life. I checked my watch for his benefit, that good old body language that said it was time for the fat lady to break out with a song.

"Merry Christmas, Nick."

"You too, Frankie."

"And I'm happy for you."

"Thanks. Same for you and all of your success."

I raised a brow. "What success?"

He said, "You're a regular Donna Trump. I heard they were thinking about renaming Ladera Heights 'Frankieville.' And you have the best house in Westchester."

I laughed so hard. "You're keeping up with me?"

He smiled. "You're smart. Beautiful. Independent. I'm proud of you."

I paused. "And your wife. She's beautiful."

"Thanks." He paused, his body language showing his awkwardness. "Maybe I'll see you around, maybe I'll run into you at the L.A. Marathon."

"And maybe I'll show up at one of your book signings."

I was ready to send him back to his beautiful wife, and it was time for me to head back to . . . back to Frankieville. It was hard getting to that awkward good-bye.

But I was ready to move on.

We gave each other one-arm hugs, and I headed toward my car.

I had promised myself that I wouldn't, but I looked back. Hard not to look back at a man who had you going *Woo Woo Woo* and popping Percodan like jellybeans.

Nick was staring. Not at my ass, but at the whole me. Admiring me from the soul out. The dreamy expression, the way he grinned at me told me that his mind was on a journey, playing what-if with both of us as the leads in that mental production.

I nodded and smiled back at him, telling him, *Yeah, what if?*

I chuckled and shook my head. Maybe wishing he wasn't married, maybe wishing I was the kind of woman who shared her natural resources. But Nick looked like he wondered how it would've been to have me as his queen. No sin in that.

I savored my small victory as I sang my way to my car and drove away, headed toward Frankieville with the top down, locks being teased by the wind, my face one big smile.

I was free from that old lover who would never love me. Letting go felt good.

Frankie was happy with Frankie right now.

Before I rushed back to the crib and threw down the Cornish hens, since I was in the area and there wasn't any mad traffic, I zoomed over the speed bumps and parked in front of Mail Connexion. Needed to check my post office box since I hadn't done that in the past few days.

My head was down and I was getting my mail out when this brother walked in. Really didn't see him or look up, not at first, was too busy tearing up junk mail, and didn't feel like being bothered.

He said, "Merry Christmas."

I sighed and looked up.

He was tall with a body that looked like it had been chiseled from stone. His locks were perfect; each one a carbon copy of the next. His skin was the color of burnt caramel and a small, silver hoop earring dangled from his left ear. He wore jeans and a T-shirt with 205 across the front. And he had on running shoes.

I cleared my throat, said, "Merry Christmas."

"Love your locks. The brown and light-brown, that's tight."

"Thanks. Your locks are tight, too."

He asked, "How long have you been locking?"

"Four years. You?"

"Little over three."

He got his mail from his box, stood at the counter, smiled, and asked me my name.

I tossed the last of my junk mail, said, "Frankie."

He laughed. "My name is Franklin. People call me Frankie."

I laughed too.

He said, "Don't mean to bother you. But I'm new in the area."

"Okay."

"So I was wondering . . . You know anybody who can tighten my locks?"

"Yeah. Cathy at Hands in Motions hooks mine up."

"Any way I can get her number?"

"Sure. She'll hook you up real good."

We walked out together, stopped in the Christmas sunshine, started talking. No mack talk, no slick dialogue, just talking the way two people talked. He was divorced. New in town from the 205, Ruebenville, the place formerly known as Birmingham. Alone on Christmas.

I said, "Well, if you don't have anywhere to eat, you're more than welcome to come and eat with me and my family."

"I'd like that. I really would."

We exchanged numbers.

My blues exited stage right.

The moment I stopped looking for my keys, I think I found them.

$\mathcal{L}$ivvy

I drove five minutes away to the other side of Ladera. Went to my home, gifts in my hands. Tony was at the hospital, that's what the schedule on the refrigerator said. After visiting my parents, after being around Tommie and Blue, I had wanted to see my husband, try to talk to him about the state of our marriage. Just tell him I had his back, that we'd work through this ordeal with Miesha and her mom. Life has had harder challenges.

I heard the whirs before it came from around the corner.

Without looking I said, "Hey, Roomba."

On cue, Roomba whirred into the room, bouncing off the wall, cleaning the carpet.

"Sorry I kicked you the other day . . . but you know how it gets sometimes."

The mail was on the counter next to a few dirty dishes. Tony had brought it in for a change. I put the dishes in the dishwasher, looked over the mail.

A present was on the counter too. A present for me, wrapped in golden paper with a red ribbon. Not the best wrapping job, but the shoddy kind of wrapping job Tony always did.

I tore the paper away.

It was a court document. From the district attorney. My heart dropped and I felt the inevitable barreling toward me. Tony had wrapped up the divorce papers, bypassed having me served, left them for me as a present. I was about to lose it, about to scream. Then I read the papers. Not divorce papers. The results from Tony's paternity test. At first I was a different kind of angry, then my jaw dropped. Over and over, I reread the results.

It said zero percent, excluded.

I had to adjust, think what that meant.

Zero percent.

The child wasn't his.

Just like that, I started shaking my head and crying.

I hurried to the phone and dialed Tony's cellular.

He answered on the first ring. "Livvy?"

"Tony . . ." I paused a long time. "I have . . . I have . . ."

"Merry Christmas."

I swallowed. "I have the papers in my hand."

"Not my kid."

"When did this—?"

"Yesterday. I got the papers yesterday. We hadn't heard anything because the kid wasn't mine. The system . . . guess it's kind of slow. Or the system is backed up."

"This . . . this . . ."

"It's real, Livvy."

I read the papers over and over, praying that what I was reading didn't change.

I kept it simple and told Tony, "Still . . . even with this . . . You did a bad thing to us, Tony."

"I know."

I paused. "I did too. I haven't been . . . I . . . I . . ." My words faded. "I've done wrong, too."

It took him a moment before he responded. "Livvy—"

"I'm not saying that one cancels out the other, or that one is greater. I'm just saying that, if you want to try, maybe we can have a second chance."

"Livvy—"

"So all I'm asking you . . . I'm asking you to not . . . to not do anything that would keep us from having a second chance."

"I'd never do anything to lose the chance to be with you."

I chuckled. "Thought you were going to have me served."

"You know I wouldn't do that. I was angry. Thought that's what you wanted."

We stopped talking.

I asked my husband, "When are you coming home?"

"Soon—" Tony started. "Soon as I can."

"I'll be here. We're going to Frankie's."

"Okay."

"And we're going to walk in together."

It was there in his voice, the sound of relief. His voice cracked when he heard mine do the same, the echo of the fissure in two hearts trying to close, the echo of two people bonding.

He said, "Thought you were done with me."

"I know."

"You changed your cell phone number."

My voice was soft, humble. "I know."

"Sent you an e-mail. It came back 'user unknown.' "

"I know. That e-mail address, it doesn't exist anymore."

None of who I was . . . none of who I had been . . . that cellular number . . . that e-mail address that Bird used . . . none of that existed anymore. Bird was gone. As if she never had been.

I said, "The fake snow on the lawn . . ."

He laughed. "I know, I know. I overdid it."

"No, it's pretty . . . and . . . it . . . it looks good under the palm trees."

"You like it?"

"Yeah. And with the frosted Christmas tree, the lights outside, with everything you've done, we . . . we have the best house on the block."

Our words were becoming easier, not as distant.

He told me, "I bought you a few presents."

The court papers were in my hand. Our reprieve.

I said, "I have the best present in the world in front of me."

"Open one of the gifts I bought for you. The small green box."

I went to the tree, found that box, and tore away the paper. It was a silver bracelet adorned with gems and pictures of me, Tommie, Frankie, and our parents.

"Tony, this is beautiful."

"I bought the same thing for your sisters. Hope you don't mind."

"Wow, Tony."

My eyes went from the bracelet and I looked at the gift I had brought inside with me, the small box that was sitting on the counter. After we had left the cemetery this morning, I had rewrapped the gift in pretty green paper and a white bow. Had written Tony's name on it. I said "I brought . . . Tony I bought you a present."

"I didn't expect anything."

"Me either."

Again there was laughter between us. I almost told him his gift was a watch, but I didn't.

Tears were running down my face. My body was so light. With every breath, another boulder rolled off my shoulders. All I could think was that not everybody got a second chance.

He asked, "What are we going to do?"

"We're going to have a wonderful Christmas. Let's start with that."

"Love you, Livvy."

"Come home, Tony. Just come home."

We held the phone for a long time, holding each other for the first time.

"Merry Christmas, Tony."

"Merry Christmas, Livvy."

Then I pushed the red button.

I smiled.

I closed my eyes. Tried to see my future. In the morning I'd wake up in my marriage bed, on my side, my husband's arm around me, his body spooning up against mine. Maybe after this Depo wore off, we'd start making other plans. But for now, knowing that I would wake up with him in the morning, and the morning after that morning, was all I needed to know.

After I moved and sat in front of the frosted Christmas tree, I remembered a moment I'd had. It was a while ago when I was watching this movie, *Frida*. In it, one of the cynical female characters said that marriage was a happy delusional, that it was about picking who you wanted to irritate the rest of your life. That was bullshit. Momma knew. It was about picking who you want to love the rest of your life, who you want to be buried with until we were all called home.

Like Momma would've said, Mine's ain't perfect.

Sometimes you gotta make your own happy ending.

But there was one more thing I had to do before I earned mine.

I grabbed my coat and my keys, stepped around Roomba, headed to my truck.

I had to go back to Manhattan Beach.

Livvy

I doubted Carpe would be there on Christmas. Doubted his wife would be on the prowl on this holy day, but I had my Mace, just in case. Didn't take long to get there. No traffic. All the businesses were closed, but there wasn't much parking on the main streets. The beach parking lots below were getting full. So many people were out in the sand playing volleyball. On the way down Rosecrans, I'd seen people going up and down that monster hill at Sand Dune Park. Joggers were on every street, burning up as many calories as they could before the big meal. A few people were in the ocean on surfboards, Boogie boards, kids and adults zipping by on the concrete trail, testing out their Christmas-new Rollerblades and bicycles.

When I parked on Highland, I sat in my SUV, hand on the door handle, heart beating fast once again, wondering if I should go back to that nest.

Silver key in hand, I walked with my leather coat wide open, defying good judgment and common sense, the scarf on my wounded neck loose. Sweat was on my neck. I felt warm.

When I opened the door to the love nest, she jumped. So did I. She wore a black thong and a red T-shirt. Her eyes sparkled when she saw it was me. Mine did the same.

But still, seeing her caught me off guard. "Hey, Panther."

"I was worried about you."

We stared at each other for a moment.

She was lounging on the bed, her suitcase open. The room smelled sweet and hypnotic, just like her. Her sensual eyes and strange grin confirmed that she didn't expect me to be here.

She asked, "Are you okay? I heard about what went down between . . . that bitch."

"I'm cool."

"If I had made it here on time, I could've helped you treat her to a beat down."

My tongue slid across my bottom lip. "It was for the best."

She asked, "You talked to Carpe?"

"His name is Michael."

"I know. And you're Olivia."

That increased my level of discomfort. I drew in a deep breath, let it out.

She got up and came over to me, gave me a two-armed hug. I found that exhilarating. It made parts of me throb in remembrance of things she'd done with her tongue and hands, things I'd never admit. Her skin was moisturized, breath was sweet as peppermint. She tried to kiss me on my lips but I turned my face, gave her my cheek, letting her know that part of my life was over. My abrupt rejection tightened her eyes, then she nodded her head like she understood.

She said, "You came back for him."

I went to the closet, went through the clothes. Feather-touched all the things he had bought me, all the wonderful gifts fit for a queen. Then I pulled out one pair of shoes.

I told Panther, "I came back for the Blahniks."

She laughed.

So did I. I had come out on Christmas day and risked my life for these Blahniks. Only a true shoe whore could understand that kind of insanity; her laugh told me she understood.

My words were laden with heaviness, the kind that comes from a great unburdening. I told her that this part of my life was over, that I'd just come back to get these shoes.

Then she wanted to see the injury on my neck, my broken nails, see all the things I wanted to forget and remember at the same time. I moved her away from that talk of the past, told her about my future, starting with the Christmas present I'd just gotten from Tony.

She said, "So, the baby's not his and you and hubby gonna work it out."

"Maybe we'll work on having our own now."

"How cute. Can you trust that guy?"

"We've been together a long time. The love was there. It's still there. Maybe we both needed excitement." I talked to her the way you talked to a person on a plane trip, the openness and honesty you gave a stranger you'd never see again. I stared at the romanticism in this room, even looked down at the spot where we had marked this territory. I whispered, "Excitement. I was special. He'd do anything to please me. That was what I got from Carpe."

She said, "He's a great guy."

"Yeah, too bad I didn't meet him before . . . didn't meet him a few years ago."

"I know what you mean. Biggest dick, best sex, we never marry that guy, so we have to take what we can get when we can get it."

We laughed. What I'd just said about wishing I had met Carpe first, I wasn't sure if I meant that. Then I would've been the broken wife who hired a private investigator to follow her adulterous husband around. Maybe, deep down, I'd had my own sex-with-a-stranger fantasy. Now he wasn't a stranger anymore. His name was Michael.

Panther said, "I'm fond of you."

Her sweet tone, her soft expression, she wasn't making this easy for me.

My eyes went to my bracelet again. To the pictures that represented my reality.

In a good-bye tone I said, "Merry Christmas, Panther."

"Merry Christmas."

Again we hugged, her softness against my softness. She smelled good, like sugar and wonderful spices. Her warmth blended with mine and my breathing became ragged. Goose bumps rose on my arms, moved up and down my spine. Once again she offered me her lips and I lowered my head, this time giving her my forehead. She leaned her head against mine for a moment. She sighed. I put a hand on her shoulder, eased her away, shaking my head. That look of rejection manifested itself in her eyes one more time.

She asked, "Sure you don't want to . . . before you go?"

The tip of my tongue slid across my teeth. "Take care of yourself."

I took one last look at this space, tossed my silver key on the bed, headed for the door.

"Keep the key, Bird."

"No."

"Never know when you might need excitement again."

"No."

"If you're worried about his wife, that can be under control in no time."

"No."

"Stay. I want you to stay. Spend some time with me."

I stalled, my hand on the doorknob, nodding and wincing, and I'd be lying if I said I didn't look at her, if I didn't remember what had been done, what had been shared, if I didn't think about it. I looked at my left arm, at Tony's gift to me. The silver bracelet with the pictures of my family. Bernard and Momma were smiling up at their little girl. Tommie and Frankie were smiling up at their sister.

I pulled the door open, winter's breeze sneaking in, chilling my warm desires.

She said, "So, you're serious."

"Take care."

What I'd done, those erotic experiences that had me trapped between the pangs of guilt and longing, I wouldn't do them over, but I didn't regret them at the same time. I imagined that time to time I'd think about this place and parts of my body would spring to life, become warm, get moist, then I'd smile.

And no one would know why. Maybe somewhere down the road I'd tell my sisters about the things I'd done this December, but I'd leave out the parts about Panther, at least the part that started after the strip club. She was the secret I'd take to my grave.

"When we bought the Blahniks," Panther said, and her tone had changed, had lost its sweetness. I turned toward her. Lips turned down, arms folded, she went on, "I told him that would take you over the edge. Shoes do that to a woman, you know."

Her new voice startled me. It had a Southern meanness in its tone.

I blinked a few times; think I might've raised a brow. "*We* bought the Blahniks?"

"Oh, please. Like he knows about shoes. I picked them out. Just like I picked out the decorations here. The music, the colors, the knickknacks; see how well it all goes together."

I laughed a laugh of uncertainty, one that echoed my sudden confusion. Still not believing. Tommie had said that out of all the human emotions, denial was the most predictable.

Panther gave me her charming smile. "I really liked you. You were different."

And yet, my perplexity ascended. I repeated, "Different?"

"Not like the others."

I looked directly at her, tried to understand. "The other women that you've . . ."

"That we've had."

"We?"

"This isn't easy because . . . I'm developing . . . I have a profound attachment to you."

My face was struggling with confusion and enlightenment.

She asked, *"Are you a woman betrayed?"*

She had recited Carpe's Internet ad. That killed the last of my awkward smile.

Panther read my expression. Then she said, "Those were my words."

"Your words?"

"I am a woman betrayed." That halted me. She was reciting my response to Carpe's Internet ad. *"I have been cheated on. I don't understand."*

I asked, "Who are you?"

"I can't fly." She went on, feeding me my words. *"I can't sit. I'm restless."*

I swallowed. Felt like I was in a twilight state, wide awake and dreaming all at once.

Her sweet smile turned into a soft laugh, a mask for her irritation.

Then, in a flash, I remembered all of us at Stroker's, when she was stripping, coming on to me, and talking to Carpe with so much ease. The way they were laughing and flirting, whispering back and forth. It was so easy for him to get her here, to bring her into our world. All of their interactions were so . . . smooth. As if they already knew each other.

I said, "His wife said he lied."

"All men lie. Women lie. We all lie."

"What are the lies, Panther?"

"You mean what is the truth."

"Okay, what is the truth?"

"What he told you, his story was an amalgamation of things."

"Amalgamation?"

"He mixed stories together. Yeah, I came out here pregnant, to be with him. I dropped out of Clark-Atlanta. Drove out here by myself. Found out he was married."

I swallowed again. He hadn't enticed Panther into our world.

He had seduced me into theirs.

Still I couldn't fathom what was going on. I said, "He told me . . . He said that he was a man cheated on, but he was . . . was just cheating on his wife."

She shrugged. "Just like you were cheating on your husband."

"It's not the same."

"All sins are equal, Bird."

She was scorned by my rejection, annoyed by my strength, now trying to weaken me by talking to me like I was nothing. The warmth I had for her dissipated. Just like that I hated her.

This was what I saw in my mind: The first shoe would hit her in the middle of her beautiful face. I'd throw it hard and fast. Then she'd run, grab her forehead, curse and yell.

Then the second shoe would hit the bathroom door with the impact of a combat boot. She'd be in there, locking the door, stunned and bumbling around while I banged on the door, while I kicked on the door and called her every name I could think of, while I looked for a knife.

But that didn't happen. Not because I didn't want to beat her ass. Not because she intimidated me. You just don't throw Blahniks like you would a pair of shoes from Payless.

My fingers loosened and the coveted shoes slipped from my hand.

Panther stood firm, her breasts high, dark skin glistening, full lips parted.

I remembered what Tony had said about wanting to kill Miesha's mother. About how he said he wouldn't do anything that would make it impossible for us to be together again. I wanted to make what we had new again, make it as exciting as what Tommie had with Blue.

She was Panther. A goddess scorned. Like a warrior, she stood her ground.

Women destroyed each other just as much as men destroyed women.

I'd like to believe that thought kept me from acting a fool. Or maybe I was just tired.

I stared at the closet filled with clothes, the boxes of new shoes.

Designer attire for a betrayed woman. A whore's wardrobe. That was all that was.

Panther had given me the most devastating, destructive, and unpredictable news she could. Shattered my illusion. That was the kind of petty thing a woman did. The way I nodded my head, the way I tisked told her what I was thinking.

I asked, "What's your real name?"

She smiled a one-sided smile. "Cynthia Smalls."

I smiled a one-sided smile too. Now she was no longer a stranger.

I shook my head. "I won't be coming this way again."

My pisstivity at myself had me heading out the door. Christmas air chilled my skin.

But I couldn't leave.

This wasn't over.

I startled her when I hurried back inside, my expression tight, mouth fixed for a verbal exchange, hands fixed for more than that. The way I pushed the door open, the way it banged the wall when I rushed back inside scared her to her feet. She jumped like she knew I was ready to take the shoes and leave her bruised body on the floor so Michael could find her ass.

Her expression stopped me where I was.

So many tears were running down her face.

The goddess in her was gone, dissipated. She was a child named Cynthia, a long way from her Southern roots, alone on Christmas, willing to do whatever she had to do to not be alone on this holiday. A stripper who would do anything for a man who didn't love her.

She pulled her long hair away from her face, stared at the floor.

She snapped, "Get the fuck out, Olivia. Go home to your damn family."

Women destroyed each other, but sometimes we tried to save each other as well.

I moved toward her. She trembled, backed away, picked up a housecoat, covered herself, lowered her head, wiped her tears away as she went into the bathroom; then she closed the door.

I asked, "How old are you?"

"Twenty-three."

"Go back to school. Get your shit together."

I stood where I was. She remained inside the bathroom.

Her voice came to me, "Olivia . . . Take care of yourself."

"Yeah. You do the same, Cynthia."

My wounded fingers sang when I picked up the Blahniks. I didn't come back to fight. It was all about the shoes. No way in hell I was going to leave them behind. I wasn't insane.

Scarf around my neck hiding my scars, I pulled my lips in and hurried back outside, brisk air drying the sweat on my face. My quick pace took me up the hill to my SUV. I placed the shoes in the passenger seat, and headed toward my home, not speeding, and never looking back.

ACKNOWLEDGMENTS

This is a work of fiction.

As usual, I was mulling over a different novel when my former editor asked me about doing a holiday novel. What I was working on, in my opinion, was a little too dark for the seasonal thing, so I put that project down, put on my Santa Claus suit, and moved on to a lighter story. Needed to do a little comedy. I've heard actors say that after doing intense pieces, they wanted/needed to do something light to maintain their sanity, sometimes just to flex their acting chops, maybe to keep from being typecast. (Sometimes it's the reverse, after doing so many light pieces some actors want to do something heavier. Artists, writers, singers—I think most creative people feel that way.)

What I love about fiction is just that, it's fiction. The writer has the freedom to change things, redo scenes until the flow is seamless, rework lies until they sound real, rewrite until what's been created is the best scene for the story. I love being able to do that. You can't rework the truth, which is why trying to write nonfiction doesn't work for me. You can't swap shit around or rewrite the real deal, not without people calling you, well, a liar. (Maybe some peeps will add some colorful expletives in front of that tag.) Which is what a good fiction writer is, a decent liar. And when two or more fiction writers are in a room, in the words of Richard Pryor, his voice bringing the character "Mudbone" to life, we sit around and "compliment each other's lies." It's our job to make it all seem real. Just like a good actor, we have to make you believe.

I have no idea what's going to happen until I start writing. Don't have a clue who is going to show up, banging on the door, begging for a part in the story. In the book you're holding, Livvy's job changed along the way. Her relationship with her sisters changed. Livvy was single; then she was married. (And Livvy wasn't her original name.) The nationality of her husband changed too. How they met came to me weeks later. Frankie's height and weight both went up and down. About halfway through I changed my mind and moved her from a duplex to a house. Her dates with the legion-of-whatever-she-called-them changed a thousand times. Tommie's tone changed and her backstory was softened up a bit. Characters from other books showed up, got deleted; then others showed up and refused to leave, no matter how much I prodded. There was even a chapter told from one sister's POV, then switched at the last minute. (Don't ask because I'm not telling. Gotta have some secrets. ☺) The point is, well, the freedom in writing fiction is that I don't have to worry about facts, not in the nonfiction sense of the word. Don't get me wrong, that doesn't make it any easier—it's still hard work. Even you have "talent," you still need to study, put in the hours, and even then if you don't have the discipline to complete a project . . . 'Nuff said. I always encourage people struggling with writer's block: do what you have to do, *finish the friggin' project*. It's a labor of love, and I have the same struggles. One day you love what you're working on, the next you're ready to kick your laptop off your desk and take up basket weaving.

Some pretty cool people have asked me, "How can I be a writer? What do I have to do?" Which I find curious. Not trying to sound . . . dunno . . . guess that logical side of my brain kicks in whenever I hear that question. I was in software development for nine years, and when I told people what I did, no one asked what it took to get that gig. (Then again, no one was really impressed—no one wanted to know how to get a job where you wore a pocket protector and sat in a cubicle and watched other people scratch their asses. Oh, the glamour! And the high-brow humor. "Is that a hard drive in your pocket or are you just happy to see me?") All that to say, peeps knew it required a lot of studying. A hella lot. They knew I had to start with the basics of computer design and learn the craft from ground up. That meant a lot of classes. (Arrgh! Pardon me, had a flashback.) The same, in my humble opinion, goes for writing. I'm not saying you need a degree from Harvard, but I always suggest finding your way into somebody's class or workshop, start with the basics, get an understanding, build a foundation. (Actors, singers, artists, dancers, comedians, anybody in the arts will tell you the same thing—what they do may look easy, but it's not a no-brainer and you have to put in your time.) There are no secrets. Just hard work. A lot of falling and getting back up. If you love writing, that's what you'll do. It's not about fame; it's about writing. I still take classes when I can, wherever I can. I love learning, even if it's just getting a fresh perspective on old ideas. Anyone who tells you they know all there is to know is a bona fide idiot. Run away from them as fast as you can. And be careful what you wish for. If you don't mind deadlines and sitting in a dungeon (sort of like being an engineer, only you don't have to watch people wearing pocket protectors scratch their asses). If you don't mind working a capella while the rest of the world goes out to play on a sunny day, this might be the gig for you. From revisions to recasting, from frustration to elation, a lot happens to a story before it makes it this far. Whenever I look back at my notes (and sometimes flowcharts) from any book I've written, the evolution of each project amazes me.

For the people who've asked me how I write in a female voice, I've tried to answer. That Q finds its way into every book signing, every interview. But here's the kicker, I've never had a good answer. Close to ten years have gone by, still no good answer. And I can tell you why. Hold the book up to your ear so I can whisper the truth. Closer. Little closer. Not that close. Don't want to get earwax on the pages. Ready? Here goes. *Because I have no idea. Serious. I don't.* There it is. I said it. Now I'm an official member of the Do Not Know How He Does It Club. To be honest, if there is some secret, I don't want to know. If a bird knew the secret to his flying, he'd probably crash. And if a bird knows, he ain't telling, cause he's too busy flying. I'm flying and I love the feeling. All I can tell you is this: I try to create characters old and young, male and female, many nationalities. The same amount of energy gets put into each one. I guess what is seen depends on who is doing the reading. Nothing wrong with that. Whatever floats your boat. Either way, cool by me. Much better than being ignored.

'Nuff said.

So far as what I was working on before the phone rang and my former editor made me an offer I couldn't refuse, the day is still young and I have plenty of ink in my printer. The Lord willing and the creek don't rise, I'll be getting back to that project as soon as I finish sending a few shout-outs to the crew. No man is an island and no writer can do it alone.

To my wonderful agent, Sara Camilli, once again, thanks for looking over every scene change, word change, from beginning to end. Thanks for pointing out a few errors along the way, and thanks for the phone conversations and listening to my ever-changing ideas while I worked my way through this one. Your suggestions were priceless.

To the people in publicity, Lisa Johnson, Kathleen Schmidt, and Betsy Dejesus, a kazillion thanks and just as many hugs. You peeps are awesome to the nth degree.

Carole Baron, thanks for believing in me. MUA!

Brian Tart, Amy Hughes, thanks for picking up the ball on this project. Much love.

Rose Hilliard, thanks for handling all of my requests with a smile.

And to my warm, close, personal friends . . .

Olivia Ridgell, thanks for the feedback, Boo! Much love to you in Chi town.

Denae Marcel, thanks for the input. Once again you've been a tremendous help.

And, as usual, I have to thank Yvette Hayward in NYC for reading the scenes as I wrote 'em. (Whaddup Jamez!)

Ronnie L. Adams, II (MD), thanks for the medical info. It was great meeting you and your few words were a great help in shaping a key character.

Amy Mason, thanks for your comments. You're a regular Evelyn Wood.

Tiffany Pace, thanks for the copyedits. You're the best. (I stopped there but, nnnnooo, Tiff got a little beside herself and wanted me to add the following.) *I don't know what I'd do without you. Your work is beyond compare. I'm learning to like the smell of cigarettes on my manuscripts. I'm giving you a raise.*

J. McDaniel, thanks for all the feedback and info on all that Derma stuff.

Dominique Simone Dickey, I love your poetry! MUA!

Audrey O. Cooper, Robert (Bobby) Laird, Travis Hunter, thanks.

To the wonderful people at Trillion, many thanks to Kathryn Tyus Adair and Laurent Zilber. Thanks to Steve Lapuk for the enthusiasm and interest in my work. And many hugs to Deborah Martin Chase and Martin Chase Productions.

In case I forgot anybody, break out a pen and get ready to fill in your name! This book would not be possible without _____'s help.

To the readers who have been hanging out with me and my imagination for the better part of the last decade, thanks. I mean that. If it weren't for you, I'd still be at the post office licking stamps. Unfortunately I can't go back because my old job has gone away, replaced by self-adhesive stamps. Technology is a beast.

Laugh, cry, get mad, I just hope you have (or had) fun reading *Naughty or Nice*.

Special thanks to the peeps who went out and bought books as soon as they hit the stands. To everyone who took the time out of their schedules to show up for the book tour, thanks. I look forward to meeting you year after year while I'm on the road.

Now, all the writer birds out there . . . get to flying.

Peace, blessings, and happy holidays.
Virginia Jerry's grandson signing off . . .☺

eric jerome dickey
07/07/03
www.ericjeromedickey.com